When his tongue continued to flick over her lips and dip into her mouth, she moaned then flattened her palms on his hard chest and pushed against him. "Stop!"

The one word was like a splash of cold water stunning him back into reality. He lifted his face from her, looked down at her now swollen lips, her passion-filled eyes, and realized what he'd done. He'd crossed the line.

He eased away from her while keeping his hands on her waist until she lowered her legs to the floor. When he knew she could stand on her own, he backed away, putting several feet between them. "Sabrina—"

She shook her head quickly. "Our emotions were running high. This entire situation has changed in a matter of hours and we have to deal with that. That's all we have to deal with. Is that clear?"

"No, it's not clear. There's something else between us that will have to be dealt with sooner or later. You know that as well as I do."

A.C. ARTHUR

was born and raised in Baltimore, Maryland, where she currently resides with her husband and three children. An active imagination and a love for reading encouraged her to begin writing in high school, and she hasn't stopped since. Determined to bring a new edge to romance, she continues to develop intriguing plots, racy characters and fresh dialogue—thus keeping readers on their toes! Visit her Web site at www.acarthur.net.

GUARDING HIS
BODY

A.C. ARTHUR

KIMANI™
ROMANCE

To Andre, Asia & Amaya
A mother could not ask for a better crew

KIMANI PRESS™

ISBN-13: 978-0-373-86073-9
ISBN-10:   0-373-86073-0

GUARDING HIS BODY

Dear Reader,

Whew! ROMANCE ON THE RUN—just the title sounds exciting. And I am more than pleased to be a part of this themed series.

Guarding His Body introduces two new families, the Desdunes and the Bennetts. They are influential families in the quiet town of Greenwich, Connecticut. Renny Bennett is an alleged playboy who left his family business to become an erotic-art sculptor. He's a quiet alpha male who you'll instantly fall in love with. Sabrina Desdune is not your ordinary heroine—she's feisty, headstrong and a bodyguard. Bree uses her military training to protect Renny and his family from an anonymous threat, while Renny uses his charm to break down all Bree's defenses. I loved these two characters and the way their differences came together to forge a strong bond.

Bree and Renny have a lot of obstacles, but their desire for each other and loyalty to their families outweigh them all. This was a fun story to write, with a touch of suspense thrown in for good measure. Be on the lookout for an appearance by one of those sexy Donovan men in this story as well!

Please do not hesitate to share your comments about Renny and Bree via e-mail at acarthur22@yahoo.com.

A.C. Arthur

Chapter 1

Renny had a death grip on his temper. Of all the Bennett children he had the shortest fuse. In the past few months he'd been trying really hard to prove his brothers and father wrong, that he could make intelligent decisions without first over-reacting. But glancing again at this tiny woman—she couldn't be any more than five feet three inches and one-twenty soaking wet—with serious dark eyes and hair pulled back into a simple ponytail, he felt his resolve slipping.

How in the hell did they expect him to take the news that she was his new bodyguard seriously?

She didn't look capable of buying herself a drink without identification, let alone protecting him from some psychopath killer!

Through clenched teeth he managed a smile and extended his hand to clasp the one she'd held out to him. "I'm Renny Bennett. It's a pleasure to meet you, Ms. Desdune," he murmured, because his mother had been a stickler for manners.

Bree hadn't missed it—even though he'd tried valiantly to hide his irritation, she'd seen the spark in his brown eyes and almost winced with its fierceness. He wasn't dressed in designer suits like the three other Bennett men in the room. No, this one was so sure of his good looks, he'd opted for crisp new blue jeans and a navy button-down shirt. His boots looked sturdy, Timberland, she thought with a shrug, the same ones Lynn had just purchased for her nephew, Jeremy.

She was an excellent judge of character. Her mother said this was her sixth sense inherited from her Creole grandmother, Ruby, on Daddy's side. Bree didn't care who it came from, it was a great tool and she had used it all her life. Now she used it to tell the true feelings of Mr. Bennett. He was thinking that this little woman couldn't possibly be a threat to anyone, so how was she supposed to protect him? She had to admit, the Bennett men did soar over her at more than six feet, but then she'd always been the shortest one in the bunch. It never stopped her from taking either one of her brothers down, nor had it stopped her from graduating tops in her basic training class when she'd enlisted in the marines.

So regardless of how Renny Bennett glowered down at her through his fake smile and brilliant white teeth, she had his number, loud and clear. "You can call me Sabrina." She tossed him a big ole fake smile of her own and clasped his hand.

Both their eyes shot open at the contact, twin bolts of heat traveling quickly through their limbs.

Sabrina pulled away first.

Renny continued to stare, dumbfounded and looking silly, his empty hand still outstretched.

"Ah, Renny, I assure you that Sabrina is very capable. As you are the only one of the Bennett men not directly involved in the business, it's most likely you're not the target. Still, I'd like to keep a close watch on you just in case," Sam said, moving closer to Bree.

"I'm sure that Ms. Desdune is good at what she does." He doubted that very seriously; she was a woman, for goodness' sake. Why on earth her brother was letting her run around playing cops and robbers was beyond him, but that was not his concern. "I simply don't think I need any protection."

"That's what they all say." Bree couldn't help it; the words were out before she'd had a chance to consider the company they were in. A quick glance to her right and she saw Sam's frown. She'd promised him she'd be on her best behavior, that she'd complete this assignment without any mishaps. The Bennetts were very wealthy and very influential in the Greenwich community. Their charity work and financial contributions around the state were well-known and much appreciated. Besides that, Sam needed this job. His security company had only been open for two years and he was making a steady amount of money, but he was getting married in six months to Leeza Purdy—Connecticut's very own Paris Hilton. But that was another story for another day.

Behind her she heard a snicker. Renny Bennett glowered over her shoulder, then lowered his eyes to her again.

Sam glowered at her, then turned his attention to their new client. "What she means is that most of our clients that receive personal attention are against it, but your father has hired me to do a job and I would not be doing that job if I didn't cover all the bases."

A muscle in Renny's jaw twitched and Bree found herself staring at his face, the finely chiseled features, strong jaw, dark bronze skin, dark eyes and thin beard and mustache giving him an air of danger. She remembered that one of his parents was Brazilian, the mother, if she wasn't mistaken. That would explain the exotic look all the Bennett sons had. They were certainly a triplet of beautiful men. When she made her way to his eyes again she realized with a start that he was staring at her as intently as she'd been staring at him. She cleared her throat and stood a little straighter, her mouth suddenly going dry. "Mr. Bennett, I can assure you that I'll guard your body as if it were my own." The moment the words were out she knew they were an even bigger mistake than her previous comment.

Sam grabbed her by the arm. "Yes, Mr. Bennett, Desdune Security will take very good care of your family. Now, if you'll excuse us we'd like to get a better look at the grounds to decide what other precautions we need to take here at the house." He pulled her to the door, barely masking his anger.

"Taunting the client is not good business, Bree," Sam scolded when they were well down the hall from the dining room.

Bree had already pulled away from his bullying grasp and was checking the locks on the windows in the living room as Sam spoke. "I wasn't taunting him. He was the one looking down his nose at me, a mere woman assigned to guard his body." And what a wonderful body that was, she thought surprisingly. "These windows are the pits." She stood back and looked at the almost floor-to-ceiling windows and held in a sigh. "Besides giving you a breathtaking view of the landscape, they aren't the best safety choice. I think we should line the entire house with a new alarm system. Possibly some motion sensors since they seem to have a lot of valuables in here."

Sam wanted to be mad at her; he wanted to continue to drill into her head the importance of this job, but he just couldn't. Bree was his baby sister. Not only that, she was his fraternal twin. They were as close as two people could possibly be and he loved her with all his being. But she could be a stubborn pain in the ass when she felt like it. Still, she was smart and good at what she did. She'd studied weaponry and hand-to-hand combat in her sixteen-year stint with the Marine Corps. Despite her small frame and wispy appearance she could beat the hell out of you without batting an eye—he'd seen it done.

He moved through the elegantly decorated room and had to agree with her. The windows were gorgeous, but wouldn't protect the Bennetts from an intruder. He pulled his notebook out of his back pocket and scribbled down some notes. "Yeah, that's a good idea. I think a security gate to get on the property would be good, too. I can't believe they have this huge estate and never thought to have one installed."

Bree chuckled. "We live in Greenwich, Connecticut, Sam. Who the hell needs security out here? We're only a step away from Smallville."

Sam couldn't help but laugh with her. Bree always hated Greenwich. Her spirit and energy fit New York or L.A. much better. That had him wondering again why she'd come back. "Actually, we're only a step down from Beverly Hills, which has its share of crime and danger. Now, I've already bugged the office phones. Mr. Bennett's direct line and the lines of Alex and Rico, as well. I doubt any calls will come in through the other staff. We need to come back and set up the lines here in the house and we need to do each of the private home phones, as well."

He looked over at Bree, who had paused at the mantel looking at the family portraits. "Are you writing any of this down, Bree?"

She didn't wince, didn't even turn before replying. "Nope."

He let out a deep breath. "And why not?"

She tapped her temple as she turned toward him. "I've got it all up here." She gave him that award-winning smile. That smile that made whatever else you were thinking fly right out of your mind.

Sam shook his head. He felt sorry for the man that fell for Sabrina Desdune.

"That's some bodyguard you've got there, little brother." Alex moved to the minibar and poured himself a drink, still grinning after what had just happened.

"I don't need a bodyguard." Renny moved to the window, looked out at the cloudy October sky. "This whole thing is ridiculous. Just call the police and let them handle it. That's what they get paid for."

Rico sat down at the table, opening a file and poring over its contents. "It's too delicate a situation for that. If word gets out that we're being stalked the publicity alone will be a nightmare. Not to mention our stockholders who'll probably get jumpy and start selling off stock. We're going about this the right way and you'll just have to deal with it."

Renny jammed his hands into his pockets. He hated when Rico talked in that highly professional, full-of-crap tone. He'd learned it from his father and now did it more often than not. Renny missed their teenage years when they'd talked like normal boys about sports and girls and everything in between. He knew he was the outcast because he hadn't gone into the family business, because he'd rather wear jeans and tennis shoes than a Brooks Brothers suit and tie. But they were still brothers.

"It was only two notes, Rico. It's not as if the house was broken into or a threat was made on our lives. Two little notes that said basically nothing." He frowned and continued to stare outside. He'd much rather be in his studio or on his deck drawing whatever came to mind. Being cooped up in this big house was stifling.

Alex jumped in, now over his petty laughter. "They said something, Renny. And we can't ignore it."

"Oh, I'm sorry I didn't realize you were finished with your joke of the day." Renny turned to face his oldest brother. They were almost the same build but Alex was about two inches taller. Alex wore a suit, like he normally did, but he didn't look suffocated by it like Renny usually did. He looked distinguished and professional. Renny admitted that he was proud of his brothers. Even though Rico was a little obsessed, he was glad they'd made their spot in the world. And now Renny was making his own.

He admitted this was a bad time for him, as well. He didn't need any bad press, didn't need the threat of some lunatic stalker hanging over his head. His gallery was opening in three weeks; his first solo show would be on display. He did not have time for this stalker or that woman.

"No, I still think that feisty little nymph was funny as hell. But I agree with Rico that we need to take this very seriously. Dad is obviously worried that this is a viable threat, so we should be, as well." Alex took a drink from his glass. "I would like to commend Rico for hiring Desdune Security. They have a good reputation for getting the job done. *And* I think your guard in particular is going to do a magnificent job on you."

"She's not hired to do a job on me. Hell, I don't know what she's supposed to do." Renny hadn't missed Alex's implications. Of the three Bennett men, Renny was the most reckless when it came to women. Because he was so absorbed in his work he didn't give them any more time than was absolutely necessary. The problem was, with his good looks and obvious colored background—green for money—women were always practically throwing themselves at him. He took from the bounty when the mood struck him and when it didn't, he ignored them.

Sabrina Desdune, however, would not be easy to ignore.

She was tiny, yes, he'd give her that. Yet she possessed something he'd never seen in the women in his life—confidence. He'd bet half his trust fund that Sabrina Desdune knew exactly who she was and what she wanted out of life. Now, whether or not that should concern him, he wasn't quite sure. What he was sure of, where she was concerned, was that she was damned beautiful. Despite her attempts to downplay her good looks, a blind man could see them. Skin the color of cocoa, a pert little mouth with full lips, high cheekbones and eyes so deep, so moving, you could sink right into her soul. And that body…any woman that wore jeans and a T-shirt like that had his vote every time.

Still, he did *not* need a bodyguard.

"She's supposed to keep you alive. It's as simple as that so don't get any other sordid ideas about her," Rico chided.

"I think it's too late for that, Rico. Didn't you see the sparks flying between those two? I'll bet he has her in his bed by the end of the week." Alex guffawed.

"I will not!" Renny said adamantly.

"He'd better not!" Rico added. "This is serious, Renny. Now, I know you don't care much about Bennett Industries, but this attack is personal. Dad has made quite a few enemies in his time and now it appears one has gotten bold enough to come after his family. You'd do well to watch your ass this time instead of that woman's."

Renny was instantly offended. "Now, wait one minute. Bennett Industries is just as important to me as it is to either of you. Just because I choose not to work there doesn't mean I don't care. I know how important it is to Dad and to the two of you. And I see how worried these notes have Dad and Mom, for that matter. That's the only reason I agreed to come here and meet with these security people in the first place. But I don't see either one of you being assigned a girl to guard you."

Alex sat in a chair, stretched his long legs out in front of him. "Nah, I could never be so lucky."

"It's not luck, believe me." Renny had turned toward the window again, just in time to see that curvy little body moving swiftly toward the SUV her brother drove. Those jeans molded over her bottom as she stepped up into the vehicle, and blood pumped swiftly through his loins. Hell, no, this was not luck, this was going to be a game of Russian roulette if he'd ever seen one. And he'd never been lucky at gambling.

Okay, so he was fine as hell with that thick, curly hair and those smoldering dark eyes that sent chills down her spine. But he was just a man. One of the species that she had sworn off for the rest of her natural life.

Turning into the lower-level garage, Bree realized that little oath might be a tad unrealistic—a woman needed some sort of sexual relief sooner or later. But she was definitely not going to get that relief from this man. He was a client. Her brother's biggest client, and she wouldn't dare muddle something that important with stupid thoughts of sex with Lorenzo Bennett.

Besides, she wasn't the type of woman he got excited over. She'd seen that in the look he'd given her when she was introduced as his bodyguard. He'd barely masked his disgust. Tomboys definitely weren't on his platter as an appetizer. She visualized him with the tall, leggy, buxom, model type. The glamorous, giggling bombshell that would hang on his every word and grace the society pages with elegance— elegance that she would never possess.

She parked her Durango, the one luxury she had allowed herself upon her departure from the U.S. armed forces, and lifted the bag from the backseat. "God, Sam, did you pack everything out of the office in here?" she muttered as she slipped the black duffel onto her shoulder and climbed down out of the truck.

She pulled a piece of paper from her back pocket and glanced at the address again. He was on the third floor. She disregarded the elevator and took the stairs. She hadn't had a chance to run this morning because Jeremy and his cute self was full of questions and stories for his auntie Bree, and she'd happily indulged him.

Besides, taking the stairs would give her the chance to check out the ins and outs of this building—this high-priced, glitzy condominium complex that she should have known the billionaire playboy would reside in. She wasn't impressed. For all the money he undoubtedly paid to live here, the security wasn't worth crap. She'd driven right into the garage and opened the stairway door and was now pulling it open without any security breaches.

There was a long hallway with only two doors to her right and one to her left. She went to the left first even though that wasn't in the direction of the door she needed. At the end of that hall was a floor-to-ceiling window giving a view of the golf course that looped around from the country club up the street. There was no way to open the window, but there was no security tape around it that would signal any alarm if someone decided to bash it in and gain entrance. She turned and came back down the hall, passing the bright green Exit sign pointing to the stairs she'd just come from. The doors were numbered with big glossy black numerals. Looking up and down the dove-gray walls, she frowned at the lack of even a security camera. She stopped in front of the door with the numbers that matched those on the paper she still held and took a deep breath.

You can do this, Bree, he's just a man. She shook her head vehemently. *Correction, he's just a client.*

The incessant knocking resonated through the thick haze of Renny's thoughts. He was focused, in a place that soothed and comforted him—that place his father called his fairy-tale land. He held his pencil in a loose grip, looking down at the paper filled with lines that were about to take shape even as someone continued to rap on his door.

Cursing, he stood from his desk and walked out of the studio. Through the CD player the smooth, sensual sounds of Brian McKnight filled the living room. He paused momentarily to turn it down a notch, then went to the door, pulling it open with all the frustration he was feeling at the moment.

Bree had been about to knock again but instead the door had flung open and she'd lost her balance, her raised arm and the top half of her body falling into what felt like a solid wall. She looked up into the stern face and dark eyes of the owner of that massive wall of a chest and forced herself to smile. "Oops. Mornin'," she said in a voice that was much calmer, much more chipper than she really was.

Renny had caught the flailing female effortlessly, but the moment his hands made contact with the bare skin of her arms he knew it was a mistake. She'd haunted him last night and that hadn't been enough. It wasn't even eight o'clock and she was here on his doorstep, possibly to torment him some more.

He steadied her, then quickly took his hands off her. She wore lip gloss today, her pouting mouth almost begging to be kissed. She wore sunglasses so he couldn't see those eyes, those deep-brown, expressive eyes. Her hair was pulled back into a ponytail again and he fought the sudden urge to pull it free. She'd twisted and turned it in some fashion so that it looped around a few times and was dangling down her back, but he knew that if he just pulled on that band it would fall, cascading down her back like a curtain of pure satiny bliss.

He cleared his throat. "What are you doing here?" he asked gruffly.

Bree tried not to take his rudeness personally and pushed her glasses to the top of her head. Without the dimness of the shades she almost moaned. He was beautiful. He wore sweatpants that accentuated his trim waist and a sleeveless shirt that was glued to his muscled chest. That funny bronze skin of his almost glistened from his face to his neck, to the bulging biceps and big hands. Through his shirt she could easily make out the imprint of impressive pectorals and a six-pack of abs. He must work out religiously to keep that kind of body.

"Not a morning person, huh?" she said airily as she pushed past him and made her way into his condo. She instantly began looking around, surveying what was needed.

Renny closed the door, lounged against it, crossing his arms over his chest, and enjoyed the view for a moment. "Normal people don't go around banging on doors this early."

She shrugged, dropped her bag on the couch and moved to the windows. She was dragging her hands along the seals as if she was looking or feeling for something.

Renny watched her intently. With every stroke he let his detail-oriented eyes settle on her fingers. She had small hands, low-cut fingernails, no rings, no watch, no polish. Her touch was swift, methodical, yet he felt every stroke as if she were slowly guiding it over him, caressing him. He shifted his stance to relieve the tightness in his pants. "What are you doing?" he asked through a slightly cracked voice.

"I'm checking out your windows. I'll need to wire the security system through here." She moved from the patio door to the phone. She picked it up, put it to her ear and listened for a second or two, then put it down and lifted it to look at the underside. "No bugs."

"I'm glad to hear that. I would hate to have to call an exterminator."

She was moving toward the bedroom now and Renny felt his groin tighten.

"Don't tell me you have a sense of humor."

He tried like hell not to watch her butt as she walked in front of him, or to imagine that she was leading them right to his bedroom, to the bed where he'd dreamed of her only hours before. "Ah, yeah, something like that. But it's still early." He heard himself stumbling over his words. This was new for him. Of all the Bennett men he was the smoothest around the women, the charmer, the home-run hitter each and every time. "What exactly are you looking for?"

She was in his room now, turning her head this way and that, taking in everything he possessed. She paused at the bed. It was a four-poster Victorian antique he'd found on a trip to Paris. It sat on a platform in the middle of the floor, covered with cream-colored bedding that his mother had picked out.

"Wow! That's a seriously big bed." Bree was used to the military twin size. Even when she'd moved off base to her own apartment she'd purchased a full-size bed since it was only her. But this monstrosity looked like it could easily fit her, her two brothers, her sister and her two-year-old nephew.

"I like big things," Renny said simply.

That remark poured over her as she found herself thinking he probably had a lot of big things in his possession. She couldn't resist; she hadn't wanted to, but it almost called to her. She stepped up on the platform, touched her hand to the thick dark wood and let it slide all the way down, then up again.

"How long have you lived here?" Bree asked, pulling her hand away from his bed. She wanted to sit on it, to feel what she knew would be soft against her back, but she digressed. She didn't turn back to face him for fear he'd see the longing in her eyes, so she stepped down off the platform and went directly to the windows on the other side of the room.

"Ah, four years now."

"And you haven't done anything about security?" She turned to him then. "Americans are so gullible."

Renny blinked quickly. "Excuse me?"

"We take our safety for granted. You simply believe you're safe and trust that the local authorities will protect you from anything bad. When what you should be doing is ensuring your own safety. Protecting what's yours."

"Listen, Sabrina, why don't you just tell me why you're

here? We can handle any business we have to and then you can be on your way."

Bree blinked at his curt tone and hooked her fingers in her belt loops, an awful habit she had that drove her mother crazy. "You are my business," she informed him. "I mean, you are my job. I have to secure your premises and then we need to go over your schedule and how we'll be traveling for the next few weeks."

"So, how long is this going to take? I have my own work to do."

"Oh, you work?" She looked clearly surprised.

Renny tried not to take offense. "Yes, I work. What? Did you think I just sat around living off my father's money all day?"

He looked angry now. His brow had scrunched together, his luscious lips growing into a tight line, and for a moment she felt concerned—for a brief moment. She moved closer to him. "Actually, I thought you spent your days scouring for what new woman you would take to your bed. Isn't that what rich playboys normally do?" Who he took to his bed should not have concerned her, yet with a fierce certainty it did.

Now he was officially turned off. How dared she barge into his house at the crack of dawn insulting him at every turn? *You're not a morning person. Your house isn't secure enough.* And now, *You're just an unemployed rich playboy.* In a minute he was going to lose all the good manners his mother had taught him and say a few things that would likely send little Miss Bodyguard running. "I'll have you know I am very gainfully employed. Outside of Bennett Industries," he said, lifting his head high and poking his chest out just a bit.

She raised a brow. "Really? And what is it that you *gainfully* do outside of Bennett Industries?"

She'd folded her hands over her chest, effectively pushing her plump breasts up a few inches so that he could see the smooth skin slipping into the crevice between them. *Damn.* He was turned on again. He clenched his teeth until he was sure he'd develop lockjaw. He'd never been this physically aware of a woman before. He preferred soft, compliant women. Women that wore ultrasexy, ultrafeminine clothes and treated their hair and makeup as if they were their only commodity.

So why was Sabrina Desdune getting under his skin so easily?

"I am a sculptor and I own an art studio." For a minute he thought he'd had her stumped. She blinked quickly. Then the corners of her mouth upturned and she gave him a wry grin.

"Bored, are we? Or are you simply rebelling against Daddy?"

That was it! That was the last insult he was going to take from her without striking back. He moved to the soft Italian leather couch and sat down slowly, stretching one arm over the back of the chair while the other one rested in his lap. "I could ask you the same thing. Running around playing cops and robbers with your big brother. What's the matter? You couldn't find a man to marry you and knock you up?"

Without another word she scooped up her bag and turned her back to him.

Damn, he hadn't thought she'd pick up and run. A part of him was enjoying their little sparring match. Besides Gabrielle, his youngest sister, he didn't have this type of exchange with anyone else. He jumped up from the chair and was at her side before she could take another step. "I'm sorry, Sabrina. I was out of line. Don't go." He cupped her elbow, turned her to face him.

Her head tilted to the side, a few strands of her ponytail draping over one shoulder. Her eyes sparked and glittered with flecks of gold he hadn't noticed before. Then she smiled. And Renny felt his chest tighten. She was quite simply breathtaking.

"Oh, you were way out of line, but I wasn't leaving." She tossed the words at him as she purposely turned quickly so that her duffel bag hit him square in the stomach. Then she moved to the matching couch he'd just vacated and plopped herself and her stuff down. "But I have a job to do and I plan to do it. We don't have to like each other and we don't have to know each other's personal business. I'll just need your schedule and then I'll show you how to work some of this stuff. Then we should be set."

Renny rubbed his hand over his midsection. The jab she'd tossed him hadn't been the least bit painful, but his ego sure was taking a beating. He was used to women falling over him, batting their eyes and doing everything in their power to attract him. Sabrina acted as if she couldn't care less whether he took his next breath or not.

The bodyguard situation was turning out to be just as bad as he'd thought it would.

Chapter 2

"So, do you want to talk about it?" Lynn set her cup on the table, picked up her napkin and folded it neatly in her lap. Jeremy was in the living room watching his morning cartoons. The sun streamed through the windows on another unusually warm October day. And her baby sister sat across the table from her, looking as if she had the weight of the world on her shoulders.

Bree shrugged. "There's nothing to talk about." For the first few months of her return Lynn had been the quiet one, the one person in her family hadn't asked a million questions about her sudden decision not to reenlist. She loved the military, loved the life of a marine. She'd served in Desert Storm, done a year in Germany, a year in Japan and was happily based in Camp Lejeune, North Carolina, when her glorious life came to a screeching halt.

"You were really happy in the service. You couldn't wait to get away from here once you graduated from high school and you only came back on holidays. So I guess I'm just a little confused as to why you're here now, doing this little security thing with Sam."

Bree looked up at her sister, the oldest of the Desdune siblings. Lynette Desdune Richardson, her mother's pride and joy. Lynn had always done the right things in her mother's eyes. She'd been a cheerleader on the honor roll. She went to college, found a guy, married him and had a baby, exactly as planned. And in the last year that guy had walked out of her life, leaving her with a mortgage and a son to raise alone. Still, Lynn was the epitome of womanhood, according to her mother. She was tall and beautiful, with the coffee-brown skin that all the Desdune siblings shared, light brown eyes, full lips and a great body—yes, Lynn was the woman that Bree had secretly longed to be.

Even though she knew she'd definitely lose her mind if all she had to do from day to day was housework and taking care of kids, the small female percentage of her wanted the love of a good man and wanted that love to spill over into a couple of kids—but that wasn't written in the scroll of her life; she accepted that. Besides, Lynn had a career now. She was an attorney at the Legal Aid Bureau. She said it was entertaining to say the very least, and Bree had to agree that her sister looked really happy. She wished she could feel that way.

"It was simply time to come home, Lynn. Don't make a big deal out of it." Bree bit into her muffin and tried to look away.

Lynn shook her head, sipped from her coffee cup, then smiled. "There's nothing out that window that wasn't out there yesterday or the day before. And you're going to have to tell someone what happened sooner or later. I just thought you'd like to share with your only sister first."

Bree frowned. "Oh, don't give me that only-sister crap, I

had to find out from Mommy that Roger had left. I didn't see that sister bond reaching out then."

"You weren't here, Bree. You were doing your own thing and nobody really wanted to disturb you."

"Except for Mommy, who wanted me to come home, anyway."

Lynn smiled. "Mommy never wanted you to go. It was only because Daddy threatened to tie her up and lock her in her room that she didn't board a plane and bring you home a million times herself."

Bree laughed with her sister. "Yeah, Mommy never did understand."

Lynn reached across the table, took Bree's hand in hers. "But I do, Bree. I know that there is something going on, something that has hurt you deeply. I can see it in your eyes."

Was she really that transparent? It didn't matter, she'd failed. She'd been so headstrong and so determined to make her life mean something, to prove to her family that she was more than just the baby of the troop, that she could hold her own. Yet when it really came down to it, she'd been a childish dreamer and as a result she was sitting here in her sister's kitchen, sleeping in her guest bedroom and working security jobs with her twin brother.

"I remember Mommy saying that there was nothing like growing pains," she began in a hushed tone. "Now I know that she was right. Again. Mommy always seems to be right."

"Not always. Remember she thought that white dress and those white pumps would look fabulous on you for your prom."

Bree smiled at the memory. "Yeah, except I couldn't walk on those stilts and I ended up wobbling right into Bobby Spencer, who was carrying two glasses of punch that immediately landed all over my dress."

The sisters laughed over the memory.

"Growing up is hard. But for the record, I think you've done a wonderful job." Lynn still held her hand.

"Yeah, whatever." Bree snatched her hand away, not willing to go any further. If she continued to sit there, Lynn with her caring eyes and tender touch would have her talking about things that were better off left alone. She stood abruptly and carried her own dishes over to the sink and rinsed off her plate.

Lynn, who was taller than Bree by a couple of inches, came up behind her, wrapped her arms around her sister's shoulders and hugged her tight. "It's okay, you're with family now, with the people that love and cherish you. Whenever you're ready to talk, just know that I'm ready to listen."

For a moment Bree's heart filled and she wanted nothing more than to rid herself of all these hurtful feelings, but she just couldn't. They wouldn't understand why she'd done the things she had and she didn't want to see the disappointment in their eyes. So she took a deep breath and rubbed a hand over her sister's arm. "Thanks, Lynn. But I'm going to be okay. I'm going to find an apartment and make a life for myself here in Greenwich. This is my home and this is where I belong. I should never have forgotten that."

When a yell from the living room pulled Lynn away, Bree stood at the kitchen sink, looking out the window in front of her.

Greenwich was her home but it had never emotionally filled her. She wanted to see the world, to find action and adventure, to live her life on the edge, and joining the marines was the closest she was ever going to get to that. Her first four years had been fantastic; she trained in the Special Weapons Division. Because that was what had intrigued her most and she'd mastered everything, from martial arts to taking apart a semiautomatic weapon and putting it back together again in less than ten minutes. She'd been having the time of her life.

Then all that had changed.

The phone rang, startling Bree out of her reverie. Hastily, she dried her hands on the dish towel and scooped the receiver off the mounting on the wall. "Hello?"

"What are you doing still home? You should be on your way to Bennett's place."

"Good morning, Sam. Yes, I've had breakfast and am about to start my workday. And how are you this glorious fall morning?" Sam's voice had been curt, laced with a bit of tension. But then if she had to spend every evening with Leeza, she'd be stressed, too.

"Sorry, sis. I guess I've just got a lot going on this morning. But really, you should be on your way out. I hear Bennett is an early starter."

Bree cradled the phone between her shoulder and her ear and looked down at her hands. "Yeah, he gets up at the break of dawn, sort of reminds me of my days on the base." She hadn't cut her nails in a few days and was surprised to see the beginnings of growth. She'd never had fingernails before or worn fingernail polish for that matter. She wondered briefly what it would feel like.

"Alex says he's opening an art gallery in a couple of weeks. You should probably check out his building and find out what type of celebration he's planning. It might be a good time for a hit."

Her adrenaline started to pump, slowly. "Really? You think it'll go that far?" She pushed her hands into her pockets, not really sure why she was thinking about nail polish and stuff, anyway.

"I think we need to be prepared for anything. This merger is worth billions of dollars. A lot of people stand to become rich just as a lot of people stand to lose their jobs. It's our duty to make sure our people are protected from whatever goes down."

Bree nodded even though Sam couldn't see her. Her brother had pored over those letters, studying every detail, the homicide detective in him never leaving the job the way Sam had. He said the Force was simply too restrictive. He wanted to really make a difference, so he set out to provide security for the citizens of Greenwich so that they wouldn't end up on the desk of some homicide detective. "Well, I'm ready for whatever goes down."

Sam chuckled. "You're always ready for anything, Rambo."

"That's why you hired me." She smiled. Sam hadn't called her Rambo since she'd been back home. She realized she'd missed the stupid nickname.

"Well, get moving before I fire you. And, Bree?"

"Yeah?"

"Be careful," he warned solemnly.

"Be careful of what, Sam? We live in Greenwich."

Sam sighed. "I know how you feel about our rural little town, but a lot of sick things have happened since you've been away fighting wars. It can get dangerous out there. But that's not what I'm talking about."

"Then what are you talking about?"

"Renny Bennett has a reputation and I don't want you getting caught up in it."

Now she was intrigued. Of course Renny had a playboy reputation. With those looks and that body, why shouldn't he? But that had nothing to do with her; she was so not his type. "Please, I'm the last person he's thinking about in that way."

"Bree, just watch yourself around him. Okay? He's smooth with the ladies and I don't want to have to walk away from this job because he stepped out of line."

"Sammy, you've clearly had too much coffee this morning. There's no chance of that happening so don't even worry about it. Now, I can't get to work if I'm on the phone with you."

"You've been forewarned," Sam said before disconnecting the line.

Bree hung up the phone and ran back upstairs to get her cell phone and keys. She walked past the full-length mirror that hung on the wall near the closet and stopped. She'd put on khakis today, a powder-blue color that her mother had picked out for her. Her shirt still resembled a T-shirt but it had a slight V-neck and was the same pale shade as her pants. On her feet were purely functional Reebok classic tennis shoes and her hair was pulled back in her signature ponytail, except it swung loose today.

She stood to the side, studied her silhouette. She didn't have a bad shape. Sure, she wasn't as curvy as Lynn and didn't look as soft as other women, her own muscled biceps flexing as she moved her hands up and down her body, but she was clearly a woman. She turned to get a frontal view. Her face was free of makeup. She never really liked the stuff, but looking at her plain face now she thought maybe some gloss would be okay. After moving to the dresser and finally finding a tube that wasn't dried out or caked up, she smeared it on her lips, then groaned.

"You're his bodyguard. This is so silly. He would never be interested in someone like you." She swiped the back of her hand over her lips and sighed. "And you don't want him to be, either."

Without glancing in that traitorous mirror again, Bree grabbed her jacket, keys and phone and left the room. She had a job to do.

Renny had a busy schedule today. He needed to go by the foundry to check on a last-minute piece he'd added to the collection. Then he needed to go past the gallery to meet the decorator and go over the details for the opening with his general manager. And he had to squeeze in time to work on

his newest piece. The piece that had been keeping him awake
at night.

It was so clear in his mind and as he'd drawn it, he'd felt
his pulse quicken, his breath hitch. He'd mounted the
armature and had just started to apply the clay earlier this
morning. He wasn't sure if this piece would ever see the light
of day. Still, he was compelled to finish it, to have the picture
of her etched forever in bronze.

She'd been with him for the past two days. From sunup
until sundown, she'd been at his condo hooking up one gizmo
after the next. He found her to be very thorough in her duties.
She checked and double-checked everything the moment she
got there and just before she left. He felt like he was on
display in his own home. She had cameras and motion sensors
outside his door, along the windows, and bugs in his phone.
It was as if he didn't have any privacy left at all. Not that it
was an issue since he never brought women to his home,
anyway. It was simply too personal and the moment they
were in his house, to their mind's thinking, they were in his
heart and in his pocket, neither of which he was allowing.

He loved women, but he didn't want a permanent one. As
in love as his parents were, Renny was in no hurry to have
those emotional entanglements. It just wasn't for him. He was
too focused on himself, his work and his gallery. He'd be no
good to a woman. His father had said as much the day he told
him refusing to work for Bennett Industries meant he didn't
have a care for his future stability. To Marvin Bennett, being
an artist was not stable, it was stupid.

Renny accepted his father's view, but didn't let it sway his
decision. He wasn't sure he'd ever be able to offer a woman
the fame and fortune that went along with the Bennett name—
because Marvin swore he wouldn't leave Renny one piece of
the company as long as he was playing around with clay and
drawing. Renny had a handsome trust fund set up for him by

his grandfather on his mother's side, so he really wasn't worried about being the proverbial starving artist, but women expected more from a Bennett. They expected to have it all once they landed him and he would ultimately have to disappoint them.

So instead, he dated, had sex and left soon after. There were no mornings waking up beside Renny Bennett, and if any woman dared to say she had, she was surely lying. A hotel or her place was the destination of choice, so he could get up and leave when it suited him. None of them even had his home number, and his cell number was changed periodically because he especially hated the ones that couldn't let go. His brothers called him ruthless as a businessman when it came to women; he called it a necessity to his own survival and didn't have any plans of changing his routine.

His bodyguard wasn't here yet this morning, but then he was leaving a little earlier than she normally arrived. It didn't matter; she had a key to his place, so if she wanted to go in and check on her gadgets she could. He really didn't understand why he needed a bodyguard in the first place, and wondered what this little woman could actually do to protect him, anyway. She had loads of energy, though. She moved from the time she came in until the time she left. She drank her water, but he never saw her eat much. Yesterday, he had convinced her to have a slice of pizza, but she hadn't sat down at the table to consume it. Instead she'd held it in one hand while she pored over maps of the city, saying they needed to have safe routes mapped out in case of an emergency. He'd gone back into his studio then. All her moving about was making him tired. He was as much of a workaholic as the next guy, but his job was more slow, more graceful, while hers seemed to be adrenaline driven, and she was really into it.

His mind had wandered out into the living room as he wondered what she was doing. Had she had enough to eat? When was she going to go to the bathroom after she'd consumed almost a half gallon of water in three hours? And was she biting on her bottom lip like she did when she was concentrating?

As he stepped through the door he shook his head. He shouldn't even have thought about her lips or the fact that he'd remembered such an inconsequential detail about her like that. He checked the locks the way she told him and even smiled up at the camera just above the entryway. He had his bag on his shoulder as he took the stairs down to his car. Pulling his keys from his back pocket, he hit the button disengaging the alarm and was just about to open his car door when he felt a jab in his back.

He turned around quickly and was faced with her wrath.

"Where the hell do you think you're going? You didn't say you were going out today. And you shouldn't be out here by yourself. You didn't even look around or check your surroundings. You didn't see or hear me come up behind you, did you?"

She was like a madwoman, spouting off questions, not waiting for answers. Her sienna eyes sparkling with anger, her chest heaving. Yeah, he found his eyes resting on her chest quite frequently in the past couple of days. He'd never considered himself a breast man before, but admitted that his fingers tingled each time he looked at the perfect roundness of hers.

"Good morning, Sabrina." He smiled down at her and she clamped her lips closed so tightly he thought she would break a tooth. She opened her mouth to speak again, but closed it just as quickly before taking a deep, steadying breath. She was even more beautiful when she was angry.

Bree instantly felt guilty. Hadn't Sam just done the same thing to her less than an hour ago? It was a good morning and she should have said that first, but he hadn't heard her come up behind him and she could have been a hit man with a gun and he wouldn't have had any time to protect himself and… he'd smiled at her. That smile that left her breathless. "Good morning, Renny."

"That's so much better." He reached for the handle and opened his door.

Bree stepped back to avoid being hit. "You still didn't tell me where you were going, and you weren't watching your back."

Renny tossed his bag into the backseat and climbed inside. "Isn't that what you get paid to do?"

Oh, no, he wasn't popping an attitude now. "Yes, it is, and that's precisely why I'm angry with you now. You should have told me last night before I left that you'd be going out this morning and I would have been here earlier. It's clear you don't have a care for your own safety, which makes my job even harder." *That and the fact that you are one mouthwatering piece of eye candy.*

"We've already established the fact that I don't buy into this whole threat and need for a bodyguard, and I wasn't aware that I had to tell you my every move."

"Well, you do. So you might as well start now." She folded her arms over her chest and waited.

Renny expelled a deep breath. She sure was a feisty little thing. He actually enjoyed getting her all riled up. Her eyes looked wild, filled with untamed passion that he'd love to tap into. He sat back in his seat, his hands on the steering wheel, because he wanted to reach out and touch her more than anything else. "I have a couple of errands to run. Is that okay with you?"

He really was infuriating. But Sam had warned her that in cases like this there were always people who didn't see the need for a personal guard—especially men. "Fine. I'll follow you."

She turned to walk away and Renny felt a sudden loss that he couldn't quite explain. He pushed on his horn. She was just at the front of his car, so the loud sound startled her and she jumped a bit. He grinned and shrugged, poking his head out of the window. "Sorry."

"Yeah, right," she snapped.

"Hey, if you're supposed to be guarding my body shouldn't you be a little closer to it?" he shouted.

Bree almost collapsed right there. How had he known she'd just been thinking about being up close and personal with his body? Then it dawned on her he didn't know, he was simply teasing her about her job again. "I'll be right behind you in my truck."

"That's not acceptable. I happen to know that my brother is paying you a pretty penny and I want him to get his money's worth. Hop in." He could see her trying to think of a reason to decline and wondered for a moment if Miss Bodyguard was feeling the heat between them as he was. "C'mon, I'm going to be late."

She didn't have a choice. It was her job and he had a point; to effectively protect him she did need to stay close. Squaring her shoulders, she took those first steps toward the passenger side door and then climbed in beside him. This was a great car, a Porsche, candy-apple-red with all the niceties that came with it—even the devilishly handsome driver. Clasping her seat belt, Bree laid her head back on the headrest and tried to remind herself that this was work, he was Renny Bennett and she was Sabrina Desdune, ex-marine, lifetime tomboy. That was it, plain and simple.

"We're here," Renny announced as he pulled into a parking lot.

Bree looked around. It looked like a deserted building from where she was sitting, so she couldn't help but ask, "Where is here?"

Renny reached over, undid her seat belt and grabbed his bag from the back. "It's a foundry." He hopped out before she could ask another question and came around to the other side of the car just as she was swinging the door open. He reached for her hand and she stared at it as if it were a foreign object.

"What are you doing?"

Renny smiled, reached in and grabbed her hand, pulling her resistant body out of the car. "You sure do keep your guard up. I'm helping you out of the car. That's what a man is supposed to do."

He closed the door behind her and dropped her hand. She was glad of that because the heat that soared up her arm at his touch was disconcerting to say the least. "Being alert is part of my training," she said to his now-retreating back.

Renny looked over his shoulder to see her following him. "You actually trained to become a bodyguard?"

Was that humor she heard in his voice? She frowned. "No. I actually trained to become a marine."

Renny stopped abruptly. Bree had been looking at her surroundings and didn't realize he wasn't moving anymore until she collided with him and that alluring chest again. He grabbed her shoulders.

"Sorry. I keep doing that," she mumbled, then tried to move around him, but he wouldn't let her go.

"You're a marine?"

He looked absolutely flabbergasted. It was kind of funny, this look men got when they were confronted with a female soldier, especially a marine. There were men who hadn't made it through the Marine Corps, so a woman was definitely a shock. Bree kind of liked the effect. "For sixteen years."

She was so tiny he would never have imagined her climbing over walls and dodging bullets, yet the thought was a definite turn-on. He was quickly realizing that there was a lot about his bodyguard that turned him on.

"Do you have a problem with that?" He was staring at her and it made her uncomfortable. His dark eyes raked over her body as if he were searching for something...and amazingly enough had found it. She battled with whether she liked it or not. Then he smiled and she wanted to melt into his arms.

"No problem at all. I guess I'm really protected now." He should stop touching her. She was steady now; there was no need to have his hands on her. Except the need deep inside him that wanted to get closer. The light blue outfit she wore today was refreshing from her normal denim and white attire. It gave her a softer look that he really liked. A slight breeze mussed her hair, the back of the ponytail swayed gently.

"Are we going into this foundry or what?" She managed to move away from his touch this time and walked around him. Her stomach was doing somersaults and they were standing out in the open where he was a clear shot.

Renny dropped his arms to his side and led her into the building. He was tall and didn't walk slowly. Usually he'd have to slow down to almost baby steps when walking with a woman, but Sabrina, even with her shorter legs, kept up with him without a problem. She didn't carry a purse, just a small pouch at her waist. She didn't wear long flourishing earrings, just simple studs. Her watch was the only jewelry that adorned her arms, and today he couldn't even see her ankle bracelet. She looked around, taking in everything and seemingly recording it for future use.

"You ever been to a foundry before?"

"No."

"Then let me give you the grand tour," a familiar male voice interrupted. This was Walt. He worked on all of Renny's projects. In fact, Renny didn't trust anyone else with his pieces.

Renny extended his hand, and Walt clasped it quickly and with a generous smile. "Hey, Walt. What's going on?"

"Nothing much. I've got this dude working me like crazy, that's all." Walt was a tall man, wire thin, with a long face and a big, warm smile. "I see you've brought me a little bit of sunshine this morning. You tryin' to bribe me?" Walt was looking at Sabrina.

Renny didn't miss the implications in Walt's words, nor did he miss the salacious look he was giving Sabrina. What was even harder to miss was the swirling heat in the pit of his stomach—something he wasn't even going to qualify as jealousy. "This is a friend of the family, Sabrina Desdune. She's helping out with the opening, so I thought I'd let her get a look at how the background work is done. Sabrina, this is Walter Hemler, foundry worker extraordinaire."

Bree gave the man a cordial smile and extended her hand. He eagerly took it between both his hands and rubbed her skin gently. "It's a pleasure to meet you, Mr. Hemler."

"Oh, no, you don't." Walt shook his head. "You'll call me Walt just like everybody else. You sure are a pretty little thing."

Bree blushed at his words. Why was it that older men always flirted with younger women, embarrassing them both immensely? "Thank you, Walt. I'm a bit curious. Do you think you can explain all this to me?" She looked around them again, ignoring the heated glare she was receiving from Renny.

"Sure thing, little missy. You just follow me and I'll answer all your questions."

Walt hooked Bree's arm in his and began walking. Each of them seemed to forget Renny was even standing there.

With his lips drawn tightly Renny followed them, not liking the exclusion one bit. He was supposed to be showing her around. It didn't really matter. He was here to check on his pieces; showing Sabrina around would only distract him. Sort of like the sway of her hips was doing right now.

"We mostly do artwork here. You know, sculptures and statues. Over there's the oven. That's where we melt the metal and fire the castings. It's hot as Satan's den over there, so I won't take you too close." Walt was busily talking and guiding Sabrina.

Bree looked around, watching as workers poured a glistening liquid into small molds and large molds, her inquisitive mind working overtime. "So, do you just come up with the ideas and pour the metal inside and then you have a statue?"

"Naw, all this starts with the artist. He dreams up the idea and then brings us a smaller model. We take it from there."

"This is really interesting. I never gave much thought to how these things were actually created."

"It's a daunting process," Renny spoke up from his spot behind them. When she turned her eyes to him he felt like sitting her down and answering any question she asked. She looked suddenly vulnerable and very childlike in this big warehouse with all this heavy machinery. A marine, no, you would never guess it of this petite woman. Not until you looked deep into her eyes. They were such expression-filled eyes that Renny found himself getting lost in them once again. She was passionate, with a strength and determination to rival any man's; he could see that clearly. An artist had an eye for detail, and ever since meeting Sabrina he'd stored away loads of details about her.

"Really?" She'd known he was close, had felt his dominating presence behind her as if he were her entire world. There was an unknown element about Renny Bennett, something she assumed other people didn't see often when they looked at him. "How do you get your inspiration?"

He couldn't tell her his latest source of inspiration and didn't quite know how to explain his pieces, so he thought an example would suit this conversation better. "Walt can show you a couple of my finished pieces and then I'll let you answer that yourself."

"Sure. Right this way. He's real protective of his stuff, so I keep it in a locked room until it's time to move it."

They walked through the center of the factory, up a few stairs and across a catwalk. Renny grabbed her elbow to keep her steady. Bree frowned but didn't say anything. She'd walked on a catwalk before; hell, she'd jumped out of a plane before, so this was a piece of cake, but she kept that to herself. Renny seemed to be real big on this gentleman thing, so she'd leave it alone, for now.

Walt used a key to gain entrance into the room and flicked on a light before inviting them in. Renny still held on to her arm even though they'd left the catwalk about twenty steps ago. White sheets covered everything in the room except the steel shelves. When it seemed no one was in a hurry to remove them, Bree took a step and pulled one away herself.

She gasped, her hand coming to her throat for an instant. Then she ran her fingers lightly over the figure. It was a woman. A naked woman, lying on a couch, one leg thrown over the back while the other dangled over the edge. One arm was draped over her head while the other extended down between her legs. Her features weren't clear, yet the excitement, the growing passion, was unmistakable.

Her skin tingled as she continued to study the sculpture. It was intricate in its design, right down to the sharp protrusion of the woman's nipples. Renny was standing right next to her now, close enough that she could hear his breathing. "What do you think?" he almost whispered.

She licked her lips. "It's, ah…very interesting."

Renny sighed. "You think it's pornographic, don't you? You can tell me the truth." That's what his father thought, that he was spending all his time making dirty sculptures so horny nutcases could pay a fortune for them.

Bree heard the disappointment in his voice and turned to face him. His hands were thrust into his pockets, his jaw clenched as he looked away from her. She touched his arm gently, knowing exactly what it felt like when someone didn't understand your life's work. "I think it's extremely passionate. It's not pornographic, more like sensually tasteful, I'd say."

Overhead a speaker blared and Walt heard himself being paged. "I'd better see what's going on out there. You two take your time. I'll be right back."

They were alone in the room when Renny finally let himself look at her. She'd touched him of her own accord, but the moment his eyes rested on hers she'd pulled away. She thought his work was passionate. "Do you want to see the rest of them?"

"I'd love to." Bree was careful to keep her eyes averted from his. This room was really small, and very hot since she'd unveiled the first sculpture.

"I call the collection Breathless Passion," he told her as he went about the task of removing the other covers.

Breathless was exactly what his sculptures made Bree feel. Each one, twelve in all, were of men and women in various stages of sexual fulfillment—together and separately. She touched them all, hadn't been able to resist. They were so real, so alluring. Renny Bennett must be some kind of lover to create like this.

One in particular drew her closer, both her hands moving over the cool, smooth surface. The woman stood with her back facing the man, one foot lifted to rest on an ottoman, one hand fingering her breast while the other reached up to wrap behind her lover's neck, pulling his head closer to hers. The man was behind her, buried deep inside her womb, his hands grasping her hips as he bent her slightly forward.

Bree's heart took on record speed as she examined the piece. For a moment she felt as if she were in the room with that couple. She could smell the distinct aroma of sex and sweat, could feel the tension rising until it clogged her throat. The place between her legs began to throb, her breasts stiffening with the erotic reverie. Then she felt it, his hands on her waist, his thumbs at the base of her back, his fingers splayed over her pelvic bone. He pulled her back to him until his hardness rested against her like a silent, but persistent, offering. She inhaled.

"It leaves you breathless, doesn't it?" Renny asked with a thickness in his voice he hadn't intended. Usually his work excited him, not to the point of masturbation or driving him to go out and find the nearest woman to sleep with, but excited him with a feeling of accomplishment. His dedication paid off. But watching Sabrina enjoy his creations, watching her touch the very bodies his fingers had molded did something to him. He envisioned her hands on him as clearly as if she'd turned and undressed him herself. His skin had reacted to each of her caresses as if they were meant only for him. And he wanted her.

Breathless was an understatement to Bree. She remembered inhaling, but for the life of her she couldn't release that breath. His hands were still and they weren't on any real prohibited part of her body, yet they sent sparks of heat through her so intense she'd closed her eyes to keep from sighing. If they were naked and she lifted her own leg he could slip inside her—they'd be just like this sculpture and she'd have the same look of supreme satisfaction on her face that this woman had.

The doorknob turned with an unmistakable click and Bree rushed away from Renny. The moment Walt entered the room she snatched her hands away from the sculpture and tried to gather her wits.

"Just a minor problem I had to deal with. So, little missy, how do you like my boy's work?"

Renny jammed his hands into his pockets to conceal his burgeoning growth from his longtime friend. He was sort of glad that Walt had picked that moment to return. If not, he wasn't sure what he was going to do to Sabrina next. She was an enigma. An ex-marine turned bodyguard. A wisp of a woman with the allure of a porn star. An ordinary female with more beauty than a supermodel. What had his brother gotten him into?

"The pieces are wonderful," she said in a slow measured tone. "I would venture to say that very creative hands brought them to life. The public is going to love them." She was looking at Walt as she spoke, but her words were meant for Renny. She'd sensed his insecurity about his work the moment they'd stepped into this room, and wondered where it stemmed from. Most artists, she assumed, were very confident about their creations, almost to the point of being arrogant. But Renny seemed a little leery, as if he were always waiting for approval—for someone to say he'd done a good job.

He was covering the pieces now, his back to her, and she felt a little deflated. He hadn't even acknowledged her compliment. Well, it'd be a cold day in hell before the magnificent playboy received another one from her. She couldn't believe she'd allowed herself the briefest second of romanticizing the man through his work. He was just what she thought he was, a manipulative womanizer. He'd touched her with such softness, such familiarity that she'd, for a moment, believed they'd had some sort of connection. That was absurd. He was Renny Bennett and she was his bodyguard. He was not attracted to her and she was definitely not attracted to him!

Chapter 3

Renny was quiet in the car, his body still adjusting to its reaction to Sabrina and his sculptures. If he let his mind wander he'd feel her soft strokes against his skin and the heat would ultimately begin to rise again. So he tried to focus. He turned on the radio. Something by Usher was playing and to his dismay Sabrina started to sing. The lyrics were a bit sexual and bam…his thoughts again turned lusty.

He rolled down his window, let some of the breeze into the interior of the car. He was losing his mind. He was not supposed to be attracted to her. You've got to be kidding. Who wouldn't be attracted to her? *But I'm no good for her. She already thinks I'm some rich playboy. She probably wants picket fences and kids in the yard.*

He stole a glance at her. She had her hands raised as high above her head as they could get in the confines of the car and was snapping her fingers, gyrating the top half of her body to the rhythm of the music. *Then again…maybe she didn't.*

Either way, she definitely didn't want a one-night stand or even an intense physical affair that would ultimately end badly. She deserved more than that. Besides, Rico would never forgive him if he mixed business with pleasure and he'd hired Desdune Security to do business with the Bennetts. Touching her was definitely out of the question. But he'd already touched her, albeit briefly. He'd already felt her soft curves against him and so help him he desperately wanted to feel them again.

"What?" she asked when she caught him staring at her. "You don't like this song?"

He shrugged. "It's okay. I'm just not a big Usher fan." But he was definitely a fan of the way the man's music had her body moving. This little woman continued to wreak all kinds of havoc on his libido.

"Then let's find something to loosen you up a little. I'm tired of you looking all grim over there." Bree leaned forward and pushed the buttons that roamed the radio stations.

"Ooh, I love this one." She swayed slowly from side to side as the smooth voices of Boyz II Men vibrated through the speakers.

Oh, hell, no! Renny's mind screamed. Was it pure coincidence or pure torture that they were singing "I'll Make Love To You" at the same time he was fighting a tremendous hard-on.

Renny gripped the steering wheel even tighter, praying his pants were baggy enough not to give away his state of mind.

"I know you like this one. All men like this one." Bree gave him a brief smile. She touched his arm and sang along with the four men of the group. Renny's muscle tensed beneath her hand and she frowned. "Are you always this happy?"

He clenched his teeth so tight his head started to hurt. "I didn't say I didn't like the song. I've just got a lot on my mind." About one hundred and twenty pounds of gorgeous female, come to think of it.

"Is it the letters? Are you worried about whoever is stalking your family?" Bree grew serious, reaching over to turn the radio down. She was being insensitive. His family was dealing with a lot right now, the merger and these threats. It had to be hard on him since he and his brothers seemed so close.

No, it wasn't that, because he thought that was some big promo scheme thought up by the execs at Coastal Technologies, but he couldn't tell her the real reason. "That and the opening."

"Oh, your gallery? Is that where we're going now?"

"Yes. I need to talk with the decorator and make sure things are moving along smoothly."

Bree sat back and looked out the window. It was early afternoon. People lined the streets either heading for their lunch breaks or to run some mundane errand; that's all they did around here. "So, what made you get into art? I mean, did you need some type of hobby?"

He cut his eyes at her once, then paid attention to the right turn he was making. Her flippant question had sounded a lot like his father. And here he'd thought she really got his work. "It's not a hobby. At least not for me. I've always been good with my hands."

Bree shifted uncomfortably at his remark. "Oh? Really?"

He knew she was thinking of his comment in the wrong context and most likely with the wrong female, but he ignored the thought. "As a kid I used to spend hours drawing. I went through so many sketchbooks and pencils that my father threatened to cut down all the trees in our backyard to keep me in supply. He didn't mind my drawing so much back then." It was only when he'd grown up that Marvin said it was time to put that task to rest.

"How does he feel about your career choice now? I mean, since you obviously don't care for the family business."

"It's not that I don't care for the business. I get all the stock reports for Bennett Industries. I know all of our products and all of our customers. I've read and reread this merger file a billion times. It's my family and my family business, so naturally it means something to me." He took a deep breath. "Sculpting just means more."

"I know what you mean," she said softly.

"You do?" He pulled into the parking lot behind the newly renovated building. "Do you have a big family?"

"I guess you could say that. There's Sam and me, we're the youngest of the bunch. Then there's Lynn and Cole, Mom and Dad. My parents are from Louisiana. They have a chain of Creole restaurants along the coast called Lucien's."

Renny switched the engine off and sat back in his seat. "I've heard of them. Actually, I've been to the one in New York. They have great food. So why aren't you in the restaurant business?"

"While I love to cook, slaving behind a hot stove for a bunch of patrons was never my idea of the perfect career."

Because she looked so vulnerable at this moment, and the hollow of her neck seemed to glisten in the sunlight that streamed through the window, Renny reached over and traced a finger over the bare skin.

Bree jumped. "Look, Bennett, I wasn't going to say anything about this touching habit of yours, but now I don't have a choice."

Renny grinned. Did he have a touching habit where she was concerned?

"Just because we're going to be working in close proximity doesn't give you free privileges. I'm not one of the women you trifle with—not that I needed to remind you of that—but regardless, I won't be fondled by you, either."

Renny blinked, wondering what she'd meant by not needing to remind him that she wasn't like other women. Of course she didn't need to remind him, he knew very well how different she was. And that, ultimately, was the problem.

But it was his problem and he'd deal with it. "Relax, Sabrina. Since the window was open some of that pollen stuff blew into the car. I was simply wiping it off of you. I have no intention of fondling you while you're working."

"Good." Bree unlocked her seat belt. "Just so we're clear on things."

Renny released his seat belt, as well. "We're perfectly clear. You're the bodyguard—"

"And you're the client in need of protection. That's all."

Their eyes locked and in that moment their circumstances didn't matter. He looked as if he wanted to say something else.

Her eyes seemed to call him, to welcome him inside her world; then she broke the contact and stepped out of the car.

Everything about the Silhouette Gallery screamed Lorenzo Bennett's name. From the high ceilings to the pure white walls and the smoky-gray moldings, it was chic and understated, masculine and smooth, artistic and unique.

The outside of the building was deceiving, sturdy brick with no flare and no excitement. Just above the swinging glass doors the simple word *Silhouette* was scrawled in bold black script letters. The moment she entered, the clean lines and sharp angles greeted her. A pewter winding staircase shocked her as she found herself traveling to what should have been the basement, but was actually the main showroom.

Stone-gray marble floors and recessed lighting flanked her as she walked through absorbing either canvases on the walls or statues on podiums. It was class personified and Bree was simply amazed.

Renny walked beside her, afraid to ask what was going through that mind of hers. She always seemed to surprise him, so he decided he'd let her comment on her own.

"This is extraordinary, Renny. Did you do all this by yourself?" Bree finally said.

"I'd like to think I had a hand in it, as well." Clicking heels and a sultry female voice interrupted the twosome.

Bree turned in the direction of the sound and nearly swallowed her tongue as she was faced with the most gorgeous female creature she'd ever seen. She had to be at least five feet eleven inches to six feet tall, limbs as fluid as liquid draped in a red crepe slip dress that accentuated her honey-toned skin. Bold, blond tresses cascaded past her shoulders while her flawless makeup let you know she was serious about her appearance. Her gaze briefly swept past Bree before resting comfortably on Renny.

"You're late," she said as her long arms twined around his neck, pulling him close for a hug.

Renny reciprocated. "I got caught up at the foundry. Is everything going okay?"

The hug was complete, but her arm stayed around his neck in a proprietary fashion that wasn't totally lost on Bree. She took a step away from Renny to assure this platinum bombshell that she wasn't stepping into her territory.

"Everything is just fabulous now that you're here." One long red-nailed finger stroked his chin as she spoke only to him.

Bree shifted from one foot to the other before clearing her throat. She wasn't drop-dead gorgeous, but she wasn't about to be ignored, either. He'd have plenty of time to cozy up to this sex goddess when she was off duty, but until then she would give her a modicum of respect.

Renny had already released his hold on Yolanda, but since she hadn't done the same he was sort of trapped in her embrace. He hadn't forgotten that Sabrina was standing there, nor had he missed the implications this little display undoubtedly sent to her. "Sabrina, this is Yolanda Tate, my general manager. Yolanda, this is Sabrina, a friend of the family."

Again he so effortlessly lied. Bree was careful to take note of that fact. She extended her hand and pasted a smile on her face. "It's nice to meet you, Ms. Tate. The place is wonderful. You've done a good job."

Yolanda regarded the outstretched hand a moment, then turned to Renny. "Are you babysitting?"

Resisting the urge to put this Amazon in a Chinese headlock, Bree lifted a brow and then pulled her hand back. "It's called a greeting. I say 'nice to meet you' and you say 'same here' or something to that effect. The handshake is optional, but I assure you I'm not contagious." She shrugged. "Just a few things I'd think a general manager would know."

Renny grinned. Clearly her size was an underestimation of any opponent. He'd be sure to take that into consideration at all times. Thankfully though, Yolanda took the bait and released him from her grasp.

"Your candor isn't amusing. Still, if you're a friend of the Bennetts I assume you know when and where to use it. Will you be visiting long?"

Bree slipped her hands into her pockets; that was the only way she could assure herself that she wouldn't take a swing at the blond beauty. "I'm sure you and I will be seeing a lot of each other since I'll be here for quite some time."

As exciting as a catfight seemed to younger men, Renny was not about to let one break out in the middle of his gallery. "I've been showing Sabrina around today. We stopped at the foundry and now we're going to look around here. She has a wonderful eye for detail and I thought I'd put it to good use."

Bree looked at him as he talked about her. Something in the way his eyes roamed freely over her body made her fidget. She clearly paled in comparison to Yolanda, so his look must be intended to agitate, not excite her.

"*She* has an eye for detail?" Yolanda looked her up and down, clearly not impressed.

"She has an exceptional eye," Renny said, still staring at Sabrina. He was talking about the intense pools of brown, how they swirled and tantalized him, and of course how she paid attention to her security detail. "We'll just take the tour and I'll speak with you before I leave." He took Sabrina's hand and led her away from Yolanda, not waiting for the woman's reply.

"Your Amazon manager is going to need some etiquette classes before the opening or you're never going to sell a thing," she commented when they were only a few steps away from Yolanda.

Renny laughed. "She's usually not so…blunt." He led them around a sharp corner.

"Is that the best you could do? I was thinking more along the lines of shallow, rude…"

Renny squeezed her hand gently. "I get the picture. But she looks good and the men will come in just to see her alone."

"Is that why she was scarcely dressed and draped all over you?" She sounded jealous. She could hear the cold tint of her voice and didn't like it one bit. "I mean, if she hangs on to you like that, they'll assume she's taken and go on about their business elsewhere." Goodness, was it hot in here, too?

His thumb played over her skin as he listened to her. She sounded jealous, but then that was impossible, or was it? He decided to find out if his bodyguard was indeed feeling the same attraction he was. "Do I detect a note of jealousy?"

She tugged on her hand, but he didn't let go. "You don't detect anything. I'm just making a point to rebut your reasons for having her around. At any rate, you're touching me again."

She was definitely shaken. He couldn't help but grin. If she was shaken, then she was affected, if she was affected, then the attraction wasn't entirely one-sided. He lifted her hand to his lips, placed a whisper-soft kiss over her knuckles and watched her eyes darken. There it was as plain as the day, desire. Dark as sin and as alluring as fool's gold. This was exactly what he wanted his art to bring to the surface. The liberation and release of pent-up desire in everyone.

"Let me go," she said softly and without any conviction. What was it about him that appealed to her? She knew and yet she couldn't quite put her finger on it. Sure, he was fine and he seemed intelligent enough, but there was something else—something inside him that called to her.

"Is that what you really want, Sabrina?"

Her name rolled off his tongue like a rush of warm water and she almost drowned in its effect. He kissed her knuckles again, this time letting his warm lips linger, his thin mustache prickling her sensitive skin. He was smooth. That was his reputation, and as of this morning she'd been forewarned. With a forceful tug she retrieved her hand and glared at him. "I always say what I mean, Bennett. Don't forget that."

And there it was, the door had been closed and from the looks of it, locked securely. She was the bodyguard again, the professional. But for the briefest moment, just like back in that room at the foundry, she'd been something else. She'd been the woman, the enigma that plagued him.

She hadn't a clue how she'd let Renny talk her into dinner. Maybe it was his plea that he needed to eat and she was his bodyguard so she had to follow him wherever he went. She'd rolled her eyes and clasped her seat belt without another word to him. They'd driven in silence and were now seated in a booth near the back of Thataway Café, one of Greenwich's trendy restaurants.

"Are you hungry?" he asked while he perused the menu.

"No."

He peeped at her above his menu and took note of the folded arms and bored expression. She was angry with him.

Funny how he'd only known her three days and her moods were already as transparent to him as if they'd known each other forever. What was even funnier was the way her anger affected him. He didn't like it, to put it simply. He didn't like when she wasn't smiling, when her eyes were brewing instead of smoldering or sparkling. He didn't like when she folded her arms, effectively closing him out of her world.

"You haven't eaten all day, Sabrina. How about a hamburger?"

"I said I'm not hungry."

He expelled a deep breath. "How do you propose to protect anybody when you're weak from malnourishment?"

She cut her eyes at him, released her arms and placed her palms flat on the table. "I'm getting sick of you using my position to your advantage."

He feigned innocence. "Would I do something like that?" He lifted his menu to hide his smirk. Sabrina was very serious about her job. The mere mention of her not being able to do it to the best of her ability had her agreeing to almost anything. He'd have to remember that in the future. "I'm going to have a bacon cheeseburger with everything on it, French fries and whatever you have on tap," Renny told the waiter who'd mysteriously appeared.

Bree picked up her menu and scanned the contents. When she looked up the waiter was standing in front of her, pen poised and waiting for her order. "I'll have a bacon cheeseburger with mustard only, French fries and a glass of water. And the gentleman doesn't want onions on his burger."

The waiter looked at Renny in question and Renny looked at Bree in the same way.

"I'm not smelling onion breath for the rest of the night. How do you expect me to protect you if I can't stand being near you?" she said smugly.

It was back, that sparkle in her eyes he was quickly becoming used to. "No onions, please."

They talked amicably after that, in which time Bree learned more about the infamous Lorenzo Bennett. He wasn't shallow like his reputation painted him. Instead he was very passionate about his work and about his family. She watched him as he spoke of his younger sisters and their future, of his brothers and their childhood escapades, of his parents and how much they loved each other. As she ate, she found herself wishing for just a moment that he was her man. She could tell he'd love her and cherish her, he was just that way. Too bad she wasn't looking for a man right now. If she'd met him two years ago, maybe…no, she would still be Sabrina the tomboy and he'd still be the gorgeous millionaire with his pick of the world's most beautiful women.

"Sabrina?"

He touched her hand as he said her name and she focused on his mouth.

"Are you okay?"

"Uh, yeah. I'm fine. What were you saying?"

"I was asking about your life as a soldier. How was it for you personally? Did you date?"

She stuck a fry into her mouth to give herself a moment to think about the question. "We had personal time to do with as we pleased, if that's what you mean."

He'd finished his food and was actually enjoying watching her eat. She didn't pick like the other women he'd dated. She hadn't ordered a salad and then acted as if those bits of leaves and vegetables had filled her up. No, she tackled that burger with as much enthusiasm as she tackled everything else she did. "I meant were you seeing anyone special?"

She'd figured as much. "Then why didn't you just say that?"

"I just did."

"Why do you want to know?"

"I'm curious."

She picked up her napkin, wiped her mouth and sat back against the chair. "It's really none of your business."

"Look, we're two adults sharing a meal. We're going to be working together until this merger is wrapped up. We might as well have some type of friendship between us." She wasn't budging. "Okay, if you answer me, then you can ask me a really personal question in return. Deal?"

She drummed her blunt fingernails on the table. "Fine. Yes, I dated. And once I had a serious relationship."

He'd thought as much. "Was he a soldier, too?"

"Uh-uh, I answered you. Now it's my turn."

He nodded in compliance. He was enjoying his time with her, more so than he'd enjoyed an evening with a woman in a long time. "Go ahead."

"Why do you use women?"

"Who told you I use women?"

She shook her head. "You can't answer a question with a question."

"Okay. I don't use women. At least I don't think I do. I see a woman I like, I ask her out. We may or may not sleep together and then it's done. That doesn't sound like using to me."

"Why do you sleep with them if you don't want a relationship with them?"

That was two questions, but he was going to answer her; it would indebt her to him in the future. Sabrina was nothing if not honorable. "I don't sleep with every woman I go out with. And I make my limitations perfectly clear from the get-go. It's their choice whether to proceed or not."

"How long do you plan on sleeping with women and dumping them?" She'd leaned forward now, her arms folded on the table in front of her.

"Until I find the right one." He didn't know why he said it. He'd already decided that there was no right one for him, that a committed relationship was simply not in the cards of his life. Yet the answer had come so quickly, so honestly that he thought there might be some semblance of truth to it.

That wasn't the answer she expected. She blinked and tried to retrain her thoughts.

His cell phone rang, effectively ending the conversation. She sat back against the chair piecing together all that she'd just learned. Renny Bennett was one hell of a man and she suspected she was being treated to something people outside his family rarely saw—the real him.

"I'll be right there," she heard him say before disconnecting his phone and putting it back into his pocket. He pulled out some bills and stood.

"Adriana is stranded. I have to go and get her. I'll call you a cab."

Bree stood, looked at her watch. "No, you won't. As long as you're out, I'm on duty. I'm going with you."

Renny started to argue, then thought better of it. She would remind him it was her job, and he didn't really feel like spoiling the camaraderie they'd just forged. "Let's go. It's getting dark and I don't like the idea of her stranded on some side road by herself."

They trudged out of the restaurant and toward his car.

"Why is she by herself? Gary is supposed to be guarding her," Bree said as she climbed into his car.

"I'm not sure. She just said she was stranded and told me where to meet her."

They drove through the city until they hit the rural roads. Streetlights were a good distance apart and like Renny said, it was getting dark. "Why would she be out here? Does she know people out this way?" They were miles away from the city and even farther away from the Bennett estate where Adriana lived. Adriana was a grown woman, so she could go about as she pleased, but Bree sensed something wasn't right.

She kept looking out the windows memorizing her surroundings even as she mentally went down her checklist. Her
gun was holstered at her ankle, a knife was in her pack along
with her cell phone and mace. Gary should have called if they
needed a ride. Why hadn't he called? She was about to reach
into her pack for her phone when Renny's voice stopped her.

"There she is." He swerved off the road, pulling up behind
the stalled vehicle.

Before Bree could stop him he'd jumped out of the car and
was heading toward the driver's side. Bree reached down, retrieved her gun and stepped out of the car, as well. She
watched as Renny bent over, looked into the driver's side
window, then walked around to the passenger door.

Her gun down by her side, Bree came up on the back of the
car, passed the driver's side while peeking in herself, then began
to make her way around the front of the car. She heard it before
she saw it, a speeding vehicle. When she turned, there were no
headlights, but she could see the phantom outline. Renny was
just standing there, looking into the passenger-side window.

"There's nobody in there. Where is she?" He stood, his
body halfway in the street as the car got closer. He turned the
moment he heard the engine behind him and was about to jump
onto the hood of the car when he felt something slam into him,
knocking him to the ground. The car whizzed by as he lay
there. He rolled over, trapping the person who had tackled him.
He heard something fall, looked to his right and saw a gun slide
over the asphalt. Then he looked down into her face.

"What the hell were you thinking?" he yelled when they
were safely inside his car pulling back onto the road ahead.
"Why would you jump out there when you saw that car coming? Are you crazy?" His heart was pumping, his mind reeling
with possible scenarios.

"I was doing my job, thank you very much." Bree leaned
over to strap her gun back to her leg.

"And what the hell is that? Why didn't you tell me you were strapped?" He was driving like a maniac, in a hurry to get to his parents' house to see if Adriana was okay.

"I'm a bodyguard. It makes sense that I'd be armed. And for your information that's what I was doing when I tackled you to the ground. The car was coming right at you. I saved your life, Bennett!" She wasn't accustomed to being yelled at by people whose lives she saved. She reached into her pack and dug out her phone.

"Why? I didn't ask you to. I would never ask you to put yourself in danger for me! I can't believe you did that! And who the hell are you calling?"

"I get paid to do what I do and I'm calling Sam to see what the hell is going on. Why would Adriana call you? She's supposed to be with Gary."

Renny didn't get a chance to ask another question before she was talking on the phone.

She spoke quickly into the phone. "Sam? It's me. Have you heard from Gary? Where's Adriana?"

"Adriana is here having dinner with her parents and Alex. Where are you?"

"Renny got a call from Adriana saying that she was stranded. But when we got out to her car there was no one there, and then someone tried to run him down."

"We've been here for the past two hours. Gary's here with her. It must have been a ploy."

Bree looked to Renny, who by his grim expression had heard the conversation. "Okay, we're on our way."

"No. Get Renny home. I'm going to lock things down here and I want you to do the same with Renny at his place. Make sure everything's working, and call me when you get there."

"Fine." Bree disconnected the line. "Adriana's okay."

"Let me guess. This so-called stalker has just stepped up his game."

Bree only nodded because the fierce look in Renny's eyes held her quiet.

He hadn't spoken another word to her during the ride back to his place, and he'd only grunted when she told him that'd been where they'd been instructed to go. Upon getting out of the car she retrieved her gun again and walked close beside him, telling him they'd take the stairs. He'd looked down at her, then at the gun in her hand, and clenched his jaw, but still he didn't speak.

Renny pulled out his keys and let them into the condo, pausing to punch the new security code into the pad on the side wall. He dropped his keys to the table and went straight to the bar in his dining room and poured himself a drink.

Bree moved to the canvas on the large wall in his living room and checked to make sure the surveillance camera she'd installed behind it was working. Beside Renny's very advanced audio entertainment center, she'd installed a tiny box that kept track of outside intruders. She checked to make sure it was running and operational. He didn't make a sound behind her and she was getting a little antsy. His silence, not the events that had taken place or the impending danger this could signal, bothered her.

When she turned he was downing the glass of brownish liquid, his eyes resting fiercely on her. She looked away, reached into her pouch for her phone to call Sam.

"Sam, we're here and everything is secure. So what happened?"

"It was definitely a setup. Somehow they got Renny's cell phone number and called with a voice-over sounding like Adriana. She was never in danger and she was never stranded. Yesterday her car was acting up so she took it to the shop.

About a half hour ago the body shop called to say the car had been stolen."

"But I don't understand, Sam. Why Renny?" Renny didn't have any connections with the business besides the family name and neither did Adriana.

"All I can figure right now is that he's targeting the most unlikely subjects. It would be too obvious to attack Mr. Bennett directly, and the loss of one of his kids would be far more devastating. We're gonna have to step up our security. We can't risk another setup."

"I agree. What do you want me to do?" Bree paced the floor as she talked; moving kept her calm. Without really thinking about it she went to his balcony and pulled the horizontal blinds closed, then moved to the other windows and made sure they were secured, as well. Renny was in the same room with her occupying space and brooding like a volcano waiting to erupt. She wondered what he was thinking, what he was feeling. This had to be a shock to him. After all, he hadn't placed much credence in this whole stalker business in the first place. A direct attempt on your life was difficult for any civilian to take.

"I want you to stay with him 24/7," Sam said with finality.

"What?" Her movement stopped.

"I know what I'm asking is difficult, Bree, but we don't have a choice. I'll try to find someone to take over for you as soon as I can, but for now it has to be you."

He was right, she knew it and it was her job—everything else she was feeling was secondary. "I understand, Sam. And don't worry about finding someone else. I'll be okay." She said the words, but her heart hammered in her chest as she acknowledged his closeness. She smelled him, felt his strength and anger just behind her. She didn't get the chance to turn before the phone was ripped from her hand.

"What the hell is your problem, Desdune? How could you give your sister a job like this? Do you know what she did out there tonight? Do you know how much danger she put herself in because of this little job you gave her?"

Renny was yelling at Sam and Bree turned to look at him, stunned at his words. Why was he still fussing over what she'd done? It was her job.

She didn't know what Sam's response was, but by the way Renny continued to yell into the phone it wasn't a good one. "This is ridiculous, and risking her life for mine isn't worth it!" Renny roared, then clicked the phone off and tossed it across the room.

He was on her before she had a moment to blink, his hands grasping her shoulders as he shook her slightly. "You will never, ever do that again! Do you hear me? You will not put yourself in danger on my account!"

His face was scant inches away from hers, she could feel his breath whispering across her face. She opened her mouth to speak, to argue with his stupidity, and then his lips stole her words.

Fierce, hot, hard, her senses reeled as she struggled to keep up with the torrent of sensation. Persistently he nudged her lips apart, the hot tip of his tongue sweeping inside like a summer storm, quick and potent. He dominated and controlled, sampled and delivered. His teeth raked over her bottom lip, soliciting a gentle moan from her.

His hands released her shoulders only to gather her up completely in his embrace, fingers splaying over her butt, gripping her cheeks intensely. Bree didn't even attempt to fight the feverish motions, but instead twined her arms around his neck, coming up on tiptoe to increase the connection. Tilting her head, she opened her mouth wider to take him in completely. He was the one to moan this time as he pushed her until her back was up against the wall.

When he had her steady he grabbed beneath her hips and lifted her, guiding her legs around his waist. His lips trailed a line of heat over her chin, down her neck and into the soft opening of her shirt. Bree held on for dear life as her mind reeled and spun out of control. She couldn't think, couldn't speak, couldn't focus on anything but the incessant throbbing between her legs.

Renny returned to her mouth, moaning as she opened for him once again. Her butt was soft and pliant in his big hands, her legs wrapped tightly around his waist increasing his hardness until he was sure he'd burst. He widened his stance, pushed against her middle, rubbing his arousal against her juncture.

That feeling shocked her to her senses and she gripped his shoulders and whimpered. "Renny, stop." When his tongue continued to flick over her lips and dip into her mouth she moaned, then flattened her palms on his hard chest and pushed against him. "Stop!"

The one word was like a splash of cold water stunning him back into reality. He lifted his face from hers, looked down at her now-swollen lips, her passion-filled eyes, and realized what he'd done. He'd crossed the line. The invisible line he'd drawn between them the moment he realized he was attracted to her and that she was also working for him. The one he'd sworn he wouldn't cross no matter how much it cost him.

He eased away from her even while keeping his hands on her waist until she lowered her legs to the floor. When he knew she could stand on her own he backed away, putting several feet between them. "Sabrina—"

She shook her head quickly. "Our emotions were running high. This entire situation has changed in a matter of hours and we have to deal with that. That's *all* we have to deal with. Is that clear?" Her chest was heaving, her lips still tingling from his touch. She straightened her shirt and made a move to get away from him.

He reached out, grabbed her elbow and spun her around to face him. "No, it's not clear. There's something else between us that will have to be dealt with sooner or later." She began to shake her head and he held up his free hand to stop her next response. "You can deny it if you want, but it'll only prolong the inevitable. You know that as well as I do."

She jerked her arm free. "All I know is that it is my job to keep you safe and alive until this merger goes through. I have every intention of doing my job. What I don't intend to do is become one of your many conquests." The words were bitter and hard and she saw the moment shock registered in his eyes and turned to anger. Rather than continue this heated conversation, she turned and walked away. She needed a moment to regain her senses, to convince herself that he hadn't just kissed her with such passion and longing that she'd been ready to surrender completely to him.

She could not, would not, surrender to another man again. It was dangerous, a game she wasn't good at and was destined to lose. Her heart couldn't bear it a second time.

Chapter 4

Memories of last night flickered in Renny's mind. A car had been coming fast and deliberately behind him. He'd heard it moments after the thought that something wasn't quite right entered his mind. She'd slammed against him with a lot of power, knocking them both to the ground. At any moment she could have shifted, her body rolling into the street directly into the path of the car.

He turned back, looked at Sabrina sleeping peacefully on his sofa and cursed softly. The reality was she could have been hurt or killed and it would have been his fault.

The phone rang and he rushed to pick it up so it wouldn't wake her. It was still pretty early and he wanted her to get as much sleep as possible.

"Hello?"

"Are you calm yet?"

It was Rico. Renny moved into his studio. He had some

words for his brother, words he knew he didn't want Sabrina to hear.

"I told you this bodyguard thing was a bad idea," he growled into the phone.

"So bad that it actually saved your life," Rico commented drily.

"Yeah, but at what cost? She could have been hurt, Ric. I can't have a female getting hurt on my account."

"But you don't mind hurting them at your whim."

Renny pinched the bridge of his nose. "That is so irrelevant to this situation. I don't want her injuries or possibly her death on my conscience."

"Sam assures me that she's a professional. Hell, she can kill a man with her bare hands. I really don't think you should be worried about her getting hurt." Rico paused. "You should, however, worry about the fact that you've pissed her brother off."

"I don't give a rat's ass about that. He shouldn't be allowing her to do this type of work anyway."

Rico snickered. "That's funny, because Dad says the same thing about you."

"I'm an artist, Rico. I'm not jumping in front of speeding cars or bullets for that matter."

"And you're not behind a desk running Bennett Industries, either. For your information, Sam's not real happy about her career choice, but he loves and respects her, just like we do you. You of all people should know how it feels to be different. Besides, we really need to focus on who's doing this."

Renny never argued with logic, so he let Rico's words stand even though he still didn't like the danger Sabrina had put herself in. "Okay. What are you thinking?"

"I'm thinking that maybe you were right and Coastal is behind this," Rico answered.

"But why? This deal is going to make both Coastal and

Bennett combined the most powerful telecommunications firm in the U.S. It would be stupid for them to sabotage that."

"Yeah, but you forget there were a few of Coastal's board members that voted against the merger. Including Dad's old army buddy."

Renny sat back in his chair contemplating Rico's words. "Roland Summerfield is not totally out of his mind. Whatever feud he and Dad had going all those years ago is probably the furthest thing from his mind right now."

"I don't know, Renny. Some things are hard to let go."

Rico's tone told him he knew something more about their father and Roland Summerfield. "I never knew the details of that feud. Do you?"

It was Rico's turn to sigh. "Let's just say money is not the root of all evil. Women are."

"What? This is about some woman?"

"Listen, I don't want to get into this right now. We'll talk about it later. I think Dad's going to call a family meeting sometime this week."

Renny wanted to talk about it now, but heard noises coming from the other room. Sabrina was awake. He needed to talk to her about last night. "Fine. You just make sure you don't conveniently forget to fill me in."

What the hell was she doing? She was in Lorenzo Bennett's kitchen about to cook breakfast as if they'd just spent a pleasure-filled night together.

Not!

Instead she'd lain on that sofa for what must have been hours, waiting for the warm rush of his kiss to subside. His touch had birthed feelings she had no idea were wrapped inside. Her skin where his kisses had fallen suddenly came alive. The stirrings of desire deep between her legs warned of Lorenzo's potency.

She cracked an egg into the bowl, then squeezed her legs together tightly to ease the pressure building there with her lurid thoughts. She wasn't going there with him. She couldn't.

"I like cheese in my eggs."

Her insides jumped, but her body didn't move. Instead she tossed him a serious look over her shoulder. "Don't get used to this. It's not part of the job." He looked so good leaning against the door frame, like a photo from one of those calendars. His jeans fit snugly over his waist and thighs, his sleeveless T-shirt molding seductively against that awesome chest and abs. Hurriedly she looked away.

"You look comfortable in the kitchen," Renny commented as she sprinkled shredded cheese into the mixture, then poured it into a hot skillet. "Maybe you're in the wrong profession."

She didn't miss the edge to his words and she sighed. She would have to defend her life's choices yet again. She'd thought that after fighting this battle with her family this drama would be over. And why did he care, anyway? For some reason, however, Renny's questioning of her choice was more than a little disturbing. She continued stirring the eggs without turning to face him. "You're a fine one to talk about career choices."

Her tone was bristly, which actually aroused instead of irritated him. "We're not talking about me."

She switched off the stove and scooped the eggs out of the pan and onto two plates. "And as I'm a grown woman, perfectly capable of making my own decisions, we're not talking about me, either."

Renny moved to the cabinet and retrieved two glasses before filling them with juice. "I guess I'm just confused as to why your brother gave you this job."

"Because I'm qualified."

"But—"

She gave him a heated glare before he could utter another word. "But what? I'm a woman?" Bree put both plates onto the marble-top table with a thunk. "Listen here, Mr. Bennett. I can protect you just as well, if not better, than any man you'll ever find, and I don't appreciate you insinuating otherwise."

Cautiously and because the heat sparkling in her eyes did something to him, Renny took measured steps until he stood in front of her. "I don't doubt your capabilities. I'm simply concerned for your welfare. I wouldn't like to see my sisters putting themselves in danger on a daily basis and I'm having a hard time digesting the fact that you're being paid to do it." While he spoke, he'd pulled out the chair behind her and now motioned, with his eyes, for her to sit down.

Bree was not impressed by his chivalry this time, but was beginning to fume at his words. At least she thought she should be fuming at his words. "Why would that bother you? You're not paying me." She sat and watched him move to the counter, grabbing their glasses of juice, then coming to sit across from her.

"Call me old-fashioned, but I'm used to the man protecting the woman, not the other way around."

"Well, I'm used to taking care of myself," she snapped.

Renny stared at her contemplatively. "You're the baby of a nice-size family. I find that pretty hard to believe. My brothers and I are very protective of our sisters. And from the way your brother came off at me last night, I can see he's the same way."

Bree picked up her fork, poked at her eggs. Sam and Cole were both overprotective, as well as her parents and even Lynn to a certain extent, but she'd won her independence from them a long time ago. "Look, this has nothing to do with this assignment or the danger you and your family are in."

Renny nodded. "You're absolutely right."

She'd half expected the argument to continue, so his words stopped her short. "Now, Sam's on his way over to drop off some of my things since it looks like we'll be roommates for a while. I want to go over your cell phone records if you have them so we can compare the incoming and outgoing numbers."

Renny had been chewing his eggs slowly. He'd thought her staying here last night was a one-time thing, but it appeared he'd been mistaken. She'd be staying indefinitely. Sleeping only a few feet away from him. Tempting him every hour of the day and every second of the night. She ate as she talked, enjoying her food in between. He realized she had a healthy appetite when she slowed down long enough to eat. But her mind worked fast, going from one task to the next. The movement of her lips captivated him and he found himself staring. "I like the color of your skin," he blurted out.

Bree was momentarily speechless. "Ookay." She paused, her fork halfway to her mouth. "I don't see how that's going to help us figure out who's after you though."

Renny lifted his glass, took a slow, lazy sip, then set it down again. "You said your parents were from Louisiana. So you're Creole?"

"My parents are Creole. I was born in Manhattan."

"Interesting," he murmured.

Her face was very interesting. Soft planes and angles that he could just imagine his fingers gliding over. She had such detail in her features, from the curve of her jaw to the strong indentation of her lips. High cheekbones and great, expressive eyes. He admitted a certain amount of ignorance in the arena of origins, except for his own, but noticed that she was darker than the pictures of Creoles he'd seen. Maybe she was more a mixture of African Creole. He'd heard of the different mixtures, especially out of Louisiana. Whatever the case, she was beautiful and he suddenly wanted to be in his studio working on the sculpture that had taken his mind away from his other work.

"Come with me." He stood abruptly reaching for her hand. "I want to show you something." She would never pose for him; he wouldn't even waste his time asking. But her inquisitive nature would not allow her to leave his studio without looking around. She'd been in there once, when she'd been planting her cameras and other stuff. He'd seen how every so often her eyes roamed to his worktable, his stands full of completed and uncompleted pieces. She was curious and he'd play on that curiosity to study her until he captured every nuance of her being in that piece.

"Show me what? I need to clean up these dishes and get ready for when Sam arrives." She didn't want to go anywhere with him. The look in his eyes was close to…almost like…a bedroom glance…a prelude to seduction. Her heart hammered in her chest at that proclamation. His hand was outstretched waiting for hers. If she took it, she'd feel that warmth already circulating inside escalate; she'd want him to hold her close again, to kiss her as he had last night. No. She shook her head. She wasn't touching him and he couldn't make her.

Tired of waiting for her cooperation, Renny clasped her shoulders, pulled her to a standing position, then took her hand. She wouldn't close her fingers around his, but it didn't matter, he had a strong grip and he practically pulled her out of the kitchen.

"Renny, I have work to do," she complained.

"So do I." *And if you'd stop being so damned stubborn I could get on with it.*

They were going through the living room now. Bree gave up the struggle and walked placidly behind him. She'd get this over with quickly, then get away from him just as fast. They were headed toward his studio. What could he want to show her in there?

The light was already on from earlier when he'd been in here talking to Rico. He moved to his worktable, sat in the swivel stool he used when he worked and pulled her between his legs. There wasn't enough light.

He reached across the cluttered table and flicked on a smaller lamp, tilting it so that it shone brightly in her face.

Bree squinted. "Is this some sort of interrogation?"

"No, I wanted you to see what I'm working on. I thought maybe you could help me out a bit."

She was positioned precariously between his legs, his hands resting on her waist. She couldn't complain about the closeness or the feel of his touch. That would be a blatant lie. But did she have to like it so much? "I don't know much about art, so I'm not sure I'll be able to help you."

"You don't have to know about art." He moved his hands to rub up and down her bare arms. "You just have to know about sex and how it makes you feel."

Her eyes widened and she was sure her body temperature rose another ten degrees. Could he read her mind? Did he know she was thinking about straddling him right here in his studio? Of course not, he was talking about his sculptures and how provocative they were. "Wha-what's the new…ah, piece you're working on?"

The darkness of her eyes intensified, her cheeks growing in color just a pinch. In his photographic mind he captured that mood before reaching over to pull his latest piece closer. "This is what I started on the other day."

Bree turned her head, expecting to see another piece similar to the ones in the foundry. Instead she saw a few wires, twisted into a form resembling two human bodies and pieces of clay covering almost all of one of the forms. She frowned a bit before asking, "What is it?"

Renny gave a quick smile. "It's not complete. When it is it will be a man and his woman."

His woman. The words echoed in her head. What would it be like to be Lorenzo Bennett's woman?

"Oh. And what are he and his woman doing?" His hands were no longer on her; he'd moved them to the base of the sculpture, rubbing absently over the half-covered piece. Her thighs touched his as she turned herself to face the sculpture.

Renny now had a profile of that pretty face, the nose that protruded and rounded at the tip, the lips that looked puckered and ready to kiss. Her hair was down, falling around her shoulders, and he reached up to push it back out of his way.

"Are they having sex?" she asked in a tentative voice.

Renny turned his attention back to the piece. "No. They're making love."

The rich timbre of his voice sent shivers down her spine, yet she didn't make any effort to move away. "Can I?" She motioned as if she wanted to touch the piece.

"Sure." He waited until her fingers were grazing the cool clay. "I'm having trouble capturing the intensity in their eyes when he enters her. You know the moment they connect, the moment she feels him filling her completely?"

He whispered, his breath warm against her ear, and Bree tilted her head to the side. She could make out the wire formations clearly now. They were lying on a chair or a bench, her legs up on his shoulders, his face turned slightly, planting a kiss on her ankle. She could almost hear the moans. She definitely felt the wetness between her own legs and could only imagine what the woman was feeling. She closed her eyes even as her hands roamed over the incomplete beings. "It's like nothing she's ever known. Nothing she could ever imagine. Her legs are shaking because he has excited her so much."

Renny turned to her and saw that her eyes were closed, that she was feeling the mood just as he'd wanted to capture it. He picked up more clay, smoothed it over the wire that would be the woman. Using one of his knives he carved away the excess, sculpting it as her words, the lull of her voice seemed to guide his every stroke.

"She feels him at her entrance, just the tip of him. He pulls away, almost teasingly. She whimpers." After speaking, Bree made a sound that sounded foreign to her own ears. "He kisses her ankle to soothe her, to promise her completion." She stopped, unable to speak for the feeling of desire overwhelming her.

In that lapse of time Renny dropped the knife, turned her to face him and took her mouth savagely. His tongue pushed her lips aside, moving swiftly to ravage the recesses of her mouth. His hands rubbed up and down her back in heated strokes.

Then she moaned and wrapped her arms around his neck.

He lifted her at the waist, pulled her legs around him and sat her astride. She held on to his neck, pulling at the hair on top of his head that was longer than on the sides. She kissed him with a hunger he thought only existed within himself and he fed her, oh, how he fed her. With his tongue, his lips, his hands all over her back, her butt, he gave her what she was asking for. The need to taste more of her grew in an instant and he pulled at the hem of her shirt until it was over her head and tossed to the floor. His hands groped her breasts as she arched backward, allowing complete access. Creamy mounds strained over the sturdy white cotton of her bra and Renny pushed that fabric away to reveal darkened nipples.

With a guttural groan he sank his teeth into their softness, laving his tongue over the rigid nipple. She grabbed his head again, pressing his face deeper into her, cradling him as if she were feeding him. Now it was his turn to feast. He cupped the heavy mounds in both hands, lifting them higher, higher until both nipples were at his lips, begging for attention.

Bree was on fire, her panties soaked from the inside out. He was licking her breasts, treating them as if they were some scrumptious delicacy, and she loved it. She loved the feel of his strong hands on her bare skin; loved his tongue moving hotly over her. She wanted this and so much more. In the back of her mind logic screamed for her to get far away from this man, the danger light flashing bright red, yet she couldn't let go. Her fingers actually twined together behind his head in rebellion.

"I want you, Sabrina. I want you now," Renny growled as he rubbed his throbbing erection against her hot center.

Bree closed her legs tighter around him, craving the same connection. "Yes. Yes," she whispered.

Renny pulled at the snap of her pants, heard the zipper slide down…

The doorbell rang.

They both froze like one of his sculptures. His hand was about to push past her panties and into that sweet waiting cove. Bree was near his ear, about to nibble until he touched her. Their breathing was erratic as they remained still in the hopes that whoever was at the door would turn away and leave.

"Bree?" The bell turned into a knock, which was followed by a familiar voice.

"Sam," Bree whispered. "Sam's here with my stuff." She wiggled off Renny's lap.

Renny stood slowly, adjusted his arousal in his pants and dragged a hand down his face. "I'll go let him in while you get dressed." His voice was pinched with the tension that surrounded them.

Bree looked at him and he stared at her before moving to the door. "We'll finish this later," he told her in no uncertain terms.

Bree shook her head. "No. We can't."

He'd reached the door by then and was about to pull it closed behind him. "We can and we will. Make no mistake about it."

Then he was gone. Bree collapsed on the stool and cast a weary glance at the unfinished statue. "You guys are troublemakers."

* * *

"Speak your mind, Desdune," Renny said when he'd made himself comfortable on his favorite leather recliner. Sabrina had pulled her shirt on, then gone into the bathroom to shower, leaving Renny and Sam alone in the living room.

Sam watched the enigmatic playboy with barely restrained fury. "Look, I know your reputation and I can't say that I'm all that thrilled with the fact that Bree has been assigned to you."

"Then why'd you do it? You're the boss. Why would you give your sister a job that could cost her her life?" Renny sat forward, his elbows resting on his knees. Sam Desdune looked like a fairly smart man. Actually, he and Sabrina looked a lot alike. She'd said they were twins and the resemblance was strong, from the skin tone to the color of their eyes. Yet Sam was taller, almost head to head with Renny. He had a good build and a strong handshake. Under any other circumstances, Renny figured he could probably like the guy.

"Bree's an adult. I can't tell her what to do any more than I imagine you can tell your sisters what to do." Sam expelled a deep breath and sat back on the couch. "She's really good, so you don't have to worry about her letting you get hurt."

"I can protect myself, Desdune. I'm worried about her."

His words weren't lost on Sam; he was worried about Bree, too. Not just because of the dangerous situation she was in, but because something had made her come back from North Carolina, and she'd come back a different woman. He was willing to bet that something was a man, but he refused to push her into telling him. In the meantime, he had no intention of letting this smooth talker take advantage of her. "Listen, Bennett, Bree can do her job better than most men I know in the business. So your concern about her is pointless. My concern, however, is not."

Renny frowned. "And what's your concern?"

"Like I said, I know about your reputation. Don't even try it with my sister. Now, this is a big account for my company, but I won't hesitate to do bodily harm if I think you're messing with her."

Considering the rumors about his personal life, Renny figured Sam had a right to take this stance. So he decided to set the record straight. "Don't believe everything you hear, Desdune. My personal life, my real personal life, is my business, and I keep it that way. As far as your sister goes," he shrugged, "you said yourself she's a grown woman." Renny didn't miss the rise in Sam's eyebrows or the fact that he was now sitting forward glaring at him.

He ignored it all. "What I do with what woman I choose is my business. But rest assured I'm not as careless as town gossip makes me out to be. Your sister is safe with me."

Sam narrowed his eyes. They were face-to-face over the coffee table, man-to-man. He'd put his concerns out there and Bennett had addressed them unwaveringly. Sam had to admit the man wasn't like what he'd heard; he wasn't arrogant or stuck-up, for that matter. Renny being the only one of the Bennett brothers that he'd never had dealings with before, Sam had been concerned that the rumors were true. But this man had a look of integrity even though Sam still didn't condone him putting any moves on Bree. "She's here on business. The sooner we wrap this case up the better it'll be for all of us."

Sabrina made her entrance at that moment. She wore tan slacks and a white button-down shirt. She had her tennis shoes on again and she'd pulled her hair back into that insufferable ponytail. Still, his breath caught as her eyes made contact with his. He wanted her more now than he had when they were in the studio. For a moment he gave some thought to his track record with women and wondered if Desdune didn't have a point. Sabrina was special, he'd be the first one to concede that point. But was she special enough to melt his heart, to be the one woman that made him want to settle down? He wasn't totally sure and until he could be he probably should just leave her alone. Returning his gaze to Desdune, he grimaced. "You might be right, Desdune."

"So you think this may have been a personal hit against Renny?" Bree asked as she lounged on the sofa beside Sam. "Why? I thought this was about the company merger."

"I thought so, too. But I got to thinking last night. Why would they call Renny? He's not even involved in the company. Getting rid of him would serve almost no purpose. The deal would undoubtedly go on."

Chills had run up her spine at the thought of someone purposely trying to hurt Renny, but Bree didn't want to address them at the moment. "What about the sister, Adriana?"

"Adriana is the older one, she's the model. She has nothing to do with the business, either. Nor does Gabrielle. So the three of them stick closely together in this family, as the outcasts, I guess you could say."

Bree frowned. "I know about being the outcast."

Because they were close, only eight minutes apart in birth actually, and because he knew she had a lot on her mind, Sam put a hand on her knee. "Bree, you are a Desdune to the bone. We couldn't cast you out if we tried."

She smiled. "Whatever. Go on about the sisters."

"Well, I checked into Bennett's financial holdings and this new gallery he's trying to open. Everything looks cool so I'm leaning more toward a possible relationship gone bad."

That was the absolute last thing Bree wanted to think about—Renny and his women. Not after he'd had her about to strip and ride him hard and fast in his studio just an hour ago. He was back in that studio now, the door closed so she and Sam would have some privacy, but her thoughts kept wandering back to him. "Come on, Sam. What woman would kill a man because he left her?" Joanne Richmond came to mind. But she was willing to kill the woman who had slept with her husband, not the husband himself. Bree shook that thought right out of her head.

"Bree, you'd be surprised what a scorned woman would do. But really, I don't have anything concrete to say that's what's going on. We're meeting at the Bennett estate tomorrow night at seven, so make sure he's there. Rico, Alex and I are going to go over the list of Coastal board members today."

"Don't rule out Bennett board members and employees. With a merger this size people are bound to lose their jobs and that can set a twenty-year veteran of the company off. Who's helping you with the investigation aspect?" Desdune Security really was only supposed to provide security services, but Bree knew this case was close to Sam. He and Rico had been friends for a really long time, so she knew Sam would do whatever he could for the man.

"You remember Trent Donovan? We worked that big case together out in Las Vegas, the one with the missing girl."

Bree sat back against the pillows. Her thoughts had wandered again to the man just beyond that closed door and the sculpture he was working on. Then she heard Sam's voice. "Ah, oh, yeah, I remember him. The girl's father was a Navy SEAL. Donovan was a member of his team. Is he still on the team?"

"No. Donovan's doing his own thing out on the West Coast, but he keeps his ear to the ground when things are happening with people he's worked with. He's really good at investigating and infiltrating. We're talking about a partnership of some kind, you know, combining the security with private investigation. He'll head up the West Coast offices and me the East Coast. This case is like a trial run of us working together."

"That sounds good," she said absently.

Sam looked at her closely. "Bree, you okay?"

She blinked, stared at him funny. "Yeah, why do you ask?"

"You seem a little preoccupied all of a sudden. Is it Bennett? Because if he's hitting on you I can have someone take your place."

"No!" she said just a little too quickly. "I mean, this is my assignment and I'm not going to let you take it from me just because you don't think I can handle the playboy in there." She hoped she rebounded well enough. There was something going on between her and Renny, and after this morning's close call she wondered if it wouldn't just be easier to act on it and get it out of the way.

Sam grinned. "Actually, I've been wondering if the playboy can handle you."

Chapter 5

"Hello?"

Silence.

"Hello?" Bree called again, this time pulling the phone away from her ear to look at the number displayed on the screen.

Still silence.

On the table behind her, Renny's house phone rang and she turned toward it with a start.

"Who is this?" she asked one final time before disconnecting the cell phone line.

Renny's telephone rang one more time before it stopped abruptly, signaling he'd just picked it up. Again she looked at the turquoise screen of her phone, trying to place the number displayed there. It was an odd area code, but with a lurch of her heart Bree realized it was familiar. "No," she whispered.

Renny had been in the studio frantically sculpting the emotions he'd seen play across Sabrina's face, the exact curve of her chin, the tilt of her head as she began to feel his entrance. His fingers moved wildly over the cool clay, his heart beating as he, too, felt the rising heat between him and the woman that was hired to guard his body. Instead she seemed to be wreaking her own special havoc on it.

The phone rang, jarring his concentration. Under normal circumstances he would have ignored it while he worked, but Sabrina and her brother were in the other room discussing the case, and too many strange things were going on. So with a low growl he snatched up the receiver.

"Renny! You've got to get over here quick!" Yolanda screeched into the phone.

"Yolanda? What's going on? Where are you?"

"I'm at the gallery. Someone tried to break in, Renny. The police are here and everything. You've got to hurry!"

He didn't say another word, simply hung up the phone and wiped his hands on the smock he never wore but always had hanging on the back of his chair. He wrenched the door open only to be stopped again by the sight of Sabrina sitting on the couch with her head in her hands. "Sabrina?" In two strides he was next to her. "Are you all right?"

Bree jumped as his hand touched her shoulder. No, she wasn't all right, but that wasn't any of his business. "I'm fine." She blinked and shifted so that he was no longer touching her. "What's going on?"

Now she didn't want him to touch her. Renny grimaced. They needed to have a serious talk about what was going on between them. "I've got to go to the gallery. That was Yolanda on the phone. She says someone tried to break in."

Bree was on her feet in an instant. "Okay, let's go." She clipped her phone back to her hip and grabbed her jacket on her way to the door. She paused and was about to put in the security code when Renny swiped her hands away.

"Go ahead, I'll do it." Why did she think she had to do ev-

erything all the time? He was willing to concede that guarding
him was her job, but that didn't mean he had to stand by and
watch her take complete control. He was still the man in this
situation and she was going to realize that sooner or later.

They pulled up in front of the gallery, Renny glaring
angrily at the three police cars with flashing lights occupying the first three parking spaces. Bree was out of the car
before he had a chance to get around to opening her door and
he cursed under his breath. So many things were going on in
his mind he wasn't sure if he was coming or going. His feet
ate up the asphalt as he vowed to deal with one thing at a
time—who tried to break into his gallery, and Sabrina, in that
order.

He managed to break stride in front of her and grabbed the
front door before she could get to it. She looked up at him
quizzically and he gave her a deep flourish with his arm, signaling for her to go in.

Once they were both inside Yolanda threw her arms around
Renny. "Oh, Renny, I'm so glad you're here. I was so frightened."

Bree was just about to go over and talk to the policemen
when Yolanda brushed past her in a flurry of winter-white and
too damn much perfume. She turned just in time to see the
woman plastered to Renny as if she couldn't breathe without
him. Her stomach twisted, heated and burned with unfamil-
iar feelings.

She turned quickly and moved to the first officer, determined to find out what had happened. "Hi, I'm Mr. Bennett's
partner. Can you tell me what happened here?"

The tallest officer, the one with the intense blue eyes, looked
down at her, quickly assessing her before licking his lips.

Is he serious? Bree thought with impatience, then figured
she might as well play his obvious delusion to her advantage.

"Is there anything you can tell me, Officer?" She took a step closer to him for good measure. Just as she thought, those crystal-blue eyes sparkled and he smiled.

"And what is your name, ma'am?"

His voice was deep, smooth and did absolutely nothing for her, but Bree kept her smile in place and even managed to bat her eyes a few times. "I'm Sabrina Desdune and you are?" She angled her head to see his badge more clearly. "Officer Mathison."

Old Blue Eyes extended his hand. "Officer Tony Mathison. It's a pleasure to meet you, Ms. Desdune."

He'd put an emphasis on *Ms.* as a way of asking if she were married. Bree suppressed a chuckle. He was so typical. "The pleasure is all mine, Officer."

"Please, call me Tony."

This crap was wearing thin. "Okay. Tony, tell me what happened."

"Ah, sure. At about 11:00 a.m. the alarm went off, a call came into the station and my partner and I were first on the scene. We gained entrance and disengaged the alarm before searching the premises. We didn't spot a suspect, so we secured the scene and waited for backup. Ms. Tate over there arrived about fifteen minutes after we got here and said she was the manager and that the gallery hadn't opened to the public yet. She's supposed to be seeing if anything is missing."

Both Officer Mathison and Bree turned to see Yolanda still wrapped in Renny's arms as she gave him a very dramatic account of what happened. Bree's hands fisted at her sides, but the moment Renny looked over toward her she put on a perfect smile and turned to Officer Mathison again. "Was there a point of entry?"

"Yes, it's in the back. Do you want to see it?"

"Definitely," she said through clenched teeth. The sooner

she got away from those blossoming lovebirds, the better. As she followed the officer toward the back of the gallery her head started to pound. She was not jealous! Renny Bennett was nothing but her client. Who gave a damn about that woman draped all over him like she owned him? She didn't, that was for damn sure! If that's the type of woman he wanted, then so be it.

Renny watched as Sabrina walked off with the cop that was ogling her as if she were his lunch buffet. His jaw had clenched at the smiles she willingly gave the stranger—the same ones he had to fight tooth and nail to get from her. He wanted to follow them, but Yolanda was being exceptionally clingy today. He wasn't an idiot and knew the games women played very well, so he was sure that Yolanda's overzealousness was for Sabrina's benefit. He'd let it go originally because he wanted to see if it affected Sabrina in any way, but she seemed to move right along to Officer Friendly without giving him a second thought.

How could she be so warm and willing in his arms a few hours ago and now so quick to jump into another man's graces? Because she was a woman, that's why, and that's what women did. Still, he didn't like it.

Grabbing Yolanda's wrists, he took a step away from her. "Yolanda, is there anything missing?"

"Um, no. No, I don't think so. I looked around twice before you got here and everything seems to be here. Most of our stock is still at the warehouse. I didn't want to bring it in until we were closer to opening."

Renny released her hands and moved around the white-painted rooms. "That was probably a good idea."

"The only place I didn't check was your office. But that's always kept locked, so I doubt they could have gotten in there." She followed him like a sick puppy. "If I had a key I could have checked it out for you," she added.

Renny didn't even turn to face her; they'd been down this

road before. "You don't need a key to my office, Yolanda. Everything you need is either at the front desk or in your office. My office is private and off-limits to anyone but me."

They were rounding the corner that led to his office as he spoke. They both stopped short.

"It's off-limits, huh?" Yolanda grimaced.

Sabrina was just rising from the floor with Officer Friendly standing right behind her. With a twist of her hand she turned the knob and the door to his office opened before them.

Anger and just a spark of pride coursed through Renny as he walked toward her with Yolanda close behind him. When he skirted around the officer and grabbed Sabrina by the elbow he wished that the two people in the room with them would disappear. Instead, he frowned down at her. "You could have simply asked for the key."

Yolanda plopped down on the leather couch to the left side of the room. "Why? I did and it didn't work."

Renny ignored her and so did Bree. "You were otherwise occupied," she said with a raised brow, then jerked her arm free.

He wanted to grab her and pull her to him, but thought better of it. "So, what are you looking for in here, Officer?" Renny looked at the tall man, hoping he could read his mind— Sabrina was off-limits to him. He didn't want him gazing at her or giving her those charming-ass smiles anymore.

Officer Mathison cleared his throat. "Ms. Desdune wanted to make sure nothing in here had been disturbed. When we realized the door was still locked she became suspicious."

That sounded liked Sabrina.

"And it's a good thing I always follow my hunches," she said as she lifted a white envelope from the floor near the door with a pair of tweezers that she kept in her personal break-in kit, which had been in her purse.

Renny's gut clenched.

"Officer Mathison, do you have a pair of gloves I could borrow?" She waved the envelope in the air for all to see.

Renny was at her side instantly.

"They're in my car," Officer Mathison said quickly. "I'll go get them."

He made his way out of the office just as Yolanda stood, coming up behind Renny and entwining an arm through his. "What's that, Renny?"

Her voice was so sugary sweet that Bree wanted to puke. "Renny, I think this will be better viewed by you and me alone." Her strong emphasis on the word *alone* was not lost on Yolanda, who tossed her an evil glare.

No longer concerned with the brewing catfight around him, Renny remained focused on that envelope. "You're right. Yolanda, can you wait outside?"

Yolanda's perfectly glossed lips didn't hesitate to pout. "But Renny, I'm a part of this business, too, and if someone broke in here to put a note under your door I should know what it's about. It's not fair that a friend of your family gets to stay and I don't."

Bree itched to punch her just one good time. The woman was a disgrace to all females with a backbone. "Actually, the fewer people that know about this, the better. We wouldn't want to give the burglar the upper hand."

Yolanda took a step toward Bree, who only raised a brow at her approach. Bree hoped she was going to get the opportunity to lay this tramp out.

"Listen here, missy. You can't just appear on the scene and—"

Renny stepped between the two women, facing Yolanda. "This has to remain private, Yolanda. You understand how I feel about my privacy."

Yolanda backed down, placing her palms on his chest. "Okay, Renny. I'll go outside, but you and I need to spend

some time together…going over business, that is." She smiled
and leaned over to kiss his cheek.

Bree rolled her eyes at the smacking sound and looked
away. Yolanda sashayed past her as if she'd won the battle.
Bree almost tripped her. Officer Mathison had returned with
the gloves and Bree asked him sweetly to wait outside, then
closed the door behind him, too. Slipping her small hands into
the much larger gloves, she opened the letter and stood close
to Renny so he could read it with her.

What's done in the dark will eventually come to light.
Like father, like son.

Of course it wasn't signed and it was typed in a large bold
font. Bree read it over again, then read it out aloud. Renny
read along silently beside her.

She looked up at him, noticed the smudge of lipstick on
his jaw and frowned. "It looks like you've managed to piss
somebody off."

The muscle in his jaw twitched. "It would appear so. The
question is, who?"

Because she couldn't resist another moment Bree reached
up and wiped his cheek clean. "I wonder," she sniped before
showing him the smudge of lipstick on her gloved hand.
"Everybody seems to love you."

She put the letter back into the envelope, then looked
around his desk until she found a folder. She dumped out the
contents and slipped the letter inside. "I'm calling Sam." And
then she left him in his office alone.

Renny sat down in his chair with a thud. This stalker thing
was becoming all too real to him. First it was the car almost
running him down and now this. He didn't like the implications. Without a thought his fingers went to his cheek where

Sabrina had just touched him. A smile ghosted across his face. She was jealous of Yolanda.

Which meant she felt something for him. Not that he'd doubted that, especially after this morning. His smile broadened. Well, at least one good thing was bound to come out of this mess.

Sabrina Desdune would be his.

It was after eight in the evening by the time Bree and Renny walked through the door to his condo again. Sam, Alex and Rico had come to the gallery once Bree reported the letter found in Renny's office. From that moment on ideas had been tossed around, the gallery was locked down tight and the infamous Yolanda, to Bree's utter relief, sent on her way. The woman was past infuriating; she was downright annoying, and Bree had already decided that she didn't like her. Something in the way the woman watched her, like she for one minute believed that Bree was competition for Renny's affections.

Bree went straight to the bathroom and closed the door with a loud thump. Well, hadn't Renny said he wanted her? That had only been this morning, but then hours later he'd been enfolded in Yolanda's arms. She gazed at her reflection in the mirror. "You are simply not his type," she murmured. Then she turned sideways, standing on tiptoe to get a full view of her body in the small vanity mirror. Okay, so she was curvy; that just meant he'd like to sleep with her. That did not mean that she was girl-friend material or even wife material for that matter. "Neither is she." She thought aloud with Yolanda in mind.

Vowing to steer clear of Renny and his insatiable kisses for the remainder of this job, she washed her face and pulled her hair free of the ponytail that was probably contributing to her growing headache. Coming out of the bathroom, she leaned on one leg taking off each of her shoes, then carrying them to the living room where her bag was. But her bag wasn't there.

"I put it in the extra bedroom." Renny's deep voice sounded from behind her.

She spun around, not really surprised to see him; she was in his house, after all. "I was fine out here on the couch," she snapped.

"Sleeping on the couch is insane when there's a perfectly good bed in the other room. Since you'll be here for a while that's where you'll be sleeping."

His tone suggested the decision was final. Bree didn't really want to argue with him. In fact, she didn't want to be in the same room with him, so she held tight to her shoes and began walking in the direction of the bedroom.

Renny extended an arm to stop her. "Sabrina, we need to talk."

She expelled the breath she'd been holding. "Forget it, Bennett. I'm all talked out for the day. I'd really just like to crash." She paused, gave him a questioning look. "That is, if you're not planning on going back out."

Renny read into that question just the way he was supposed to. She was referring, once again, to Yolanda. The entire time they were at the gallery Sabrina hadn't missed the opportunity to jab at his relationship with Yolanda. At first he'd found it amusing; they were, after all, at the gallery and Yolanda's presence was overwhelmingly felt there. But now they were in his apartment and he didn't want to think about the break-in, the letter, his brothers or Yolanda. He'd been impatient all day, wishing all the formalities could be done with so he could be alone with her.

While the anonymous letter seemed to frighten everyone else, Renny didn't really give it that much thought. He wasn't about to run scared from someone who was too afraid to sign his name to a damn letter. They were all baffled by the culprit, but Renny refused to give the person any more of his time. If and when this person got bold enough to approach him face-to-face, he'd deal with him or her swiftly and in a manner that made police brutality look innocent. But in the meantime there was something—someone—else dominating his thoughts.

"I'm not going anywhere. I thought we'd have some dessert and talk."

They had ordered pizza while they were still at the gallery brainstorming, so dinner was already out of the way, much to Bree's relief. "I don't want dessert." She moved his arm out of her way.

Renny grabbed her elbow, stopping her departure again. "Then we'll have a drink by the fire."

Bree looked over her shoulder. "There is no fire."

Renny gave her a half grin. She was so stubborn. "By the time you go into your room and change, I'll have your drink and the fire ready."

She wasn't really sleepy and she knew she'd only sit in that room, wondering what he was doing, so she reluctantly nodded and then stared down at his hand on her arm. "You can let me go now."

He released her arm and watched her disappear into the guest bedroom and close the door securely behind her.

"I really don't know if I can let you go, Sabrina," he whispered when she was gone. He went to his own room, pulling his shirt over his head as he moved to the master bath. A quick wash of his face and he changed into sweatpants and a T-shirt. He normally slept nude, but he had company in the house, so that was out of the question…unless she insisted. With a bold grin he made his way back into the living room, fixing Bree a glass of champagne and stoking the fireplace. Renny preferred lighter drinks, at the distinct criticism of his brothers. Wines and champagne were more his speed. He heard her door open just as he was dropping a fleece blanket onto the floor. He reached for a couple of pillows as she entered the now-dim living room.

"I should check the locks and stuff before we go to bed," she said in a nervous whisper. She didn't know what she'd expected at his suggestion of a nightcap in front of the fire, but this cozy, intimate setting was definitely not it. The entire house was dark save for the orange glow coming from the indentation in the living-room wall surrounded by a brick ledge. That ledge was lined with linen napkins, a crystal bowl full of strawberries and a bottle of champagne accompanied by two flutes. This was more a romantic setup than a casual nightcap, and she was instantly alarmed.

"I've checked them already." He stood in the center of the blanket, his hand extended to her.

He looked so damned good standing there in the midst of that intense blaze. Her heart hammered and she took a step backward.

"Maybe this wasn't such a good idea," she heard herself saying. "I mean, I don't think Yolanda would approve." She lifted her head defiantly. How dare he try this evening of seduction on her after she watched him kissing another woman?

Renny gritted his teeth, wanting to yell that there was nothing between him and Yolanda, but then he resisted. If she wanted to play that game he'd play along until she couldn't stand it anymore. "Yolanda understands."

Appalled, Bree could only stare at him. "She understands what? That you're a careless womanizer? That she means nothing more to you than the next passing piece of ass?"

Her eyes sparked and Renny swore at any moment one of those fierce flashes would land directly at his feet. Was it possible that a woman could be even more attractive when she was angry? "It's not the next passing piece. I'm very selective." He held back a grin, knowing that it was only a matter of time before Bree threw something at him. Her chest heaved with her growing anger, her breasts moving enticingly.

"Selective?" Bree yelled as she took a step closer to him. "You are despicable! My brother was so right when he warned me against you." She drew nearer to him with every word she spoke. "You think every woman is just ready to bow at your feet and do your bidding. Well, Mr. Lorenzo Bennett, that's where you're mistaken! I wouldn't bow at your feet—"

Renny lifted a finger to her lips to silence her. "I don't want you to bow at my feet, Sabrina." Then he dropped a quick kiss on her lips, on her neck, on her cotton-covered breasts and down to her stomach. "I'd much rather kneel at yours."

He'd buried his face in her stomach as he fell to his knees in front of her. Every other word flew out of Bree's mind as his hands held her waist. "I don't play like this, Renny." Then she moaned as he lifted the hem of her shirt and kissed her bared belly.

Renny paused, looked up at her darkening expression. "I think we both know I'm not playing." His tongue found her navel and delved inside.

Bree held on to his shoulders, closing her eyes to the wonderful sensations. Then with every ounce of control she had left she pulled away and walked closer to the fire before taking a seat on the blanket. She stared at the flames even as she heard Renny come to sit beside her. He didn't touch her this time. He simply waited.

"I've never been into casual sex," she said bluntly.

Renny reached around her, pulled the bowl of strawberries from the ledge and set it between them. He took a particularly plump one off the top and with a finger on her chin turned her to face him. "It might surprise you, but neither am I." He held the strawberry by its stem and traced the edge over her lips.

"But? I don't understand?"

"Shh. Just listen to me for a minute." He continued rubbing the fruit over her lips and felt a lurch in his groin when her tongue snaked out to lick it before she captured it between her teeth. Juice streamed down her chin and when she would have wiped it away with her fingers he leaned forward and licked it off. She didn't move, only watched him intently until he pulled back. "Here, drink this." He offered her the flute full of champagne.

"Over the years it seems my reputation has preceded me. I've often found that when people don't know enough about you, they begin to make stuff up. And because I'm not in the forefront of the family business with my father and brothers, they've never really heard enough about me."

The champagne was cool and refreshing going down, highlighting the sweetness of the strawberry. Bree cradled the glass in her hands and watched the man beside her transform yet again. No longer was he the gorgeous billionaire with the tarnished reputation. Now he seemed to be more the vulnerable man wounded by some circumstance of life. "So they made up what they wanted and are determined to have everyone believe it's true."

He gave her a wry grin. "Something like that."

Bree completely realized that this could be a ploy. But something told her it wasn't.

Bree lifted a strawberry from the bowl and mimicked his previous movements on his lips. When juice spilled from his mouth, she smiled as she leaned in closer to take care of it for him. But he wasn't as restrained as she was; he grabbed the back of her head, slanting her mouth over his and thrusting his tongue inside.

Bree was drowning in the sweetness of the kiss. While his tongue was persistent, his hands on her demanding, the fruity taste of the berries mingled with the sense that this was more than just a kiss…more than just a seduction had her eager with anticipation. He must have moved that bowl from between them because the next thing she knew—and without pulling his lips from hers—she was lying on her back, his toned body stretched atop hers.

Every part of her tingled, from her ankles to her knees that were now tangling themselves around his legs; to her thighs and her pelvic area that thrust simultaneously with his. Renny's hands moved from her hair and neck to her breasts, kneading them both with a fluid expertise she'd never experienced before. He invaded every part of her, his words about not being the playboy the public made him out to be floating through her mind, even as his tongue mastered hers. She ran her hands up and down the back of his head, to his strong shoulders, then finally beneath the hem of his shirt to touch the muscles beneath. She whimpered when her skin made contact with his.

The moment he felt her hands on his bare back, Renny's body went into overdrive, taking his mind right along with it. He'd admired her for the past week, had watched the motions and gyrations of her body as she moved around him. He'd tasted the sweetness of her kiss and knew he'd never be able to stop there. A few feet away the fire crackled, champagne grew warm, the scent of strawberries wafted through the air, but none of that mattered. All he could concentrate on was her, the feel of her softness beneath him, the beat of her heart against his chest, the sensations her fingers erupted in him.

He trailed moist kisses across the stubborn jawline he'd become so familiar with, down her neck until he reached the hollow at her shoulders. Her shirt stopped his downward progress and with a savage growl he grabbed the hem of it and pulled it over her head. She wasn't wearing a bra, her unbound breasts pert and glowing in the dim light. With a move so slow, so tender he almost moaned, Renny dipped his head and took one pebbled nipple into his mouth while cupping the other breast in his hand. She wasn't too big that her small frame was disproportioned, nor was she so small to seem boyish, but her mounds fit perfectly in the palm of his hand and he kneaded in rhythm with each breath she expelled.

He touched her breasts as if they were priceless gems that he didn't want to break. He licked them with featherlike strokes of his tongue, then squeezed them until her center throbbed. With the pads of his fingers lightly passing over each nipple, Bree was in heaven. Somewhere in the back of her mind she knew that she should proceed carefully with him, her last relationship having ended badly, but she couldn't stop him and didn't really want to.

Renny devoted all his attention to her breasts as she squirmed beneath him, unable to sate every desire she felt creeping through her system. She struggled only momentarily to get his T-shirt up and over his head, but when she did, she did not hesitate in lifting slightly so she could take each of his beaded nipples into her mouth. His hands threaded in her hair, steadying her movements, and she felt his ragged breaths firsthand.

"Sabrina," he whispered.

Bree loved the way he said her name, the *S* sound sending marvelous chills up and down her spine. She rubbed her cheek over the hardness of his chest, for once in her life feeling a safety that she couldn't explain. His shoulders were broad, his muscles toned and delectable; her hands and mouth couldn't get enough of him, and her motions became frantic. When her hands roamed lower she felt his bulging desire and jerked away.

Renny still had his fingers entwined in her hair and noticed the moment she began to retreat. He pulled her head back gently, looking down into her eyes. What he saw there had him clenching his teeth in anger. She was afraid.

His brave little bodyguard, the mouthy spitfire that kept him on his toes daily was afraid of his desire for her. Only another man could spark that type of fear, and for a moment Renny thought he could actually kill a human being. He tamped down on his temper and asked her quietly, "What is it, baby?"

Bree had never felt such conflict in her life. On the contrary, she'd always been so sure of her decisions, so clear on her goals. But now, this time, in this man's arms she wasn't sure. Her track record proved her decision-making skills were dulled when it came to men, yet she felt this overwhelming sense that Renny was different. "I…I can't. I mean, this is probably a mistake." She tore her eyes away from his because he looked at her with such concern, such soul-shattering compassion that she wanted to cry for the mistake she'd made in the past and the one she was probably making again.

Renny slackened his hold on her hair, let his hands fall to cup her face. "I won't hurt you, Sabrina."

That's what they all say. Bree shook her head. "I just don't think I can do this, Renny. It would be a mistake."

Her voice hitched as she spoke and he knew he could never pressure her, could never push her to do what she simply wasn't ready to do. Though the throbbing in his pants was persistent, he was in control and as he pushed her onto her back he vowed to find out what had spooked her so and drive it from her mind. "You don't have to do anything, baby. Just lie here and let me relax you."

Those big expressive eyes looked at him as if he'd just spoken a foreign language and he couldn't help but smile. This was the Sabrina he knew. The intelligent one, the careful, no-nonsense one that took her job seriously. But as he touched her, as he'd kissed her, he'd gotten a sense of the other Sabrina. The passionate one, the desirable one, the one that made his blood simmer and boil. "Trust me, sweetheart."

She shouldn't. Trust was something earned and not to be given haphazardly, she'd learned that already. Yet he hadn't lied to her, his past could be easily checked out if she really wanted to, but she felt inclined to just believe him. She lifted a hand to his face, her fingers outlining his lips, feeling the tickle of his new growth. "You are not what I expected," she whispered.

He captured a finger between his lips, drew it into his mouth and suckled. Her eyes grew dark and he knew that she was allowing herself to feel the heat between them again. Whatever had scared her earlier was losing this battle. He wouldn't push her, but he would give her a taste of how things could be. "Stop expecting so much. Just feel."

He kissed down the length of her arm until his lips found her breasts again. He didn't spend a lot of time there, though he could have entertained himself with those twin mounds all night. Instead he moved to her belly, kissing her navel and lavishing moist kisses to each side. When her breathing increased, the subtle movements of her hips turned more frantic. Renny slipped his fingers beneath the elastic band of her pajamas. Lifting her hips slightly off the floor, he removed the pants first, leaving her panties in place just in case she grew afraid again.

He pulled her foot up toward his mouth and licked the heel, then her arch, and finally moved his tongue eagerly over each toe. He stole a glance at her to make sure she was okay. She'd lifted her arms until they had fallen on the pillows above her, her eyes slightly open. Taking that as a good sign, he kissed all the way up to her inner thighs, lavishing each side with long strokes of his tongue. He could smell her scent and all the blood in his body moved quickly to one spot. He was harder than he'd ever been in his life and thought for sure he'd embarrass himself at any moment.

"Oh, Renny," Bree whispered.

The sound of his name so soft in the air made him more eager to please her. He spread her legs, licked her center one time through the cotton of her panties and heard her immediate intake of breath.

Her panties slid down her legs quickly and he touched her with a finger first, opening her swollen lips, spreading her essence throughout her center. He lifted that finger, looked down at her, then placed it into his mouth.

Bree was watching every move he made, not wanting to miss a thing. She'd never felt this way before, never had a man do the things to her that Renny was doing. Somewhere in the back of her mind Bree realized that allowing this intimacy was wrong, but she couldn't bring herself to stop him.

Renny lifted her legs, placed them on his shoulders, then looked up at her one last time. "I would never hurt you, Sabrina. But I am going to make you scream." With that said his tongue slipped between her legs, moving with long, bold strokes from top to bottom and back again.

Bree gripped the blanket beneath her trying to hold on to any scraps of dignity she had left. This…what he was doing now…had most definitely never happened to her in all her thirty-four years. The sensations ripping through her now roared at a rapid pace and she felt as if a tornado had settled deep in the pit of her stomach and was just starting its spiral out of control.

"Oh, Lorenzo."

She was calling him by his full name. His tongue moved quickly, still stroking her moist folds. She was almost ready for the true assault. Her thighs shook on his shoulders the second he took her tightened bud between his teeth.

His name tore from her mouth faster. "Lorenzo. Lorenzo. Lorenzo!"

She lifted her hips to meet his thrusts and Renny slipped a finger inside her opening. She moaned, a long guttural sound that signaled her release was near. He'd told her he would make her scream and dammit, that's exactly what he planned to do.

He slipped another finger inside her even as his mouth continued to work her. Bending those fingers inside her in an upward motion, brushing her upper walls, he summoned her release.

Bree could hear her voice, heard his name rushing from her lips in an ultrafeminine tone and couldn't do a damn thing to stop it. He probably thought she was a raving lunatic. But then, if he but stopped this sweet torture, she wouldn't be acting this way. His fingers were so deep inside her she would swear they were in the vicinity of her lower stomach. And his lips tightened, then released the hold on her only to allow his tongue to take over the torment.

Her pitch grew louder as her thighs tightened around his head. She was so sweet, so responsive to him. Renny would give anything to sink his manhood inside her depth, but that would have to be for another time. Right now it was all about Sabrina and winning her trust. His fingers moved faster, his tongue keeping up the pace when she groaned again, his name wrenching from her almost as if it were painful.

"Lorenzo. Ooooohhhh, Lorenzo. Yeeeeesssss!"

Bree shook uncontrollably as that tornado grew and took shape, whipping about everything inside her, swirling until she was dizzy with bliss, then blowing away just as abruptly as it started, leaving her floating slowly back to earth.

Renny slowed his movements, her climax melting over his lips and fingers. Her thighs stilled and he let them fall from his shoulders slowly. He kissed her now-trembling thighs before moving upward to her navel, then to her breasts again. She wasn't moving, but her breathing was erratic. For a moment he laid his head on her heart, wondering what it would feel like to have his own special place there.

He moved until he was level with her face and dropped a soft kiss on her other swollen lips. Bree stirred, opening her eyes as if she were in a drunken stupor. Looking at him was different now. Amazingly, she wasn't embarrassed by what had just happened between them, but she was baffled by his unselfishness. They both knew he could have had his way with her and she would have been powerless to stop him. But he hadn't. He'd stopped himself. That one action proved to her above any background check she could ever perform that Renny Bennett was no playboy. He was a man. A man any woman would be lucky to have. But was he for her?

Renny saw the moment questions began to race through her mind and held back a frown. "No. Don't do that, baby. Don't question yourself or me right now. Just feel." He kissed her lightly again. "Just feel." His lips, more persistent now, parted hers until his tongue touched hers again.

Chapter 6

Bree was warm, and she snuggled back against the source of heat. She'd been dreaming a wonderful dream of swimming in clear, blue water, walking on white beaches, eating exotic foods…and making love to a gorgeous man. A smile played over her lips and she moaned as that man came up behind her, lifted her hair and dropped a kiss on her shoulder, then moved to her neck. "I love you," he whispered over and over again, filling her with such joy and contentment that she wanted to cry.

She shifted again and felt a thick erection at her bottom. She eased farther back, enjoying the feeling. Between her own legs throbbed and she was ready to open up and allow that erection in. A hand clasped her left breast and she moaned. She was so ready.

Her dream lover's lips were on her shoulder and her neck and he whispered in her ear. "Sabrina, don't forget that I'm only a man. If you keep rubbing against me like that I won't be responsible for what happens next."

Bree's eyes shot open with a quickness. It was the right voice—the one of her dream lover—but he wasn't saying the correct words, nor were they standing on a white-sand beach. Her body froze as she took in her surroundings, and memories of where she was and how she'd come to be there came flooding back.

She rolled to her back only to look up into those sexy dark eyes that had invaded her most private thoughts. "Renny?" she gasped in a sleep-fogged voice.

"You'd better not be waking up naked with anybody else," Renny joked, then dropped a kiss on her forehead.

Bree lifted the blanket, saw that she was in fact naked and groaned. What had she done? Her eyes flew back to his face while the question lodged in her throat.

Renny recognized the fear instantly and his light mood shifted. What had he done to frighten her this time? "Last night was beautiful, wasn't it, sweetheart?" He traced a finger along the line of her jaw waiting for all the memories to sink in. She probably assumed since she was naked and he was partially so that they'd gone all the way. But once her mind had a moment to clear its sleepiness and retrace their actions, she'd calm down. She'd fallen asleep so comfortably in his arms last night after they'd finished off the strawberries and champagne and talked about their childhoods. He'd held her all night thinking of how right she felt in his arms. As a matter of fact he'd just been thinking—before she'd rubbed her butt against his groin, disturbing his train of thought—that Sabrina seemed to fit into his life. That thought frightened him a bit, but not as much as it should have, not as much as it would have just a month or two ago.

"We…we slept here?" she asked tentatively. She remembered his kisses last night, his touch, him asking her to trust him before… She wasn't so much embarrassed as she was aroused by the memory. Still, this was new for her, she'd never had a morning after—even if it wasn't technically after sex.

His finger moved lazily over her shoulder. "Mmm-hmm, you said you didn't feel like moving. I agreed." He hadn't been looking forward to returning to his own bed alone. His gaze grabbed hers and held it seriously. "Sabrina, last night was just for you. I've never done that with anyone else."

She blinked quickly, her brow rising without the question ever leaving her mouth.

Renny sighed. "I told you how people create their own stories. I've dated plenty of women, but I can count on one hand how many I've been intimate with in any way."

He was Lorenzo Bennett, sexy billionaire with a great body and an even greater car. The reality of his words were ludicrous; still, she found herself believing him. "I, um…it—" she cleared her throat "—it was a first for me, as well."

"Good," Renny whispered as he descended on her lips. "I don't much like the thought of any other man knowing you that well."

The words sounded like ownership in her mind and she wanted to back away, but his lips touched hers and she lost the thought.

Bleep, bleep, bleep.

A chirping sound interrupted the kiss, and Renny looked around the room where they still lay on the floor. "What the hell is that?"

Bleep, bleep, bleep.

Bree squirmed from beneath him. "It's my phone." Completely forgetting she was naked, she threw the blanket aside and moved to the hall table where she'd thrown her jacket and searched the pockets for her cell phone. She really liked kissing Renny, so whoever was calling had better be important. She didn't really look at the number before pressing the talk button, figuring it was early in the morning and was most likely Sam checking in. "Hello?"

"You always were a morning person."

The voice stilled her heart and if it weren't for the table behind her she would have fallen to the floor. "What? What do you want?" She wouldn't have to look at the number now. It was the same one from yesterday. The one with the North Carolina area code.

He was quiet and then said, "I miss you."

Bree closed her eyes, swallowed hard. Her head was spinning. This was not happening. She had been perfectly clear when she'd left North Carolina. Hell, the circumstances had all but dictated there be no other choice. Why was he calling her now? Why was he saying these things? "This is not good. You calling me is not good at all."

"Please, Sabrina, we really need to talk. So much has changed."

She shook her head, her eyes still closed. "Nothing has changed for me and I don't want to talk anymore." Her insides swished and swayed as all those memories came flooding back. The pain, the betrayal, the embarrassment. Her head started to throb, but she wouldn't let it get the best of her. She opened her eyes, about to tell him never to call her again, when her voice caught. Renny was standing right in front of her, a questioning look on his face. Again, her surroundings had gotten away from her and she struggled to stand up straight. "Please don't call me again." She didn't wait for a response, but clicked off the phone instantly. Renny's eyes bore into her with a fierce glare that left her breathless.

"Who was that?" Of its own accord, his jaw clenched even as he willed his hands to stay still at his side. At first he'd been caught up in the pleasant sight of her totally naked walking across his living room without a care in the world, as if it were the most natural thing to be naked in his company in his home. Then he'd watched her contentment flee as she spoke to the person on the phone.

He'd instantly become alarmed and went to her. She'd closed her eyes as if whatever was being said was too painful for her to face. For a brief second he could swear he saw her tremble. And that was not acceptable.

"Uh…just someone…a fellow soldier from the base." She managed the words, but couldn't help feeling the heat radiating from his closeness. It wasn't the same heat she'd felt only moments ago; this was of anger, raw and real. The last thing she needed was Renny getting involved in her situation. He had enough to deal with on his own. Her military dilemma was just that, hers, and she would not inflict her mistakes on anyone else.

"A female or male soldier?" He really didn't have to ask, he'd known it was a man, most likely the man that made her leery of all other men.

Bree licked her lips. "He's a male. We didn't part on the best of terms." She squared her shoulders. "I'm really not into keeping in touch with people from my past. Anyway, I'd better get dressed and check in with Sam. Are you going to work this morning?" She remembered the piece he was working on and almost cursed herself for bringing the provocative memory into their conversation.

She was so confused at this moment. Not only had she allowed Renny—well, almost begged him—to continue touching her last night, but now she had to figure out where that put their relationship in the light of day. And she'd awakened in his arms, content and almost looking forward to whatever was going on between them; then Harold had called.

Renny caught her by the shoulders just as she was about to brush past him. "Tell me what he said to upset you."

His grip wasn't tight, but she knew better than to try and break free of it. "It was nothing. Forget about it. I'm chilly."

She really wasn't; his touch alone had warmed her right down to her toes.

Renny frowned. He couldn't make her tell him, but he could find out on his own. He figured that knowing the man that had hurt her would give him some insight as to how he could heal the wounds. Suddenly, healing Sabrina was very important to him. He moved his hands up and down her arms. "Sorry. You're probably right. Go on and take your shower. I'll fix us some coffee."

Bree managed a smile. "That sounds good."

Renny let her walk away, but as soon as he heard the bathroom door close and the water running he returned to the table where her cell phone sat. Picking it up, he summoned the call log and jotted down the number of the last call received. It wasn't a Connecticut area code. Moving quickly to his office, he booted up his computer and continued to stare at the piece of paper he'd written the number on.

After putting in the appropriate pass codes he went to the desired Web site and punched in another pass code. Technology was amazing. You could find out just about anything on anybody in the world by typing a few lines into the Internet. He typed in the telephone number and waited only a couple of seconds before a name and billing address came up.

Colonel Harold T. Richmond, Raleigh, North Carolina.

Her commanding officer? A private acquaintance? An old boyfriend?

Questions roared through Renny's mind as he heard the water shut off a few rooms away. She'd be back out shortly. Renny printed the information and exited the site. Turning the computer off, he folded the paper, reminding himself to make amends with Sam Desdune long enough to have him check this guy out.

Bree nursed her cup of coffee, thinking about the call she'd received a while ago. She couldn't believe Harold was calling her after all this time and after all that had happened. Before leaving North Carolina she'd told him she never wanted to see or speak to him again. That message had seemed plain and simple to her, but apparently Harold hadn't gotten the translation. Well, she'd told him again. Now hopefully he'd listen.

She wondered what Renny thought of her telephone conversation, knowing that he'd heard it since he was standing right in her face as she'd talked. He looked at her as if he were going to snatch the phone away from her ear at any moment. That's why she'd hung up on Harold as fast as she did. The last thing she needed was to have to explain to Renny about Harold and what had happened in North Carolina.

He'd let the subject drop, and when she'd emerged from her shower he hadn't brought it up again. He simply sat her down with a cup of coffee and a bagel and went off to get dressed himself. In the shower she'd had time to contemplate what had happened between them last night. As magnificent as it was and as much as she longed for him to do it again and again and to even go further the next time, she knew it couldn't be. She couldn't sleep with Renny.

They would never make it as a couple and she realized with Harold's call that that's what she wanted in her life. She wanted a man she could call her own, a man to share her thoughts and dreams with. And even though Renny wasn't the proclaimed playboy, he wasn't the settling-down type, either. He liked his privacy and his freedom too much for that. Besides, she'd never be able to stomach him working with Yolanda on a daily basis.

Thoughts of Yolanda caused her to remember Renny's art and the piece he had still unfinished in his studio. She left the kitchen and made sure she still heard the water from the shower running before making her way through the closed door. Flicking on the light, she looked to where she knew the piece sat. Moving slowly, Bree approached the figures, feeling their heat as she drew closer.

This man and woman were so in love, so in tune with each other that it was difficult to tell where he began and she ended. From the smooth curves to the beginnings of the facial features, the power in their union was undeniable. Bree rubbed her hand over the spot where they were joined and felt her own nipples tighten. Closing her eyes, she imagined riding Renny this way. The hard length of him that she'd felt pressed against her back all night and this morning offered a good estimate of his size, and she shivered with need.

Licking her lips, she now had both hands on the sculpture, grazing over the naked bodies. She'd wrap her legs around Renny and take him in completely. She'd start moving slowly, giving her body time to acclimate itself to his size. He'd hold her hips, guiding her over his shaft in long easy strokes. She bit her bottom lip even as her center began to throb.

Throwing her head back, she let the sensations wash over her until she could hear their combined heavy breathing, could smell the musty scent of their sex. He'd encourage her with lurid talk of all the things they'd do together as his manhood thrust deeper and deeper inside her. That twirling began in her stomach and she knew a release would come soon.

Renny watched her from the doorway, saw the moment she slipped into the same position as his sculpture and wanted nothing more than to be there with her. He moved slowly. Sabrina didn't hear him, she was too far gone. His hands slipped around her waist, pulling her back against his hardness. Her tongue snaked out of her mouth tracing her lower lip, and as he watched her he did the same. Her head fell back against his chest as tiny moans escaped her. He leaned forward, dropping wet kisses along her throat, around to her neck.

His hands moved from her waist to her breasts and squeezed gently. He wanted this woman so badly. He wanted to pull down the jogging pants she wore and bend her over his worktable. He'd enter her from the back, kneading her butt until she screamed his name. Each thrust would be filled with all the wanting, all the longing she brought out of him. He knew how passionate she was now, how responsive her body was to his touch, so he knew without a doubt she'd be wet and waiting for him. He bit her neck as desire formed a stranglehold around him. "Sabrina," he growled.

Bree heard her name and knew it wasn't the sculpture speaking. Her eyes flew open at the realization that she was no longer alone. Renny was there with her, touching her, kissing her, calling her name, and she almost melted inside. Instead she straightened slowly and turned to him. "I'm sorry. I must have gotten carried away," she whispered.

Renny felt her shift and allowed her the space to turn around, but still kept her captive between him and the worktable. "I think that's supposed to be my line." He grinned.

Bree smiled in return, glad he wasn't going to embarrass her by asking what the hell she'd been doing fantasizing about a statue. "Whichever." She tried to move away. "I'll just get out of your way so you can get to work."

Renny held her still. "Stay."

It was a simple request and she really didn't have anything to do in the other room, but being close to him was driving her mad. "You have to finish this piece and then get ready for the opening." He was moving his hands up and down her arms, scattering her thoughts.

"This piece is personal," he told her as he shifted their bodies so that he was sitting on the stool and she was sitting on his lap. "You give me inspiration to work on it, so I need you to stay in here with me."

She loved the feel of his arms around her, enfolding her. She also admitted that she liked to watch him work. His hands were masterful, and with each touch of the clay she could imagine him touching her. "How could I inspire such a pro-vocative image for you?" She was no Yolanda.

Renny chuckled. Was she serious? Did she have no clue how sexy she was? It was probably the fact that she'd grown up a tomboy and nobody ever bothered to tell her she was a girl instead. Being in the military most likely further diluted her sexuality. He picked up some clay, began to form the woman's breasts. "When we first met you had on a T-shirt. It wasn't too tight as to be offensive, yet it fit across your breasts like a hand in a glove."

Bree took a deep breath, expelled it.

"That night I thought if I had just reached out and cupped my hand I could have fit your breast right in my palm." With deft movements he made the curve, then replaced one crafting knife for another and detailed the nipple.

"Oh, great, so now my breasts are small enough to put in your hand." She bristled, but wasn't really offended.

Renny dropped a kiss on her earlobe. "That's a good thing. I don't like excess."

"Yeah, right."

"The first time you came into my studio was the first time I saw those breasts uncovered. I not only felt them in my palm, but I tasted them, too."

Bree watched as his large hands moved over the small model intricately detailing the woman's anatomy.

"Your nipples were so tight and so tingly in my mouth I knew that this model had to have the same thing. They were perfect and I want my sculpture to be perfect."

Bree sighed. "You're really into perfection, huh?"

"Definitely."

"Then you'd better let me go," she said quietly.

Renny didn't miss the change in tone, the moment outside thoughts intruded on their time. "The thing about perfection is that it's not always blatant, not always apparent for the eye to see. For true perfection one has to look closely, to study, to delve deep until it's found."

"Yolanda's perfect." Bree almost pouted.

Renny frowned and picked up another knife to mold the woman's backside. "Yolanda is a perfect gallery manager. She's a nice-looking woman, but she is not a perfect woman, at least not by my standards."

Bree shifted on his lap, resting her elbows on the work-table now as he created. "And what are your standards? Breathing? Passably pretty?"

Renny shook his head. "Nah. I like strength in a woman, intelligence and a sense of self-worth, self-respect. I like a woman that doesn't need me to define her."

Bree was quiet. She knew what she was and knew without a doubt she'd still be exactly that after this job and Renny Bennett were out of her life.

"What about your standards for a man?"

"I have to be able to trust him," she said definitely and without hesitation. "The best-looking packages can offer you everything, but when you find out he's offering it to other women, as well, it sort of loses its appeal."

Had this Harold guy cheated on her? Renny reminded himself not to push. They were making progress. She was comfortable with him and he didn't want to mess that up. "What if he's not what he appears to be? Could you still trust him?"

"If he was honest, appearances wouldn't matter."

"What if he appeared rich and fabulous, but was really talented and ordinary?"

"Ordinary has its own appeal."

Renny dropped the knife, pulled her closer to him and cradled her. "Do I appeal to you, Sabrina?"

Bree once again rested her head against his shoulder. "I think too much, Renny."

Bleep, bleep, bleep.

Dammit! He was going to toss her cell phone right out the window.

Bree reached down and retrieved the phone from her hip. "Hello? Hey, Sam."

Renny trailed a finger down the nape of her neck. She'd pulled her hair into that ponytail again, but he actually liked the way her silky hair brushed over his hand.

"Tonight at seven sounds good. We'll be there." Bree shrugged her shoulders in an attempt to ward off Renny's wandering hands.

He replaced his hand with his mouth simply because he liked to watch her squirm. She enjoyed him touching her just as much as he liked the feel of his hands on her. But he could tell she was trying to not let her brother know what was going on over here.

"She's always worried," Bree was saying in reference to Lynn. She hadn't spoken to her sister for two days and she'd already reported to Sam that she was worried about her. "Yeah, I'll call her as soon as I hang up with you."

Renny's hands had moved to her waist and were now going up and down her thighs as she was still sitting on his lap. She was so soft even though she could stand to gain a few pounds. She had a healthy appetite, but she didn't stay still long enough to eat regularly. That thought bothered him. She seemed to be so busy taking care of her career that she never stopped to take care of herself.

"Yeah. Bye, Sam." Bree disconnected the line, put her phone back on the clip at her hip. "You know I can conduct a conversation a lot better without your hands roaming all over me." She removed his hands from her thighs, instantly missing the warmth they'd provided.

Renny ignored her comment and cupped her breasts instead. "I thought you were calling someone else as soon as you hung up."

She sighed. Why did his touch have to feel so damned good? "You'd love to keep my mind occupied so you can have your way with me, wouldn't you?" She lifted her hands to his to remove them from her breasts, but instead found herself kneading right along with him.

"You like it. I know you do."

Bree groaned. "I'd be lying if I said I didn't. Still, we should stop. I'll need all my wits about me to dodge my sister's questioning. That's who I'm supposed to be calling."

Renny released her breasts, but continued to hold her against his chest. He liked the feel of her against him. A little too much, his mind screamed. "Why would you dodge her questions?"

"She's convinced I'm hiding something and I don't want to talk about it." Bree caught herself the moment she ended the sentence, probably a moment too late. He was going to latch on to that statement like a dog to a bone and then she'd be dodging his questions, as well.

Renny stiffened only slightly, then looked up at her, tweaking her nose as he smiled into her worried face. "Why don't we pay her a visit together? She wouldn't dare harass you if I'm there."

Bree cocked her head to the side, her ponytail swaying to her shoulder, her brow drawn in question. "Why would you want to go with me to visit my sister?"

Renny's gaze had fallen to her lips and he traced the outline slowly. "Because if we stay here and I continue to try and work on this sculpture I'll need my inspiration." He dropped a quick kiss on her lips, then hovered only inches away. "And since you are my inspiration and I can't seem to keep my hands off you, I'm convinced working is shot to hell for the day."

Besides, if her sister thought she was hiding something, and Renny was sure she was hiding something, the two of them definitely needed to meet, and the sooner the better.

* * *

Lynn lived along the coast of Greenwich Harbor where the ferry transferred citizens to Long Island and back every weekday. It was a nice forty-minute drive from Renny's condo and they chatted amiably on the way.

Renny was actually a very funny, very entertaining guy as Bree soon learned. He'd grown up in Greenwich near the old Bush-Holley House until his parents purchased their estate in the upscale Old Greenwich neighborhood. Bree had grown up in Belle Haven, about fifteen minutes from Lynn's home. Funny how they'd been so close but never met until now. While they talked the radio played in the background, Bree stopping to sing every now and then. But it was when she'd dance in the confines of the passenger seat that Renny would glance over at her. His gaze had darkened and Bree felt her mouth water. He really was attracted to her—that she still couldn't believe.

"Okay, which way now?" Renny asked when he'd turned into the complex where her sister lived.

"She's just around this bend, number twenty-seven." She pointed and Renny made the turn heading to the top of the hill.

He released her hand to park the car and Bree made sure her cell phone was on her hip and powered up. The pants she wore today were a little too tight for her gun to go in its holster at her ankle, so she'd strapped her knife there instead. As cozy as this felt she was still on the job. While she was busy doing all her checking she hadn't even noticed that Renny had gotten out of the car and was now headed toward her door until he pulled it open and extended a hand for her to get out. She didn't think she'd ever get used to this, but smiled the moment she released her seat belt and placed her hand in his.

Afraid someone might see them, Bree tried to pull her

hand away from his, but Renny held on tightly as they walked toward the front door. She should say something. She should tell him that whatever was going on between them needed to be kept between them. Since there was really no future in this "thing" they had going, there was no need for anyone else to know about it. But she didn't have time before the front door swung open and Lynn's smiling face greeted them.

"Isn't this a surprise?" She looked from Bree to the man who was undoubtedly holding her hand. "Was she lost? Are you returning her to the address on her identification?" Lynn asked cheerfully.

Bree rolled her eyes. "Very funny, Lynn. This is Lorenzo Bennett, my client." Bree hadn't hesitated, but felt Renny stiffen at her words.

Lynn extended her hand to him. "Mr. Bennett, it's a pleasure to meet you."

Still bristling from the introduction as her client, Renny let Bree's hand go when she'd tried to pull away a second time. He realized that the title shouldn't bother him, since that was his official position in her life. But he assumed that Bree had also realized that after last night they'd officially crossed the line of business. At any rate, he didn't want to get into that here at her sister's house. "You can call me Renny. And the pleasure is all mine. Sabrina has told me a lot about you."

He examined the sister, this taller, more mature-looking version of Sabrina. They had that same mocha skin color and almost the same eyes except Sabrina's were bigger, filled with more emotion. Her sister's slanted at the ends, giving her a more exotic look, the look that had garnered his sister Adriana such celebrity as a model.

"Bree hasn't told me a bit about you, so come on in so I can get to know you for myself."

Bree instantly felt small and unwanted. Lynn's tall frame linked with Renny's fantastically masculine one looked almost comparable as they moved into the living room and she was left to close the door behind them. She couldn't look like anything more than Renny's little sister when she was on his arm—another nail in her coffin, no doubt.

By the time she headed into the living room, Lynn and Renny were already seated. Lynn in a high-backed Victorian chair that she'd gotten at an antique auction and loved almost more than her own child and Renny in the beige cushioned sofa. Bree was about to take a seat on the ottoman near the window where Jeremy usually sat when Renny caught her glance and patted the spot on the couch beside him. She chewed on her bottom lip in thought before giving in to the urge to be near him. Whether it looked good or not, she couldn't deny that she liked when he was close to her and after last night found herself longing for his touch.

"So your family is in some sort of danger and my family is assigned to guard you?" Lynn asked, noting the possessiveness in Renny's motions. Something was definitely going on here, something that went way beyond the business of security. Her little, confident, usually mouthy sister was docilely sitting next to this man with almost a moony look in her eyes. Oh, yeah, something was going on.

"Something like that." Renny dismissed the comment, not wanting to discuss what was going on with his family with Sabrina's sister. "Sabrina and I were tired of being cooped up in that house, so we decided to go visiting. This is a great house you have here." Renny looked around the room with its welcoming feel. The toy trucks scattered on the floor and the baseball glove he'd spotted on the table in the hallway gave away the fact that a child lived here. He'd taken in the neighborhood and the grass-filled yards as he'd entered the complex. It was a great place to raise kids.

"Yes. I like it. Where do you live?"

Bree caught Lynn's smile just as her sister's eyes moved

back to Renny. Aw, man, this was not good. Lynn had picked up on something already. She'd known it was a mistake coming here with him.

"I live a few blocks from Town Hall, the condos on Lake. But I come from a big family, so I'm used to the country living. I actually miss it sometimes."

"Really? You think you'll have a big family of your own someday?"

"Renny's opening an art gallery," Bree interrupted. "He's a really talented sculptor."

Lynn held back a chuckle. "That sounds exciting."

"It is actually." Renny relaxed and went into a spiel about his gallery and what type of art he planned to showcase.

Bree heard footsteps in the distance and rose to head her nephew off. She'd successfully shifted the conversation away from Renny personally to Renny's business. That was safer for the moment because Bree was deathly afraid of what was going through her sister's mind right now.

Tiny legs took one step at a time as Bree rounded the hallway. He looked down at each foot as it made contact. He was in deep concentration as he'd only mastered coming up and down steps on his feet a few months ago. She crouched down and tapped on the bottom step to get his attention. Huge chocolate-brown eyes looked up and a small smile played over his lips. The tiniest teeth she'd ever seen were revealed, and his round belly rumbled with the laughter he was about to release. Unable to wait another moment, Bree took the last three steps and scooped him up into her arms.

"Mmm." She inhaled the sweet baby scent of him and kissed his chubby cheek. "I think you've grown in the two days I've been away." Holding him back so she could look into his face, she smiled down at him.

"Ah-huh, I a big boy," Jeremy said and pointed to his chest.

Bree warmed all over, adding this gorgeous little boy to the list of things she envied about her sister. "You sure are."

As much as Bree loved him, Jeremy was all boy, so being wrapped in his auntie's arms receiving numerous hugs and kisses was not his idea of fun. Before long he was squirming out of her arms until she'd had no other choice but to put him down. Then just like that he was off. She giggled before following behind him only to be stopped short by the sight of him jumping onto the couch beside Renny, who extended a hand for him to shake.

Visions danced merrily through her mind. Renny with a child. Renny with a son. Renny with their son. She and Renny in a house like this with their own children.

A hand went to her throat as she battled for air.

Lynn spotted her and figured enough was enough. She and Renny had spoken in the moments that Bree was out of the room and there was no doubt in her mind that something much more personal was going on between them. Rising from her chair and trusting that her son was in good hands, she made her way over to her sister, grabbing her by the wrist as soon as she was close enough. "Let's go to the kitchen. You've got some explaining to do."

Bree followed only because she felt the sudden urge to be away from Renny, away from the weird feelings he was evoking in her. She soon found her eagerness to be away from the man a curse and rolled her eyes as Lynn plopped down into one of the kitchen chairs looking at her expectantly. "Tell me you didn't sleep with this man, Bree," Lynn began. "Tell me I'm not picking up some serious vibes from the two of you."

"I…um…I don't know what you're talking about, Lynn." Bree turned her back to her sister, going to the refrigerator to get something to drink.

"Then I'll ask an easier question. Is that or is it not a passion mark on your neck?"

Bree screeched, her juice box falling to the floor as her hands went to the exact spot on her neck that Lynn was referring to.

"Mmm-hmm." Lynn nodded. "After you pick that up you come over here and tell me what the hell is going on with you."

Chapter 7

Golden rays stretched over the horizon. Violent strips of orange and yellow surrounded the last burning embers of the sun as it made its descent for the day. Bree watched the spectacular display from the car window. Like she imagined the huge orb was also experiencing, she felt intense heat, then waning despair.

It had been so clear for Lynn to see, her attraction or connection to the man sitting across from her. *Of course, this high-school hickey on my neck sure didn't help matters.* Still, Bree wasn't sure she wanted it to be so obvious. If Lynn saw it, then Renny had to see it, too. Maybe he was taking advantage of what he'd seen. He always looked at her as if he could read right into her mind. What if he'd recognized the signs of wanting and acted?

No. He wasn't like that, he'd told her so. Harold had also told her a number of things—most of which turned out to be colossal lies. Could she be on the road to betrayal again?

She couldn't think. For the first time in her life she couldn't get a handle on her own feelings let alone the feelings of a man she'd only known a few days. His presence was undeniable, though, both in her life and in her mind. And after watching him this afternoon with Jeremy she was afraid.

Bree and Lynn had prepared a lunch of sandwiches and soup while Lynn continued to grill her about Renny. She'd told her sister of the steamy kisses and of the man's magnetic touch, but she'd left out the pleasure his tongue had brought her the night before. Lynn didn't need to hear all that. It had felt good to talk through some of the things she'd been feeling, but without Lynn knowing the full truth about North Carolina, it would be hard for her to understand Bree's dilemma.

She would have to figure this out alone. And she planned to do just that. But when they walked into the dining room to place the food on the table she'd seen Renny on the floor playing with Jeremy and his Matchbox garage. Two heads were huddled together in a far corner of the room, one full of brown curls, the other close-cut dark ones. Big fingers and little ones pushed the tiny cars up and down the ramp and into colorful parking spaces while lips protruded making the obvious sounds of an engine revving.

In an instant her heart swelled to the point she knew she'd make a fool of herself, so she quickly headed back to the kitchen. Throughout the duration of the afternoon, Renny and Jeremy acted as if they were the only two people in the world. Except for a few glances and smiles tossed her way from Renny, Bree and Lynn were left to their own devices.

"He's not your ordinary playboy, is he?" Lynn asked when Renny quickly agreed to Jeremy's plea for him to put him down for his nap.

Bree watched as Renny lifted her nephew's small body, leveling him over his shoulder and directing him to hold out his hands. Up the stairs the makeshift jet went, complete with sound effects and plenty of turbulence thanks to Renny's bobbing knees. "No," Bree whispered. "He's not ordinary at all."

Bree watched as they approached the Bennett estate. The tallest evergreens she'd ever seen stood guard until separated by the new iron gate and security guard. Renny rolled his window down enough for the guy to get a good look at him, then proceeded through the entrance. "I don't know that I'm ever going to get used to that." He drove past the basketball net that he and his brothers still utilized and pulled into the six-car garage right behind his brother's Mercedes.

"I was shocked your father didn't have something like that in place already. He's a very influential man, he should be more aware of his security."

The engine died and Renny turned in his seat to look at her. "We're not like that, Sabrina. We're not the rich, society page snobs everybody makes us out to be. We're just a family, that's all."

Bree wasn't sure why her words had struck a nerve with him, but the sullen look on his face said that's exactly what she'd done. "I didn't mean it that way. I just meant that security is a big issue. Just because we live in America doesn't mean that things don't happen. And it happens to poor people and middle-class people and rich people."

"I guess being a marine you've seen a lot of things," he remarked when her hands fidgeted in her lap.

"I've seen way more than I ever wanted to," she said quietly.

He lifted a lock of her hair. For some reason she'd taken her ponytail out when they were at her sister's place, but he wasn't complaining. It now fell just past her shoulders in a dark brown curtain that entranced him. "You need some new memories," he told her as he let the softness glide through his fingers.

She gave him a puzzled look. "What does that mean?"

Renny let his hand slide to the nape of her neck as he pulled her closer over the car's console. "It means that every time you start to reminisce or remember you get this really haunted look about you. I don't like that look. So I'll just have to provide you with new and improved memories that will only make you happy." His lips brushed across hers.

In her lap Bree's hands stilled. The familiarity of his lips on hers came rushing back. "You've given me a few already." She nipped his lower lip and he grinned.

"The best is yet to come." He took her mouth quickly, fiercely claiming her lips, her tongue, pulling her deeper into his mouth, into his space. His hands delved into her hair as he held her still for his assault.

Bree's hands came up to his wrists as she gave as much to that kiss as she took. Her heart hammered against her chest, her thighs pressing tightly together to ward off the throbbing at her center. She pulled away before she was further tempted to ride him right here in his car, in his parents' driveway. *What is it with you and riding this guy?* she questioned herself even as she licked her lips and lowered her head. "We'd better get inside."

It was a damn good thing she stopped because he was afraid he couldn't. Dragging a hand down his face, Renny tried to think of something other than the sexy woman sitting beside him. He couldn't go into his parents' house with his erection tenting his slacks. He jumped out of the car into the cool night air hoping that would ease his arousal and opened the door for Sabrina. "Just a warning, the Bennetts are a testy bunch. My sisters are loud and opinionated. My brothers are dominant and full of testosterone. So be prepared."

He held her hand and Bree found herself enjoying the feeling of strength emanating from his palm to hers. "And here I thought you were the worst of the bunch." She grinned up at him and he nudged her slightly.

* * *

"I'm beginning to think you like making an entrance more than I do." Adriana grinned as her long, bared arms came around Renny's neck.

She was gorgeous, Bree surmised instantly—tall, long legs, golden skin, spectacular eyes and perfectly puckered lips. Her ivory jumper hugged all her curvy areas and dipped low in the front to show off the best ones. Bree swallowed, hard. No wonder she was a model.

"Somebody's got to keep them on their toes." Renny was smiling down at his sister. "I take it you have your car back." He was glad to see for himself that she was okay. The thought of something happening to her had been frightening to say the least.

Adriana waved a hand. "Please, I told Daddy there was no way I was driving that thing again. They could have done anything to it while they had it at that shop. My new toy arrives Monday by four." She flashed him a brilliant smile.

"I take that to mean Dad's pocket took a big hit on this one, huh?"

"You got that right." Adriana lifted a glass and helped herself to a drink.

Renny grinned, knowing his sister all too well. Out of the corner of his eye he saw Sabrina backing away. With a quick extension of his arm he had her by the waist, pulling her back to his side. "Adriana Bennett, this is Sabrina Desdune, my bodyguard."

Adriana choked on the wine she'd just sipped and Bree cast Renny a heated glance. She didn't know what she'd expected. She wasn't a part of the family, nor was she his date, so he really didn't need to introduce her at all. He touched her intimately, pulling her to him possessively, and yet he'd called her his bodyguard. This was the first time he'd ever done that.

"It's nice to meet you, Adriana." Bree smiled at the woman.

"You're a bodyguard." The woman was small and looked about as strong as Adriana knew she wasn't.

"Yes, she is," Alex interrupted. "And a very good one, I might add. She tackled this big goof to the ground to keep him from getting run down." Alex wrapped an arm around Bree's shoulder and pulled her against him. "I didn't get a chance to thank you for that."

Renny didn't miss the trick. While it appeared Alex was looking down at Bree, he was actually looking down the gap in the front of her shirt. Renny frowned; Alex had taught him that long ago. He immediately grabbed Sabrina's hand and gently removed her from Alex's clutches.

Bree felt like a bone between two dogs and she pulled her hand from Renny, then cast Alex a heated glare. "I merely did what you're paying me for."

Adriana smiled. "Anything for money. You sound like my kind of woman." Linking her free arm with Bree's, she balanced her wine and stood between her brothers. "You and I are going to get along just fine."

With that Bree found herself being whisked away by the beautiful sister, leaving the brothers in the middle of the room without a clue as to what had just transpired.

"Whew, I've never seen Alex and Renny vying for the same woman's attention before," Adriana said when she and Sabrina were off to a corner of the large living room by themselves.

Bree caught her words and gave her a puzzled look. "What are you talking about?"

Adriana laughed. "Tell me you're not serious? You weren't just the victim of a jealous tug of war over there?"

Bree looked back to the center of the room where Alex and Renny still stood. "No." She rubbed up and down her arms with the memory of being stretched back and forth. "I don't really know what that was."

"Then I'll enlighten you. I watched you and Renny from the window when you pulled up. I saw you walk up to the house and enter this room." Adriana raised her brows as if she expected Sabrina to understand her meaning.

It took Bree a moment, in which time she thought about denying everything she knew was going through the woman's mind. She was here on business, which meant she had no right lusting after her client. Still, she did and apparently that was obvious. "I sure hope the rest of your family isn't as observant as you."

Adriana laughed again, the melodic sound making Bree smile, as well.

"Girl, you're probably the only one that thinks I'm observant. The rest of them think I'm a flake obsessed with clothes and makeup."

Bree relaxed, finding herself enjoying Renny's sister much more than she had anticipated. "Anyway, Renny was right. I'm his bodyguard."

"And soon to be his lover." Adriana emptied her glass and signaled Raphael, the butler, for another one. "If you're not already."

Bree frowned. "No, we haven't gotten that far yet."

"Then my big brother's slipping and he better get his act together before Alex the Great steps in."

Bree looked at Alex and his dashing good looks. While she could clearly see where a woman would be attracted to him, she realized quickly that she wasn't. No, there seemed to be only one Bennett man for her.

Alex was looking at Renny suspiciously while Renny tried to avert his gaze. "You couldn't resist, could you? After all that bickering about your bodyguard being a woman. I'll bet you're damned happy she's a woman now, aren't you?" Alex had a drink in his hand now as he watched his brother stewing.

He'd seen from the moment Renny and Sabrina walked through that door that his brother wanted her. It was something in the way Bennett men swaggered when they were near a woman that whetted their whistle, and Renny had definitely swaggered. Alex had decided to test the waters by lightly coming on to Sabrina himself. From the steely glare Renny had tossed him, he'd known he was right.

"It's not like that, Alex," Renny grumbled.

"Like hell it's not. You're almost seething because I touched her. I sure hope she's good at everything she does, because we're paying her and her brother an awful lot of money to keep us safe and now, apparently, to keep you satisfied."

Renny looked at his brother. Alex was only about an inch or two taller than him, so they were just about eye to eye. He recognized the teasing glint in his eyes and felt his shoulders relax. "I only know she's good at being a bodyguard. We haven't done anything else," he admitted.

Alex let loose a loud sound, the smile across his face full and almost obnoxious. "And you're this uptight about her. Man, you better sleep with her and quick before you kill somebody."

Renny was about to respond when a hush fell over the room. The patriarch of the family and the other siblings made their appearance. Sam and a man Renny didn't know came in behind them.

"Good evening, everyone. Before we get started I'd like to introduce you to Trent Donovan. Trent's an investigator from Vegas that I've known for years and have had the pleasure of working with. Since we've had some new developments I thought it'd be good to bring Trent in. He's not local so he'll be looking at this from a different angle." Sam slipped his hands into his pockets and looked around the room.

Bree recognized Trent Donovan, handsome man that he was, from her parents' last anniversary celebration a couple of years ago. Time had been good to him. Trent had a soldier's body: hard, buff and absolutely delicious. Of course, with an ex-Navy SEAL, she expected nothing less. However, her gaze soon found itself shifting to the left, raking over the broader body, the darker skin and the sexier mouth of Lorenzo Bennett. If she didn't know better she'd swear she was falling for him.

"I'd like to start by asking Mr. Bennett—Lorenzo, that is—about his business dealings, relationships, enemies," Trent stated as he pulled out his notepad.

Rico grinned and clapped Renny on the back. "Every single man in the county's an enemy since all the available women are making a play for him."

Renny's eyes immediately went to Bree, who frowned at the remark. He made a mental note to give Rico one good punch before the night was over. "I don't have any enemies that I know of, either personal—" he glared at his older brother "—or business."

Trent seemed to ignore the underlying implications of both men and continued with his questions. "How about this gallery you're opening? Other than the break-in, have you had any problems in that area?"

Renny shook his head, remembering back over the past year in which his plans had been set into motion. "No. No problems."

"That gallery's a waste of time and looks to be at the root of this threat against you," Marvin Bennett added.

Bree's attention turned to the older man. His sons definitely took after him in the looks department, from their broad builds and muscular chests to the feeling of complete domination simply by being in the same room with them. Marvin was darker than his boys, half his face covered by a dark, foreboding beard. His eyes were those of a shrewd businessman, his touch, as witnessed by the way he held his wife's hand, that of a loving father and husband.

"Dad," Renny warned in a low menacing tone.

"I think the gallery is just fabulous and I can't wait until it opens. Renny's pieces have already doubled in price since the whisperings of the gallery began." This was the youngest sister, Gabrielle.

She'd bounced into the room with loads of energy and effortless beauty. Her long legs crossed quickly as she took a seat in the chair right next to where Renny stood. Dark, exotic eyes swept the room while long manicured nails raked through her vicious, yet stylishly short haircut. "I've been keeping track." She shrugged when questioning eyes rested on her.

"I don't think this has anything to do with my gallery." Renny cast his sister a grateful look.

"I'm inclined to agree with you," Sam added. "However, that doesn't mean somebody wouldn't use that to get at the top prize."

All eyes shifted to Marvin Bennett.

"I believe it's this merger and all this publicity it's bringing." This smooth, slightly accented voice was from Beatriz Bennett, formerly Beatriz de Carriero, from Pirata, a tiny village in Brazil.

Bree was instantly drawn by her serene air, her dark alluring eyes. Her skin was the same shimmering bronze complexion of her sons, her hair thick, black and wavy coming neatly to a chignon at her nape. She wore an elegant yet understated turquoise suit that seemed to illuminate her very existence. Diamonds at her ears, her neck and on her hands stated her husband's success even as the look of pride and love stated her dedication to her family.

"If anything, Lorenzo is just a pawn in these business dealings. I have expressed this to Marvin on numerous occasions."

Beside her Marvin didn't flinch even though he'd hoped his wife would keep this between the two of them. He'd been feeling out his own suspicions, but didn't want the rest of the family to know about them. Besides, when he heard about the break-in at Renny's gallery, he figured this was the perfect time to put his son's hobby to rest. He belonged at the realm of Bennett Industries with his brothers, not making horny little sculptures for the public to gawk at.

"I agree with Mom. I think Renny is a means to an end and he's the best one of us to attack." Raphael had just passed Rico and he motioned for the butler to bring him a stronger drink.

Trent nodded. "Because he's not directly involved with the business he'd seem the most unlikely, the most vulnerable. His gallery's opening in less than two weeks. That will provide publicity and opportunity."

"Maybe you should postpone the opening, Renny," Adriana suggested.

"Uh-uh." Gabrielle shook her head while rising. "He's not backing down from this creep. That would be like giving in, and Bennetts don't give in."

"We won't risk his life," Beatriz said to her daughter. "It might be a good idea to postpone the opening until after the merger goes through."

Bree watched Renny taking in all the conversation around him. He hadn't moved, nor had his facial features given away what he was thinking. Still, Bree knew that postponing the opening was not an option for him. This was his dream and even the thought of it not happening in the time that he wanted it to was not acceptable. And she agreed. "No. A postponement will only be that. If all this were simply about the merger, then why would it only be focused on the Bennetts? Coastal's owners sought you out for this merger. Why not put the pressure on Glen Rickman or a member of Coastal's board?" With one arm folded beneath her breasts and the other bent tapping a finger to her chin, Bree walked around the room. She did her best thinking while she was moving. "Because this is personal. This vendetta has to do with the Bennett family, or should I say Mr. Bennett personally? The merger was simply the means to put this plan in motion."

The moment he heard her voice she had his complete attention. Renny's eyes followed her as she moved across the room.

"So let's go over persons with a personal vendetta against Mr. Bennett." Sam had his notepad out and silently applauded his sister. For all that she seemed fragile and delicate on the outside, he knew better than anyone that Bree was intelligent and strong and probably capable of cracking this whole case on her own. Sibling rivalry wouldn't allow him to concede that point just yet. "Pissed off anyone lately, Mr. Bennett?" Sam raised his eyes in the older man's direction.

It was quiet inside of the car as Renny and Bree made their way back into the city toward Renny's condo. Just as discussions about Mr. Bennett's enemies had gotten under way, Raphael announced dinner and they'd all moved to the dining room. Renny had claimed Bree's arm as soon as the progression from one room to the other had begun, making sure she sat next to him. Adriana was on her other side, giving her knowing smiles throughout the meal. Alex, too, kept an eye on Bree throughout dinner until she knew unmistakably that he'd seen the same thing his sister had.

Oddly enough by the end of the evening she found she wasn't overly bothered by it. In fact, she could say that by the time she and Renny prepared to leave she'd almost felt as if she'd enjoyed a family dinner. She, Sam and Trent were the only outsiders there. The other guards had been given a few hours off since all the clients were relatively in one place. After they'd come up with a few suspects, one Bree still hadn't mentioned, the discussion had turned to the merger and what it would mean to the family. Bree noticed with some surprise that Renny contributed to this conversation as if he were an employee of Bennett Industries. He had been right when he told her he had an interest in his family business; he simply had another interest, as well.

She thought of his sculptures again and felt anticipation bloom as the opening of the gallery grew closer. Exactly when she'd become interested in art she hadn't the faintest idea, but she was definitely proud of Renny's work and anxious for the world to see what she saw. When the car came to a stop she didn't even move to open her own door, for she knew he'd be right there reaching for her hand and she'd gladly give it. She was as independent as they came and as capable as any man, but when she was with Renny she slipped easily into the role of female, allowing him to comfort and protect her as needed. And as she stepped out of the car and he held her close to his chest for a moment, his arms encircling her waist, she wondered exactly when this change had occurred.

"You're tired. Come on so I can tuck you in." He laced his fingers through hers and they went through the parking garage doors and up the steps to his condo.

On the way, Bree wondered if they would sleep together on the floor in front of that mesmerizing fire again or if they'd go their separate ways, sleeping in the beds assigned to them. All of a sudden the latter didn't seem so appealing.

She was busily thinking of the impending sleeping arrangement when they approached the door and she felt Renny stiffen beside her. When he paused, she looked up at him, then followed his line of vision.

The door was ajar.

In an instant Bree was reaching down to her ankle to retrieve the gun she hadn't been able to strap on because of the cut of her pants. Cursing to herself, she moved in front of Renny with an arm behind her pushing him back. She kicked the door open just as Renny grabbed her arm, pulling her back out of the way. "What the hell are you doing?" He scowled.

"Uh, my job." She tossed him an insolent look. "Someone could still be in there."

Renny frowned, knowing this was neither the time nor the place to have this conversation with her. Besides, he wasn't all that sure he'd win the battle. "I realize that. That's why I'm going in first. Stay close behind me." He barked the order and didn't give her time to reply as he'd already stepped into the apartment first.

Bree held back her curses, keeping them tucked in her memory bank for later when she'd let him have it. They both eased into the room and Bree quickly looked over at the alarm pad behind the door. All the lights were off, meaning the system had been disabled. That was a grade A system; disabling it was not easy. When they came to the living room Bree left Renny and veered off toward the kitchen. The place was a mess, broken glass and overturned furniture making their progress even harder.

The kitchen actually looked untouched with the exception of the knives that had been aimed at the cabinets and still clung to the wood with a death grip. Suspended from one particularly sharp blade was a slip of paper with something scrawled on it. Bree took one step to examine the writing and felt herself being pulled back once again.

"You're a terrible listener. I told you to stay with me." Renny gave her a fierce look, his heart still hammering from when he realized she'd gone off alone. He was first to get closer to the note and lifted his arm to grab the knife down for closer inspection.

"Don't!" Bree swatted his hand away. "Fingerprints," she told him as if he should already have known. Pulling on the hem of her shirt, she opened a couple of drawers until she found a box of sandwich bags. With deft maneuvering she retrieved a bag and slipped it on her hand, then grabbed the handle of the knife and pulled it from the wood cabinet. The paper stuck to it and she didn't bother to extract it but moved to the marble table and set it down. Renny was behind her reading aloud over her shoulder.

"You may own the telecommunications world, but everybody is not a possession for you to claim. Some lessons are better learned the hard way."

They looked at each other with puzzled glances.

"I don't own the telecommunications world. My father does." Renny was thinking aloud, keeping in mind the suggestion that this was a personal vendetta. But supposedly the vendetta was against his father with him being an easy target. This sounded personal—toward him.

"Okay, so what have you or your father taken that didn't belong to you?" Bree drummed her fingers against the marble top.

Renny retrieved his cell phone. "Desdune? You'd better get over here. We have another letter."

After two walk-throughs Renny decided that nothing was missing, but everything was almost completely destroyed. His audio system had been smashed, the stuffing ripped out of his sofa, his chairs; the mirrors were smashed, his clothes strewn all over. With bated breath he'd entered his studio only to find his stands overturned and supplies thrown about. But that wasn't what he was concerned about. He'd searched frantically, first on the table where he'd left it, then beneath the structure and beneath some of the other rubble tossed haphazardly throughout the room. He'd found it and released a heavy sigh. Most likely the intruder had swiped everything off the worktable at one time. The piece must have rolled and fallen to the floor without the culprit giving it another thought.

Thankfully he picked the half-finished piece up off the floor and stared down into the eyes that held the very soul of his work. Sabrina's eyes. He found a plastic bag in the kitchen and wrapped the piece carefully. He'd take it to the foundry for the time being.

Without a clue as to who could have done this, he wandered through his house barely suppressing the anger that bubbled inside. This was going too far now. This was his home, his private space, and he didn't like the idea that it had been invaded.

"Renny?"

Sabrina's voice echoed from the back of the condo and he quickly left the studio to find her. She was in his bedroom standing at the end of the platform that held his bed. Her head was tilted as she leaned over the mattress.

"What? He decided to take a nap in between wrecking the place?" he asked in a dry tone as he made his way up onto the platform.

Bree disregarded his lame attempt at humor. "You didn't sleep in here last night. And this morning we dressed and went to Lynn's."

"Yup." He shrugged and turned about to plop down on the bed.

"No!" Bree ran around to the side of the bed he stood on and grabbed his arms in an attempt to stop him. "Don't sit on it! I think somebody was in this bed."

Her eyes were huge and he could swear the wheels of her mind were clearly visible as she thought this through. "What do you mean?" He righted himself and turned with her so they both were staring down at the rumpled sheets.

"There's a stain there, in the center." She pointed and felt Renny lean in to examine it, as well.

He was confused. He saw the darkened spot and frowned at Sabrina. "Somebody pissed on my bed?"

She shrugged. "Either that or they handled some *other* business."

It only took a second for her words to register. "What! Tell me you're not serious? You think somebody…"

Bree held up a hand to keep him from finishing his sentence.

That was exactly what she thought. "I didn't say that. But it seems to be an awfully small spot for it to be urine. Besides, urine has a distinct odor." She inhaled. "I don't smell it."

Reluctantly Renny inhaled, then dragged his hands down his face. "You've got to be kidding me. This just can't be happening."

Bree continued to stare at the bed, at the way the sheets were twisted and the pillows were propped up at the top with an indentation that said someone had lain there. Someone had lain there all right and apparently had had a good time. But were they alone? Images entered Bree's mind uninvited, a man and a woman, making love on Renny's bed. One, or maybe both of them reaching climax, expelling the secretion on the sheets. A sign. A message. Whatever it was Renny didn't like it and she was having a really hard time swallowing it herself.

She'd thought of her and Renny in that bed. Now that thought had forever been tainted. Besides that, if someone came in here and jacked off on his bed, then it was definitely personal and more so to Renny than to his father. That worried her.

She startled at the sound of the doorbell.

"I'll get it," Renny said gruffly, then left her alone in the room.

With the note tucked securely in a Ziploc bag and Trent overseeing his assistant as he dusted the apartment for fingerprints, Sam had the duty of breaking the bad news to Renny. "You can't stay here, man."

Bree had seen it coming and had, in fact, been thinking of a place to hide him.

"I'm not leaving my home because of some maniac with a vendetta." Renny slammed a fist on the coffee table.

"Look, I know how you feel, but Bree installed some pretty high-tech security gear on this place and whoever is doing this still got in. We don't have much on the tapes and I've got a sneaky suspicion they're not going to lift any prints. You're like a sitting duck here."

Sam's words stirred more than anger in Bree. Something clenched in her chest as she thought of this person returning and Renny being here. "He's right, Renny. You can't stay here."

As much as he hated to admit it, they were probably right. He looked at Bree and wondered if wherever he went she would still be staying with him. He could probably handle the fact that he wouldn't be sleeping in his own bed for a while if he knew she was going to be sleeping somewhere close by. "I guess I could call a hotel." He'd get them a suite because he clearly planned to keep his bodyguard with him.

"No," Sam said quickly. "That's too open, too obvious. We need to put you someplace where he won't think to look for you."

"That's true." Bree stood thinking of a suitable place. "What about your apartment, Sam? Since you've been staying with Leeza."

Sam shook his head. "Leeza's got a sick aunt and uncle staying there."

Bree frowned. It figured Leeza would have everything where Sam was concerned on lockdown. "If I had my own place we could put him there."

"Why don't you have your own apartment?" Renny inquired. She deserved her own house, her own space, unless she had no intention of staying in Greenwich.

His question startled her and she blinked twice before answering. "I just haven't had the time to look for one."

"I've got it. Pack your stuff," Sam instructed them.

"Where are we going?" Bree asked her brother, who was already headed toward the door.

"Lynn owes me a favor and I'm about to call her on it."

On the entire ride to Lynn's house Bree thought of a million reasons why this was not a good idea and she'd spoken them to Sam, who, of course, ignored her.

"It's our only option, Bree."

"But what about Jeremy? Are you forgetting that this is a potentially dangerous situation?"

Renny grimaced at her words. She had a point there. He didn't really feel comfortable staying with Lynn and her young son, bringing to them the same danger that he was supposedly trying to get away from.

"They'll never find him here. Even if they do know that my firm is working for the Bennetts, Lynn has a different last name. They won't make the connection." Sam turned into Lynn's complex.

"And what if they follow us back here one day? I mean, they are most definitely watching us. That's how they knew Renny's place would be empty tonight." She was grasping, she knew, but Sam had no idea what being at Lynn's with her perfect little house and her perfect little son and Renny was going to do to her. This afternoon had been proof that Renny Bennett was slowly picking the lock she'd secured around her heart, and spending more time with Jeremy in a house that she wished was hers was not going to help.

"I'm not going to let anything happen to Lynn or Jeremy, you know that. If things get too hairy we'll reevaluate and find a safer place. But for right now, at least for tonight, we don't have a lot of choice."

Her head fell back against the seat in defeat. Seconds later she felt a hand on her shoulder and didn't bother to open her eyes to see whose it was. The instantaneous heat swarming through her body said it all.

Sam climbed out of the car and headed straight for the house. Renny stepped out of the backseat and helped Sabrina out of the front. Cupping her face in his hands, he stared down at her. Night had fallen, casting them in a blanket of darkness except for the scattered porch lights around them. A light breeze trickled through the air, ruffling her loose hair.

"Why do I get the feeling there's more going on with you than the danger this arrangement might impose on your family?"

Probably because you seem to see right through me, making you all the more dangerous. She closed her eyes, willing her mind to stay quiet. "I just don't want anything to happen to them, that's all."

She was lying, but he knew she wouldn't tell him anything until she was perfectly ready. He gave her a crooked smile and dropped a juvenile kiss on her forehead. "But you're the bodyguard, remember?" He let his hands fall to her sides and clasped her fingers in his.

"Very funny," she chided, but let herself fall into step beside him. His firm grasp of her hand was both comforting and terrifying. Things between them were definitely changing.

Lynn wasn't exactly jubilant over the idea of her new houseguests, but she understood that Sam had her cornered. Besides, the thought of Bree in danger was enough to bear with her halfway across town. At least having her stay here she could keep a closer eye on her. As for Renny, she wasn't sure how she felt about him staying yet. He'd seemed like a genuinely nice guy and he definitely had a thing for her little sister, as well as a way with Jeremy. She'd like to keep a closer eye on him, too.

"Okay, you two are going to have to share the guest room," she announced when Sam had finally left with strict instructions to lock up tightly.

All the color drained from Bree's face. "What? Why?" Nervous fingers came to her throat as she tried to mask the creak in her voice.

Renny hadn't missed it, nor had he missed the instant her eyes had flashed toward him. Was she afraid to be alone in a bedroom with him? The mere thought made him want to leap for joy, but she looked a little flushed. Poor little Sabrina, last night was only the beginning. She had no idea what he had in store for her, whether they shared the same bedroom or not.

"Uh, because I have a young child waltzing around the house who is not going to understand some strange man sleeping on our couch. Not to mention I paid too damn much money for him, no matter how good-looking he is, to lay his long, heavy body on my furniture indefinitely. No offense," she tossed at Renny.

He hid a smile. "None taken."

Bree ran her fingers through her hair until her short nails scraped over her scalp. Could this situation get any worse? There was one bed in that guest room, a full-size bed at that. No way she and Renny could share that bed without touching…without touching a lot. Memories of their touching last night, spooned together on the floor in his living room, had her cheeks burning. *Get a hold of yourself, Bree. He's just a man and this is just a job.*

Lynn didn't miss her sister's flustered state, either. She looked over at Renny, who seemed to be enjoying himself immensely. She'd bet five dollars she could decipher his thoughts. "You're two consenting adults. I'm sure you can handle this." She looked at him sternly.

"I can handle it." And he would handle Sabrina. She was simply a little tense and he knew just how to relieve her of that affliction.

"Mmm-hmm." With upturned lips Lynn looked at Bree. "You've got this, right, Bree?"

Bree met her sister's gaze, squared her shoulders and felt her defensive mask slipping into place. "Yeah, I've got it."

Chapter 8

The sound of the bedroom door closing echoed in Bree's head, causing her heart to pound a little harder. This was ridiculous. She was acting like a scared virgin on prom night. Well, she wasn't a virgin and whatever Renny Bennett had to dish out she could certainly take it. At least that's what she thought until she turned around to see him leaning against the dresser, arms folded over his chest, eyes fastened intently on her.

He looked dangerous, his skin seemingly darkened by the night hours and the dim light in the room. His eyes all but smoldered, his lips firm, determined. She took a deep breath. *You can handle this,* she told herself until it became her mantra.

"Come here, Sabrina."

His voice was quiet, but deep with that underlying forcefulness that she'd come to recognize as second nature to him. She felt her legs moving—traitors—taking her closer to where he stood.

"We both know that something's going on between us. Something that goes way beyond this lunatic that's after me and my family. I won't lie. I want to explore what that something is." He broke into a small grin. "Badly."

Bree folded her arms over her chest for lack of anything better to do with her seemingly too-long limbs. They were close, but not touching. He was talking to her with the patience of a teacher and she felt like his pupil, afraid that she didn't know enough to pass his class.

He saw her nervousness and knew that it wasn't easy for her to be afraid of anything, or to admit that she was afraid. But that's what she was. He could see it so plainly, yet would never have believed it. On the outside she was strong, witty and almost as arrogant as he could be. On the inside there was something totally different, something totally contradictory. And that's what he wanted to discover, that's what he wanted her to share with him. Reaching out, he lifted her chin with a finger. "But I promise not to do anything that you don't want or you're not ready for. Understand?"

Bree bobbed her head up and down until the very thought of how she looked repulsed her and she let her arms fall to her sides. "This something between us is purely physical. I know that just like you do. I'm almost wondering if it just makes more sense to go ahead and get it over with."

Renny laughed then, a deep rich sound that Bree found herself enjoying.

"You sound like you've made the decision to have a tooth pulled."

"No. I'm just a logical person. And logic tells me that this 'thing' between us isn't going to go away until we deal with it. So…" She trailed off hoping he'd finish this god-awful sentence for her.

She was definitely a treasure, one that he was so profoundly grateful had fallen into his lap. "So I'll grab some blankets and make a nice pallet on the floor and you take the bed."

Bree blinked in confusion. Weren't they about to have sex? That's what she'd thought they'd decided. "You…you're going to sleep on the floor?" She gave him a puzzled look.

Renny grabbed a pillow from the bed and snatched the folded comforter from the edge and tossed them to the floor. Pulling the hem of his shirt, he lifted it over his head and threw it on the nearby chair. "I'm not into forcing women to do my bidding, Sabrina. You've admitted that there's something between us and that we'll eventually have to act on it. So whenever that time arises we'll do it. Until then, I'll sleep on the floor."

She looked at him, astonished that he wasn't proposing they jump into bed together right this very moment. Good, the best way to deal with Sabrina was to keep her guessing. "Besides, your sister said these walls are paper-thin." He flashed her a smile, then removed his shoes and jeans and crawled under the blanket on the floor closest to the door.

Speechless, she looked at him another moment before shrugging and going to the far side of the room to change into her nightshirt. In a few minutes she was beneath the sheets in the bed and she leaned over to the nightstand to flick off the lights. "Good night," she whispered, still not believing he was sleeping on the floor.

"Good night, Sabrina."

Colonel Harold T. Richmond walked into the lobby of the motel with his duffel bag in hand. The moment he'd heard her voice he knew he had to come. They had unfinished business.

Sabrina'd come into his life like a breath of fresh air, reminding him of his youth, of the things he'd once longed for. She was so different from the other women he'd known, so vital, so full of energy. He'd wanted her instantly, had needed her writhing and begging beneath him. And for a time he'd gotten just that.

Then things had changed. People had interfered and now it was time to get her back. He had a plan that would secure their future. They didn't need the military and their dictating ways. They didn't need the approval of commanding officers or the people around them. Where they were going and with the money he was about to make for them, they'd have it all and the world around them could go straight to hell.

Bree tossed and turned in the bed. The sheets twisted about her legs until she felt caught and defeated. Her skin felt slick and warm to the touch. Her breasts felt full, her nipples hard and tender. She blew out a deep breath and tried to calm her erratic breathing. She couldn't have been dreaming about him because in the hour she'd lain there she knew she had yet to fall asleep. He was so close, she could smell him, could feel his dominating presence sharing that small room with her, and she shivered.

One hand moved to an aching breast while the other splayed over her stomach on its way down to the spot she needed touched so badly and she licked her lips hoping she hadn't bit herself to the point of bleeding.

"Sabrina?"

His deep whisper startled her and her eyes flew open, her hands halting where they were. He stood at the foot of the bed looking down on her. The sliver of moonlight that crept through the curtain landed in a dramatic slash over his face. She should answer him. She should ask him what he was doing awake, what he was doing standing at the end of that bed as if he'd heard her mental cry. Instead she lifted her arms to him, beckoning him to join her. That was all she could do, all she wanted to do.

Renny had lain on that floor wanting so badly to touch her,

to hold her. He'd sworn not to do anything she didn't want, not to push her if she wasn't ready, yet his rigid erection had rested on his thigh, insisting that he make an effort on its behalf. He'd finally acquiesced to simply asking if he could sleep beside her; that would have to be enough for now. If he could only touch her he'd be all right. This distance wasn't working. He was never going to get any sleep.

When he'd heard her tossing and turning he'd been elated. She was having just as hard a time as he. Again his thickening manhood expressed a need to find warmth. Mentally he'd tried to calm his counterpart down, citing the oath he'd made not to push. But that only made him throb harder. Then she whimpered. He'd heard it, remembered the sound from last night when his mouth had first touched her nether lips, and all conscious thought fled from his mind. He'd pushed the covers away and stood to climb into that bed with her. She lay on her back, her eyes closed tightly, her legs spread apart, and it took every ounce of control in him not to climb on top of her and strap in. He'd hesitated and then her hand had touched her breast and he'd wanted to whimper himself.

Tiny beads of sweat had already begun to dot his forehead. No way in hell was he about to stand here and watch her masturbate. That would be like dying a very slow, very torturous death. And again his erection wasn't trying to hear it. So he'd called to her, his obvious question voiced in her name alone. She hadn't answered even as he'd held his breath in anticipation. Instead she'd reached for him. The horny man inside wanted to leap on that bed and rip her clothes off, but the mature, focused part of him took slow measured steps until he was at the side of the bed where she lay, taking both her hands and bringing them to his lips to lightly graze her knuckles.

"You couldn't sleep either, huh?" Bree finally managed when he'd sat on the bed beside her. Sexual tension crackled throughout the room but she tried to keep things light. It was just sex…right?

Renny smiled, rubbing his thumbs over the backs of her hands. "That's an understatement." Because he couldn't resist, because his brain screamed that he wasn't touching her nearly enough, Renny leaned over and lightly brushed her lips with his. She responded, as he knew she would, by pressing her lips against his. It was a chaste kiss, as kisses went in this century, yet that simple connection spoke volumes.

He pressed his mouth to hers again, this time opening his lips slightly so the soft underside now connected with hers. She followed his lead and the intimacy was extended. With the next meeting of mouths his tongue extended, requesting hers follow suit. Sabrina didn't let him down; their tongues touched tentatively at first, then in one fluid movement rubbed together as if reunited after a long hiatus.

Bree drew in a tight breath, eased her hands from his to wrap them around his neck, pulling him closer while opening her mouth to his assault.

Renny recognized her acquiescence and moaned as his palms found her breasts and kneaded them through the sheet and her nightshirt. He needed that contact, feeling as if he'd been sexually starved for years. Beneath his hands he felt her heart rate increase and he took the kiss deeper and deeper.

Kissing had never been so erotic. As his tongue slid across her teeth, down and over the insides of her lips, into the deepest crevices of her mouth she moaned, unable to control the fire steadily building inside. Renny mastered her mouth. From the moment their lips first touched and with every stroke thereafter, he dominated her and to Bree's astonishment she not only allowed the domination but reveled in it.

Abruptly, he pulled back and broke the kiss, despite his burgeoning desire. He lifted his head only inches and waited while her eyes fluttered, then tried to focus on him. "If you don't tell me you want me, Sabrina, I'll have to stop."

Warning bells *bbrrnnged* in her head, red panic lights lit up behind her eyelids and she rose on her elbows to peer closely at him. "Don't stop!" she said breathlessly. "I mean— um, I mean, you don't have to stop if you don't want to."

His knuckles stroked lightly over her cheek as the desire in her eyes and the airy way she spoke answered his question. Still, he wanted to hear her say it, needed to watch her lips move as the words escaped her mouth. "Say it, Sabrina. Say you want me."

Bree narrowed her eyes. So he wanted to tease her, huh? Well, two could play that game. She leaned in closer, traced her tongue over the outline of his lips and heard him catch his breath. "You sure you want me to say it, when I could simply show you?" Her palms went to his chest, roaming over the rigid planes of muscle that she'd been attracted to from day one.

Renny closed his eyes and opened his mouth to speak, but her tongue thrust inside before the words could come. She kissed him hungrily, the kind of soul-searing kiss that was designed to bring a man to his knees.

Even as she made love to his mouth her hands moved down his chest to his abdomen, where she found the hem of his shirt and lifted it over his head. Before he could mourn the loss of her lips on his she'd lowered her head to drop kisses on his taut nipples. Renny groaned, his hands burying themselves in her hair. He wanted her desperately. "Say it, Sabrina! Now!"

Bree lifted her head enough to look him in the eye, then her hand slid lower, below the band of his shorts, her fingers moving until she found his heated arousal. "I've always been more of a show than tell girl."

The moment her hands closed around his shaft Renny lost sight of all things normal. He ripped the sheet from around her, grabbed her shoulders and shifted until he was lying on the bed and her body was splayed across his.

Bree smiled down at him, her hands still coaxing his now massive arousal. She couldn't believe it, her mouth was actually watering with each stroke she made. Her thighs were already damp with her own arousal as she found herself anticipating his entrance.

Renny's hands cupped her face roughly and pulled her down so that he could ravage her mouth once again. When she whimpered he slowed the tempo, made the kiss intimate instead of demanding. His hands slid down her back, lifting her nightshirt and moving to the rounded globes of her butt. She wore bikini underwear. Not the thong that the outwardly sexy women he usually ran with wore and not the briefs the pristine, wannabe virgins wore, either. Just a simple bikini that had him growing even harder as his hands slipped inside them. He traced the crease of her buttocks and felt her shift beneath his touch. So she liked that. He'd have to keep that in mind. Continuing south, he spread the soft pliant globes until his finger found her wetness and sank inside. "Sabrina." Her name was ground from his lips.

Bree was quickly losing her train of thought. He seemed determined to control her, to bend her to his will, and right about now—as two fingers entered her steamy center—she was all for it.

Her head dropped to his shoulders as he stroked her. He had her legs spread wide, straddled over his, while his fingers worked inside. In the next instant she was undulating her hips to the rhythm he'd created, her juices dripping onto his hand.

"Oohh," she moaned.

"Say it, Sabrina," Renny whispered in her ear. He wanted nothing more than to enter her at this exact moment. She was ready—his fingers went deeper, finding her spot, then working it until his entire hand was wet—damn, was she ready! And he was so hard he thought for sure he was going to lose it and come right in her hand at any moment. "Tell me what you want so I can make it happen."

Her entire body was shaking, her mind filling with those puffy clouds that beckoned her to take the plunge. She'd seen those clouds only once before and it had been under this man's expert tutelage. There was no reason why she shouldn't take that glorious trip with him again. "Yes," she panted, moving her hips in quick succession. "Yes. Please, Lorenzo. Please."

Oh God, she'd called him by his name again. He had no idea why that was so damned sexy to him, but just the sound of it coming from her had him thrusting three fingers inside her in a hurry to bring her to her first climax, to have her limp in his arms, defenseless and content.

It only took a moment, then Bree was soaring coasting right through those clouds, mumbling in his ear as she went. "I want you, Lorenzo. I want you so badly. Please, don't make me beg."

If he ever heard another love song it would not have been as sweet as the lyrics she'd just spoken. When at last her shivering had subsided he eased his fingers out of her and rolled her until she lay flat on the bed. "You don't ever have to beg me for anything, Sabrina. I'll give you whatever you want." His lips moved over hers as he pressed her into the bed, his tongue filling her mouth.

Breaking away from her was torture, but he knew it would be over soon. He stood, removed his shorts and watched as Sabrina's eyes followed the length of him. "Like what you see, Sabrina?" His arrogance had returned as he noticed sheer appreciation on her face.

Bree licked her lips. "I'd like it a whole lot more if it were over here with me."

She tossed him a sexy-as-hell smile and Renny scrambled over to the chair where he'd thrown his pants and retrieved two condoms from his wallet. That's all he had with him, so tonight would only whet his appetite for her. First thing tomorrow morning he was going to the drugstore to stock up—something told him that one night with Sabrina Desdune was hardly going to be enough.

Bree hurriedly pulled her nightshirt over her head and slipped her panties off. When she looked up again Renny with that godlike body was coming right at her. On his knees making his way across the mattress he looked like a dark panther coming in for the kill. Her heart skittered to a halt as his eyes darkened even more, then picked up pace as he reached out one arm, wrapped it around her waist and pulled her to him.

"Don't even think about running," he growled.

One hand wrapped around his extended erection while the other retrieved the condom from him as she brought it to her mouth to rip the package open. "Not until I've gotten what I want."

In no time he was sheathed and she was lying back on the pillows, legs spread wide inviting him to come inside.

His eyes found hers. They were hot and consuming as he watched her and she watched him. The need was mutual, the want undeniable. This tightening in his chest and the slow murmurings of something foreign in his gut were his own trial and he'd deal with that later. His palms fell to her thighs as he stroked them possessively. His thumbs traced the outer folds of her center and she gasped. He wanted to taste her, wanted to take her next climax in his mouth as he'd done the night before, but his burgeoning erection had another idea.

Without another moment's hesitation the broad head of his erection tapped her entrance and eased in a fraction.

Bree moaned. Those damned clouds were darkening now, that tornado forming in the pit of her stomach again. She bit her lip to keep from begging him to enter her completely. He leaned over her and she spread her hands over his back, holding him to her, urging him with her hips.

Eyes closed, Renny savored every inch of her scalding sheath, noting and reveling in the tightness. He wasn't a small man, he knew, so he moved extremely slow as he made his way deeper and deeper still.

Sabrina didn't make a sound, but her fingers tightened, then relaxed on his back, signaling that she was adjusting to his size. "More?"

Bree moaned, settling her hips deeper into the mattress. "More," she acquiesced.

With one long stroke Renny was snuggly inside the burning center he'd been craving for some time now. Sabrina locked her legs around him and he orchestrated the dance that would make her forever his.

One long stroke, three shorts ones. He kissed her neck. She murmured something indistinguishable.

Two long strokes, two short ones. His tongue laved her ear. She squirmed beneath him.

Almost complete retreat. She dug her nails into his back. He grinned, dropped a quick openmouthed kiss on her lips, then raised himself up on his knees. "You ready, baby?"

Bree's hands went to her aching breasts as she nodded. "I am so ready."

His hands slid down the length of her legs and he lifted and placed each ankle on his shoulder, then thrust himself completely inside her again. She lifted her hips up off the bed, preparing for his next assault. For the next ten minutes Renny stroked her slowly, milking every bit of juice from her sweet cherry. He looked down at her toying with her nipples and craved the touch of them on his tongue, but he had other business to tend to. She seemed to take him and his size well. Well enough; he thought to step it up a notch.

He moved to a sitting position, pulling her on top of him.

He gave her a minute to take him in from this new direction, and when she did he held on to her hips, moving them in conjunction with his rhythm.

Bree had never been on a ride like this before. And as she'd only had one other lover in her life, she wasn't sure she could master it without looking like a fool. But every time Renny looked at her, that glistening heat of desire in his eyes bolstered her courage until she grabbed hold of his shoulders and switched the rhythm to one of her own.

Renny wasn't shocked. He'd known from the first time he'd kissed her that she held her passion on a tight leash. He was just glad he was the one she'd decided to let it loose on. He grabbed her butt as each globe jiggled with her ministrations. Her breasts bounced in his line of vision and he opened his mouth to grab hold of a nipple just as it swiped past his lips.

Bree's head lolled back until he grabbed her hair, forcing her lips down on his in a brutal assault on her mouth as his thickness continued to thrust deeper inside her. The heat between them swirled into a churning inferno and with each stroke, each track her tongue made over his jaw, each silky line his hands made on her dampened skin they threatened to erupt.

Renny's mind was clouded, filled with the sounds she made, the feel of her tight walls closing around him, the energy she sapped from him with her salacious movements. He gave her all her hips ardently asked for, took all he wanted in return.

Perhaps it was the one link they shared—going against their family to fulfill their own dreams. Or maybe it was their differences that culminated—she was headstrong and energetic where he was more grounded, stubborn and focused on his purpose. No matter what had brought them together he thanked those forces and planned to worship them for all time.

With her insides swirling, her breath coming faster and faster and her center dripping until she thought she had nothing left, Bree pushed on Renny's shoulders, watched as he fell backward on the bed, then began to ride. She moved frantically, caught up in the intense sensations rippling through her, gritting her teeth to keep from screaming.

Renny guided her hips, felt his own release struggling to the surface as she moved up and down on his shaft. He grunted in place of yelling out as he watched the beautiful play of passion on her face. They both realized where they were and held back the sounds that would signal their ultimate satisfaction. His was coming fast and he wanted Bree right there with him. Moving a hand from her hip, he found that puckered bud in her center and rested the pad of his thumb on its plumpness. She bucked wildly as he applied more pressure.

Her arms shook as she braced her hands on his chest, still gyrating her hips fiercely. With each downstroke Renny felt her milking him, pulling his release from his center, egging him on even as his fingers played her like a finely tuned instrument. They were going to come together. Any minute now they'd both feel that splendid release.

When it came Renny felt more than just the release of fluids; his mind connected with hers, his feelings seeping out to cocoon them in its warmth. He couldn't explain it, couldn't describe the ethereal emotion strumming throughout his body. He only knew that it was intense and all-encompassing. She fell on his chest as tremors finally overtook her body. He cradled her, rocked her even as the last spurts escaped him.

He kissed her neck, her ears, lost his fingers in the depths of her hair, murmuring something, whispering what he wasn't quite sure.

Bree felt his fingers against her scalp, moaned as her walls continued to constrict around him, her release dripping all over him. He was saying something, but she couldn't comprehend what. Every ragged breath she took, every conscious thought that wandered through her cloud-filled mind was of him, of the feel of him inside her, the feel of his hands on her. That was all she had, all she needed.

They didn't talk last night. They'd simply fallen asleep in each other's arms. By the time they awoke this morning, Lynn and Jeremy were already downstairs and Bree could smell the coffee brewing. Sun slanted through the slit in the curtains, draping its fiery rays over the bed.

Renny's heavy arm was still wrapped around her waist, where it had been throughout the night, his front cradled into her back. She never realized how much she liked this simple position. When he held her like that she felt safe, cherished. That was weird because she'd never had reason in her life to be afraid before and she knew that her family loved her completely. Yet this was different, this comfort was more.

"Mornin'," he whispered in her ear.

She hadn't known he was awake, but the sound of his gruff voice first thing in the morning held its own appeal, as well. "Mornin'." She smiled despite herself. They'd crossed the line last night, entered into a whole new realm and she wasn't quite sure how they were going to deal with it. But at this very moment her thighs ached and she craved a shower. The rest would have to wait until later.

She pushed the covers away, sliding her legs to the edge of the bed. Renny groaned. "Where are you going?" He loved the feel of her soft curves against him and had slept more peacefully last night than he ever had in his life. She felt as if she belonged in his arms. And he decided he didn't want to argue that fact. If it was where she belonged, then that was where she would be.

"We can't stay in bed all day. What will Lynn and Jeremy think? Besides, the opening's only two weeks away. I'm sure you have lots of stuff to do, so we might as well get started early." She moved to the closet door where her robe hung and thrust her hands through the silky material. Her skin tingled as she knew he was watching every move she made. She turned to face him, caught the glimmer of admiration in his eyes as she did. Could he really be looking at her like that? Did he really want her as much as it seemed? That still baffled her. She was so clearly not what it appeared he would be interested in, yet last night he'd made love to her as if she were the answer to his every prayer. "What are you looking at?"

"Perfection," he answered without hesitation. She was perfect; from her mussed hair, to her swollen lips, to the gentle curve of her waist and the plump jiggle of her bottom. He pushed the covers away, exposing his naked body. "Somebody wants to say good morning." He smiled mischievously.

Bree returned his smile even as her eyes wandered down to his sex jutting up asking for its own attention. Her tongue snaked out, lingered over her lips even and her center dampened.

"Don't be rude, Sabrina. Come on and say good morning."

He was splendidly naked—and she definitely meant splendid! Bronze muscles, ridges and planes of gorgeously toned skin lay against the light tone of the sheets and she found her feet moving in his direction.

Renny couldn't wait another minute. As soon as she was close enough to the bed he rolled over and tugged on the belt of the robe until it loosened and the material fell open. Wrapping his hand around her waist, he pulled her onto the bed and covered her body with his own.

Hastily Bree reached over onto the nightstand to grab the last condom and tear it open. He rose enough for her to slip it on him, then spread her legs with his knees and sank into her warmth.

"Now, that's a good morning," he murmured in her ear just before tracing her lobe with his tongue.

Bree moaned, opened her legs wider, acclimating herself to his size and length. "Mmm, it sure is."

Bree and Renny were showered and refreshed as they both took the stairs and entered the kitchen.

Although they didn't touch and remained a reasonable distance apart, Lynn knew something had happened in that room last night. She was a woman, after all, so she'd figured her sister would succumb, no matter how strong she was, to the alluring male trailing behind her. Lynn wasn't quite sure how she felt about that, but respected that it actually wasn't any of her business…as long as Mr. Cassanova didn't hurt her baby sister.

Briefly she wondered if Bree had shared her troubled past with him. Then his gaze locked with hers as Bree moved to the counter, retrieving a cup and filling it with coffee.

"Good morning," Renny said cheerfully.

Lynn nodded. "So it is."

Renny didn't miss the speculative tone or the questions lingering in Lynn's older eyes. She was worried about her sister, worried he would repeat whatever had gone on in her past. Finding out what had happened to Bree in North Carolina took on a new urgency. "Did Sam stop by this morning?"

Lynn tilted her head. She was sure they were both thinking about Bree, but couldn't figure out why his gaze had suddenly grown sullen and he'd asked for Sam. "He called and wanted to talk to you, but I told him you were still asleep."

"Can I use your phone?"

"Sure." Lynn nodded toward the phone hanging on the wall near the refrigerator.

"Thanks," he said quickly and turned to go into the living room. He needed privacy for this conversation. Sam had told him he'd do a search on the name and number and see what he came up with. Obviously he'd come up with something and Renny couldn't wait to find out what.

Bree had heard the pleasant exchange and wondered what Renny and Sam had to talk about. She took a sip of her coffee to see if she'd sweetened it enough. She couldn't stand bitter coffee.

"You think they're close to finding out who this stalker is?" Lynn looked down at the law journal she'd been perusing, very much aware that her sister was wondering why Renny went into another room to make the call.

Bree shrugged. "I guess." Her mind really wasn't on the case this morning even though she knew it should be. She simply wanted a few more minutes to bask in the afterglow, to feel the sweet remnants of being well loved. Well, *sexed right* was probably the better term—there was no love between her and Renny, just an undeniable attraction that they'd decided to act on. She couldn't be fool enough to wish for love anymore.

"Bree!" Lynn called in a higher tone; then she stood and snapped her fingers in front of her sister's face. "Earth to Bree."

Bree blinked and tried not to flush at being caught daydreaming. "Sorry, Lynn. I guess my mind was elsewhere."

"Yeah, up in that bedroom with that man." Lynn turned so that she mimicked Bree's stance, bottom pressed against the countertop, arms folded over her chest. "So tell me what happened."

Bree had already decided that sleeping with Renny would be her secret, no sense in everybody knowing about something that would be over as soon as the case was wrapped up. But she was brimming with so many emotions this morning she had to tell somebody. She took another sip of her coffee, then licked her lips slowly, choosing her words carefully. "We had sex," she said simply.

Lynn chuckled. "Is that all?"

Bree shot her a puzzled look.

"You're daydreaming about having sex?" Her smile lingered. "I'll admit I haven't had any in a while so I'd probably be a little glazed if I got some, too. But you definitely look like you have more than a night of sex on your mind."

Bree shrugged. "Not really. It was good." She'd looked away from Lynn, but could feel her intense gaze still on her. She smiled. "Real good."

Lynn laughed. "I'll bet it was." Then she nudged her sister. "I want all the details. Just let me refill my cup."

Bree went to the table and took a seat. Lynn followed her momentarily. "Okay, shoot."

Bree couldn't help but smile as she remembered. "Well, to start he said he wasn't going to do anything I didn't want. And as much as I wanted to jump on him…I just thought it was best that we kept our relationship simply business."

"I can see the logic in that." That was Bree for you, always logical. As fine as Renny was, Lynn was sure she'd have thrown logic to the wind a long time ago.

"And I probably would have been firm in my resolve if it hadn't been for the other night. If he had never touched me…if I didn't have some idea of what I was missing, I could have resisted him."

Lynn frowned. "Yeah, right, Bree. Are we talking about the same guy? How long do you think you could have resisted that?" She pointed in the direction of the living room. "You'd have to be straight lesbian material not to get wet around him, and even then you might think about backtracking."

The sisters laughed.

"I guess you've got a point there. But you know it's still

just business. I'm not naive enough to believe it's anything else. Just a sexual attraction that two adults have acted on."

Her words sounded hollow and just a touch nervous as Lynn listened to her. "It doesn't have to be, you know. You're single and he's single. There's really no reason why you can't pursue this. Unless…" Lynn purposely paused.

Bree looked at her then and wanted to share her fears with someone, wanted to tell her what Harold had done to her and how those scars kept her from believing in love again.

"You ladies mind if I join you for a cup of coffee?" Renny made his way into the kitchen. His conversation with Sam, while not very revealing, still had him reeling a bit.

"Sure, help yourself," Lynn answered, all the while watching Bree's reaction.

There was a knock on the door and Bree hastily took advantage of the opportunity to regain her composure. "I'll get it," she told Lynn when she was about to rise.

Bree was out of the kitchen before anybody could stop her. Renny took a seat at the table across from Lynn. The woman had been watching him, assessing the situation, he figured, since he'd come in last night. They'd had a brief conversation earlier yesterday in which the older Desdune daughter had not pulled any punches in telling him she knew he had a thing for her sister and inquired as to his intentions. This morning her look was different. Without a doubt she realized that things between him and Sabrina had changed. The question was how she felt about that.

"So, what now, Cassanova?" Lynn raised her brows as she watched Renny prepare his cup of coffee.

He didn't stop his movements, but did glance at her momentarily. He took a sip, then sat back in the chair and stared her directly in the eye. "Now I convince your sister that I can make her happy despite whatever happened in North Carolina.

"I know that there was a man involved and that he hurt her deeply. The particulars I'm still trying to figure out. It all depends on how soon I can convince your sister she can trust me enough with this information."

"Why would you want to know about her past if you know it concerns another man?"

Renny looked at her seriously. "Because I can't fix what he messed up if I don't know the whole story. And I won't live in his shadow."

"Hmph." Lynn considered him. "So, what else do you know about this guy?"

Renny had just opened his mouth to tell her what Sam had learned when they heard a crash and then a bloodcurdling scream. The sharp sound echoed throughout the house until Renny swore the windows shook.

Lynn stared at him. He stared at her. Then simultaneously they both got up from the table and ran to the living room.

Bree stood in the hallway, the door behind her closed, a card in her shaking right hand. At her feet was a broken vase, from what Lynn could see a very expensive vase, water and at least two dozen bloodred roses.

Renny wasted no time stepping over the mess, pulling her into his arms. He cradled her head into his chest just after he'd smoothly slipped the card out of her hand. "Calm down, baby," he crooned as her body shook beneath his embrace.

"Bree, honey, what is it?" Lynn took a step closer. Renny's back was to her, but she could see Bree's face clearly, could see the shock in her sister's eyes, the look of dread etching her dilated pupils.

Lynn bent down to pick up the shards of glass before Jeremy came from the den where he was watching television.

"It's…him…he's…he's here." Bree tried to take a deep

breath, tried to calm the sickening vibrations that moved throughout her. She was panicking, and panicking was weak in her book. Closing her eyes, she mentally willed herself to get it together. The flowers were beautiful and she'd momentarily been caught up in their fragrant aura until she'd read the card.

Behind her back Renny flipped the small card in his hand and read the inscription.

To my one and only love. I cannot live without you. The time has come for us to be together. Loving you always, H.

His instincts told him to crumple the piece of paper just as he planned to crush the man that had hurt her so. Instead Renny slipped it into his pocket and continued to rub his hands up and down Sabrina's back until he felt her muscles relaxing. "It's okay, baby. Everything's going to be okay. He can't hurt you anymore. I won't let him hurt you anymore." And with those words he realized that he wouldn't, couldn't, stand by and let someone terrorize Sabrina or even think that he was going to have her. He wanted Harold Richmond and he wanted his ass served on a platter for what he'd done.

"I'll get something to clean the rest of this up." Lynn carried pieces of glass in her hands as she made her way down the hall. "Take her to the couch so she can sit down," she ordered on her way out.

Renny moved slowly, guiding Sabrina over the water and splayed flowers farther into the living room, where he gently lowered her to the couch before sitting down beside her. "I want to know what he did to you, Sabrina, and I want to know now."

Bree heard his words, heard the deadly seriousness behind his enunciation and cringed. His eyes were fierce, his lips stretched into a thin line as he watched her closely. She wanted to tell somebody, she really did want to share this awful part of her life, but the pain was stifling and had her shaking her head. "It…it doesn't matter anymore. It's in the past…he's in…the past." She took another deep, steadying breath. Harold was her past, a deep, dark, demented part of her past that she didn't want anything else to do with.

"I'm fine," she said in a shaky voice. "I guess the flowers sparked some memories and just threw me for a minute. But I'm good now. We can leave whenever you're ready."

He'd watched her slip that mask back into place, the one that boasted of her control, of her seriousness and her desire to be taken that way. Veils lowered over her eyes, blocking all view of any emotion. Her lips barely trembled now, her hands still and staunch on his leg. It was all a show, all a facade to convince people that the strong, untouchable Sabrina was back. But he knew better. She couldn't hide her feelings from him, not after last night. He clamped his hand down over hers and took a deep breath. Demanding and forcefulness would not work with her. He had to get around her defenses another way.

"Baby, I know something happened in North Carolina. I know that this man did something to you." She blinked and looked away from him. With a finger to her chin he guided her face and her gaze back to his. "You can trust me, Sabrina. I want to know your secrets so I can make it better."

Bree closed her eyes and took another deep breath. The last man she'd shared her secrets with betrayed her and cost her the career she'd worked so hard for. She wouldn't make that mistake again. "Renny, there are no secrets for you to know. And if there were, they would be mine and mine alone. I don't need you to make anything better."

Her words sliced through him with intense heat. Never before had he been cut down so quickly, so seemingly easily. He'd been serious when he admitted that he wanted to make things better for her because that's really what he wanted. He liked seeing her smile, liked seeing her eyes blurring with passion, then brightening with release. He liked hearing her laugh and watching her competitiveness.

He did not like seeing her scared and shaken at receiving a phone call or some flowers.

Clamping down on his own temper, he watched her before he dared speak again. This was important to him and when something was important he took his time. Like one of his sculptures, he molded and shaved until it was just right, being careful not to move too fast or cut too swiftly. It was an art, this patience he had come to master over the years, one he would use to obtain the ultimate prize.

"I know he did something to you. It's just a matter of time before I find out what. And if he comes near you—"

Bree stood abruptly, cutting him off. "If he comes near me, I will handle it. I'm *your* bodyguard, remember?"

He stood and faced her. He would concede this round. He wouldn't push her any further. A tiny vein pulsed in her neck and he knew she was still edgy from the card and the flowers. But he would find out what had happened and he would take care of Harold Richmond whether Sabrina liked it or not. But there was one thing he needed to make perfectly clear, right now. "Don't give me that bull about you being my body-guard and me being simply your client. All that's changed as of last night and you'd better get used to it."

Over her head he'd watched Lynn appear in the entryway and because he wanted to grab Sabrina by her shoulders and shake, hard, he moved around her, taking long measured strides until he was out of the room.

When he was alone in the kitchen he picked up the phone, immediately dialing Sam's number. Richmond was making the move Sam had just spoken of, and while neither of the men knew what to expect from this guy, they both agreed they needed to be prepared.

If Sabrina was that frightened by a note and some flowers, then Harold Richmond was to be taken seriously.

Chapter 9

Renny hadn't mentioned the flowers or what had happened between them last night all day long. They'd gone to the foundry, where he'd allowed her to pick out a few of the pieces that would be shown at the opening. He'd seemed cordial enough with her then and on the ride to the gallery they'd held steady conversation. Still, Bree sensed the tension.

Okay, so her past was barreling toward her. She would not let it defeat her. The next time Harold called her, and she knew without a doubt that there would be a next time, she'd tell him for the last time that it was over and then she'd threaten to use some of the maneuvers they'd learned together against him. She didn't need Renny for that.

Now as she wandered through the gallery she wondered what exactly she did need him for. Before that knock on the door, before those flowers and that stupid card she'd been convinced that she and Renny were embarking on a very satisfying affair. But his words and his attitude after the flowers had given the impression of more. That was silly, she knew, because Renny was not into relationships. While she'd go along with the fact that he wasn't the womanizer the press had painted him to be, he was clearly a bachelor, at least for the time being. He liked his solitary style, that was evidenced by the distance he'd moved away from his family, not to mention his decision not to go into the family business. His life was his art and now this gallery. There was no room for a wife and kids.

Bree didn't even know if she wanted to be a wife with kids.

"Don't you have a job or something? Or is freeloading off family friends your career?"

The shrill tone came from behind her. She turned to face the blond bombshell with the stilts she called shoes and the claws she called nails. She looked down at Bree as if she were an inconsequential bug to be squashed, a thorn in her side that she had no problem getting rid of. Bree squared her shoulders and gave her the go-ahead-and-try look. "For your information, I have a career that doesn't include chasing men that clearly don't want anything to do with me in that way."

Yolanda gave a bland chuckle. "Oh, please. Spare me. I see how you look at him and let me just save you the trouble. He is definitely—" she looked Bree up and down "—not interested in you that way." Flipping her hair behind her shoulders, she rolled her eyes. "I suspect he's simply too kind to send you on your way. I, on the other hand, am not that caring."

Bree prayed the sting of Yolanda's words wasn't evident on her face as she took a step closer to the woman. "And that means what, Yolanda? Are you coming to put me in my place?" At her side her fingers itched to slap her just once. She'd love to see the look of shock register on that carefully made-up face.

"That means—" Yolanda took a step, meeting Bree head-on "—that I've worked long and hard at what Renny and I have together and I'm not about to let some little tart mess that up. So…"

Tart? Bree was incensed and despite her conscience telling her to walk away, to not give this woman her time or energy she was ready to show Yolanda just what this "tart" was made of. "So what?" She took another step until she was close enough to inhale the woman's overstated perfume.

"So," Yolanda looked down on her with a smirk on her face as if she'd already won the battle and with one long manicured finger poked Bree in the arm. "So you need to go and find yourself someone in your league. Oh, like that nice police officer or some other public servant. Yeah, that's more your speed." She threw her head back and laughed.

Now, Bree thought, she'd gone too damned far. The comments were one thing, but touching her was well beyond her limits of control. She could have broken her pretty little neck or at the very least cracked the bone in her perfectly pert nose. But she had the good sense of a well-trained soldier to gauge what sort of force was necessary and what wasn't. Besides, she had no desire to end up in jail. So instead, Bree grabbed Yolanda by the wrist, twisted her bony little arm behind her back and pushed the smart-mouthed Amazon. Yolanda twisted and flailed her arms, unable to hold her balance in her high heels, and careened into the blessedly empty podium behind her. As she fell, a delayed yelp escaped her and Bree almost laughed. Instead she went to stand over her. She knelt down, the ball of her foot on Yolanda's wrist so she couldn't level herself to get up. "It seems you're the one not up to speed. Like I said before, there's no future between you and Renny other than this gallery. I'd hate to have to prove my point again."

Yolanda yelped again as Bree applied pressure with her foot. "Sabrina?"

She turned at his voice, cursing that he'd caught her in this position. Suddenly she felt like a jealous schoolgirl, embarrassment creeping up her neck like a spreading virus.

"What's going on?"

He came closer, taking his eyes off her momentarily to look at Yolanda, who was now trying to get up off the floor. Bree stepped to the side so that she was no longer blocking or hindering her. When he looked back at her he seemed to expect an answer, an explanation of some sort. She was in no mood to give him one, mainly because she wasn't sure why she'd done what she'd done.

Hadn't she already deduced that there was no future between her and Renny? But they were having an affair and she at least had a right to have him all to herself for however long that lasted. She couldn't do that with Blondzilla hovering around him all the time. Squaring her shoulders, she stared right at him. "You should have your employees checked out. She's terribly clumsy."

With that said she walked away quickly without looking back. No way was she going to tell him she'd pushed her and threatened her to stay away from him. She was definitely going to spare herself that embarrassment.

The rest of the afternoon passed without incident and that was mostly thanks to Gabrielle. She'd come to the gallery looking for a birthday gift for a friend and even though they weren't technically open for business, Renny had relented. Gabrielle walked Sabrina around the gallery, the two of them conversing over paintings and sculptures and the two new life-size statues that Yolanda had secured for the opening. While bronze was his preferred medium, Clayton Justinian was quickly proving that the originality and weathered look of stone were still winners in the sculpting world. Renny would have to call Clayton to let him know how much both women enjoyed the twentieth-century African-American gods he'd provided on loan for the gallery's opening.

He was used to Gabrielle's bold sexual comments, but Sabrina's had been a surprise. He liked the idea of her sexuality, her passion being a secret that only they shared. When she boldly stroked the muscled buttocks of the sculpture named Samson his gut had clenched.

"A firm buttocks is definitely essential, don't you think, Gabrielle?" She'd been speaking to his sister, but her gaze had breezed by him as if by accident. Only he'd known she meant for him to see what she was doing. "I mean, there's nothing like the feel of tight muscles beneath your hand as you guide. It makes the contact so much more intense. Would you agree?"

Gabrielle, who had been lost in the striking form of Gladiator, moaned her agreement. "That's certainly true. But you know I'm partial to nice strong legs and arms that can hold you up and support your weight as you ride in a standing position."

Sabrina's hand had paused over Samson's thigh as she tilted her head. "You know, that's a good point."

As he'd watched her fingers moving slowly over Samson's naked form he wished it were him standing on that podium. He'd grown quite uncomfortable standing there watching her and listening to the conversation, so much so that he'd had to thrust his hands into his pockets and politely excuse himself. He had no desire to stand in his erect glory with his sister in the room.

They'd shared a lunch of soup and sandwiches in his office, to which he'd had Yolanda, to her chagrin, order but not share. The tension between Yolanda and Sabrina was thick. Gabrielle found it amusing. Renny, however, wasn't sure how he felt about it. On the one hand he was mildly flattered by Yolanda's misplaced interest in him—but he'd never given her any reason to think they were anything more than coworkers. The flip side was that her interest had apparently uncovered something about Sabrina that he was sure she'd rather have kept to herself.

She was fiercely protective of those she loved, those she felt belonged to her. She must consider him one of those people, why else would she have knocked Yolanda down? The purely male part of him had suffered from severe ego inflation as he'd watched his new lover knock the tall, gorgeous Yolanda on her butt, then proceed to threaten the woman. He'd been looking for Sabrina and when he heard their voices had stopped to see what they were speaking about. The tone of the conversation had first amused him, but then he'd heard something in Sabrina's voice shift and before he could make his presence known she'd attacked. He smiled now with the memory; it was very impressive indeed.

Now she and Renny were on their way back to her sister's house, where they would share a bed again tonight. She had no doubt that Renny's concession to sleep on the floor was a noble act of the past. Last night had been comfortable, a little too comfortable if she told the truth, and he would most assuredly be in that bed beside her for a repeat performance. She was game for whatever he was for the moment. If this was all she could have of him, so be it. She'd realized this afternoon that after she'd told Yolanda in no uncertain terms to step off she'd meant it. For the duration of this affair she wanted Renny Bennett all to herself. Now, after this job was over and after they'd had their fill of each other she'd happily turn him over to Yolanda. Well, maybe not to Yolanda, but certainly to the next woman in line.

"Ah, Sabrina, about Yolanda—" he began as he eased the car into the left lane.

She expelled a deep breath. Dammit, she'd thought he was going to let that ride. "What about her?" She tried to sound nonchalant, but could hear the edge in her own tone.

"There's nothing going on between us," he said seriously.

Bree looked over at him, wanting desperately to believe his words. "Look, don't think that I'm jealous or anything.

It's just that when I'm sleeping with someone I expect to be the only one, at least for the duration." Her hands fidgeted in her lap as she tried to keep her composure. If she wasn't jealous, this warm swirling in the pit of her stomach must be indigestion or something.

Renny wasn't sure he liked what she'd said. Outside of the blatant lie of not being jealous, she hadn't said they were in a relationship, she'd only admitted that they were sleeping together. Was that all she thought this was? "There was nothing going on between Yolanda and me before I slept with you and there will never be anything between her and me."

Bree shrugged. "Whatever. Just know that while I'm involved with someone I don't get involved with anyone else. That's just not the way I work. So I expect the same from you. What you do after that is your business."

"What I do after what? After we're finished sleeping together, you mean?" He couldn't help it, anger clawed at him with each word she spoke. Could she really be that unaffected by the night they'd spent together? Here he'd been trying to pinpoint the emotions she'd set off in him all day, trying to give them a name so that they could move on from there. And she was simply thinking of it as sex.

"Yes, that's exactly what I mean."

He clenched his teeth. "And when do you suppose that'll be? Tomorrow? Next Friday? Or maybe in a month? Are you at least planning on sleeping with me that long, Sabrina?"

His tone was definitely that of an angry man, and Bree couldn't quite figure out what had set him off. They were having sex now, that was true enough. As for the duration, she didn't have a clue how long it was going to take to wrap this case up and she didn't dare hope it would last beyond that. "I don't know an exact time span and I didn't think I needed one."

"Obviously you think what we shared is monitored by

some damned clock." A car cut him off and he slammed on the brakes, banging his hand against the steering wheel, muttering a course of very explicit curses.

"Are you all right?" Ever since she'd met him, Renny had always seemed in complete control. Except for that time when she'd saved his life. But other than that he'd been the epitome of calmness. Now he looked as if he was barely holding on.

He took a deep breath, slowly lifted his foot off the brake and continued to drive. "I don't take sex lightly, Sabrina. I thought I told you that already."

"You did. And neither do I. That's why I'm telling you that I don't share my lovers with other women."

He pulled into the parking lot and slowly switched the ignition off. "Is that all we are?"

His eyes were intense, his lips drawn into a tight line, and Bree felt something akin to guilt snake through her skin. "I…I thought…I mean, after last night I assumed—" She was confused and was beyond pretending any differently.

"You thought and you assumed, but you didn't feel, did you? You didn't simply allow yourself to feel what was happening between us. If we're lovers and that's all, that's because you won't open yourself up to the option of anything else. Just like you refuse to open up to me about anything personal in your life."

Bree was quiet. She didn't know what to say, how to counter his bitter words, and she didn't want to accept that they might be true.

Her silence infuriated him. "You know what, Sabrina? You've had it all wrong from the get-go. You thought I was the player, that I was the one who slept with women and toyed with their emotions, then dropped them without malice. But you're the uncaring one, you're the one that does what she wants with people, then chooses when she's done with them." He climbed out of the car and for the first time since he'd known her, didn't open the door for her. Instead he made his way to the front door without looking back.

She stalked up the walkway prepared to enjoy dinner with her sister and nephew and to ignore Renny Bennett, if need be. She wouldn't discuss this with him again. Either they were lovers or they weren't, it didn't make a difference to her. But when she stepped into the house she heard voices and before she could make them out clearly she felt thick arms encircle her and sweep her up off her feet.

"Bree! You're safe now, little sis. And whoever's bothering you will have to face me should he be man enough," Cole Desdune whispered into her hair as he swung her in a small circle.

After a round of introducing Renny to her parents and her brother, Cole, Bree frowned because her father dismissed all the women from the room.

When the females were out of the room, Bree's father, Lucien, turned to Renny again. "What do you know?"

The man wasn't looking at him with speculation and reserved judgment in his eyes anymore, but Renny still felt he hadn't quite passed Mr. Desdune's checkout, so he moved slowly away from the window, dropping his hands to his sides. "He's an ex-marine just like Sabrina. I haven't been able to pinpoint their connection and she's not saying much. I know that he left North Carolina two days ago and that those flowers were purchased from a florist here in Greenwich."

"Bree's pretty stubborn. Getting information from her is going to be hard if she doesn't think you need to know." Cole took a seat in one of those high-backed chairs that Renny thought looked way too uncomfortable.

"She's as pigheaded as her mama can be at times and it

drives me crazy." Lucien sighed. "But if this man has come here, then he has a plan and we need to find out what that is."

Renny wholeheartedly agreed. "Sam's trying to get more information, as well as trying to find out where this guy is staying." Renny dragged his hands down his face. "Like I said, I'll be with her most of the time, so I'll keep a close eye on her."

Lucien looked up at Renny, his eyes narrowing on the young man. He was from a good family, that he already knew. And he wasn't a bad-looking guy. He even looked like he could take a good tussle and give an even better ass whuppin'. Still, he didn't easily trust men with his daughters. "And why is it you'll be spending so much time with her again?"

There it was, that deadly look again. Renny swallowed hard and squared his shoulders. This was the first time he'd had to deal with the father of a woman he was interested in. Truth be told, this was the first woman he'd really been interested in. "Sam's company was hired by my family to take care of some security issues we're having."

Cole grinned. "Lynn says there's some lunatic stalking your family because of that big merger I keep reading about in the papers."

Cole reminded him of Gabrielle, blunt and itching to keep things going. Still, he liked the big fella and he smiled back at him. "Yeah, apparently somebody doesn't like the idea of Bennett Industries and Coastal becoming the largest communications entity in America." He shrugged. "But it's not a big deal. The merger will go through in a couple of weeks and then everything will be back to normal."

"And then you'll be out of my little girl's life?"

Renny couldn't tell if that was a statement or question coming from Lucien. He decided that honesty was the best policy in this regard even though if he said the wrong thing he was positive the much larger man would break him in two, with his not-so-small son grinning while he did. "I have no intention of leaving your daughter after the merger."

Lucien nodded and the room was deathly quiet for a few minutes. Then he rubbed his beard and rocked back on his heels. "So she's wrapped you around her little finger, too?"

Renny finally let his stance relax. A physical confrontation with Mr. Desdune didn't look imminent. "Something like that." He grinned.

Cole stood and moved closer to Renny, clapping a meaty hand on his back. "Watch out, she's got claws and fangs and she's not afraid to use them. I know, I taught her everything she knows."

Taking the other hand Cole had extended to him, Renny shook it casually. "I'll keep that in mind."

Chapter 10

The evening had progressed with Sabrina's parents soothing and talking to her about any and everything that had nothing to do with her job or her personal preferences. On more than one occasion she'd looked up at Renny balefully. He could see her straining to keep her cool, to remain respectful and not upset their dinner.

While he completely understood her parents' need to protect her—because he felt it within himself—he also realized how stifling this situation must have been throughout her entire life. He wasn't the youngest of the Bennett clan, but he was the youngest son and at times it seemed there was great emphasis put on him and what he wasn't doing to uphold the family name.

That part of him completely sympathized with Sabrina and for the first time he realized just what her independence meant to her. Throughout dessert he thought of his pledge to make her happy, to prove to her that she could trust him. But her declaration that they were simply lovers still irked him. If he wanted a lover he could have had his pick, but lately he'd begun to realize that he needed something more. Something stable and nourishing. He needed a woman that would encourage him, as well as kick his ass when he was wrong. Sabrina fit that description to a tee.

She'd scrutinized and argued with the choices for the Breathless Passion collection, as well as being instrumental in the final placement in the gallery. He suspected that had been the straw to break Yolanda's back, but he'd indulged Sabrina because he was amazed at how enthused she'd been about his work. Nobody had ever cared that much about his gallery or his pieces. She seemed to see the same vision he did. And that had warmed him.

"I'm trusting you with something very valuable, son. Don't make me regret it." Lucien had cornered Renny in the hallway just as he, his wife and his son were leaving for the night.

Renny gripped the older man's hand, having found some common ground with him over the course of dinner, and gave a curt nod. "You can depend on me, sir."

"I hope so." Lucien released his hand and turned to his wife. "Come on, Mama. We'd better get going."

Marie Desdune came to stand in front of Renny after shooing her husband away. She lifted a hand and cupped Renny's cheek. "Something tells me you're good for my Bree."

If that was her blessing, Renny was elated, but before he could speak Sabrina had made her way between them.

"Stop touching him, Mama, he'll think you're twisted or something. You've been ogling him all night as it is."

Marie looked down at her daughter and gave a knowing smile. "Nonsense, Bree. I just know a good thing when I see it."

Renny smiled. "Good night, Mrs. Desdune. It was a pleasure to meet you." He'd placed a protective hand on Sabrina's shoulder mostly because he hadn't touched her in the past few hours and he itched to do so.

"Likewise, Lorenzo. I enjoyed spending the evening with you." She looked at Bree again. "And I'm happy to know my daughter is in good hands."

Bree frowned. "Ah, I'm the bodyguard, which means he's in my good hands, Mama." She felt like a complete idiot saying that since he loomed over her, grasping her shoulder like he was ready to jump in front of a speeding train to save her. When had the tables turned? Her mind whirled as she felt like she was losing the one thing she'd called her own—her career, her skills—they were quickly becoming overshadowed by Harold and his stupidity and Renny and his dominance. Men—she was beginning to hate them! Except as Renny massaged her shoulder she felt her bones melting, her body giving over to the feel of his touch once more.

Before they'd gone to the gallery he'd stopped at a drugstore and purchased three boxes of condoms. That should hold him for a week or so, he thought, smiling to himself.

Bree entered the room finally. She'd stalled long enough in the bathroom. Actually she'd stayed in there until the thought of hiding had almost made her sick. There was nothing to hide from. She was a woman and he was a man. She had a job to do and he had a gallery to open. They were attracted to each other and pretty damn good in bed. Those were the facts and she could work with them. Anything else was irrelevant and she wouldn't bother thinking about it.

He was stretched out on the bed, his lean body oiled until he looked like one of his bronze sculptures. She took a steadying breath before removing her robe and sitting on the opposite side of the bed. Before she could speak, his hands were on her shoulders, massaging gently. Thankfully, she relaxed against his movements, letting her head loll back as she did.

"You have a nice family," Renny murmured. He didn't want her falling asleep on him and he knew from the sounds she was making and the way her breathing was slowing down that at any minute, she'd be out.

"They're great as long as you don't have an opinion of your own." He was close, his knees at her sides as his hands moved to her neck, his thumbs applying pressure at her nape.

Renny grinned. "They love you."

She expelled a breath. "I know. And I love them, but sometimes they can be a bit overbearing."

He agreed and sympathized. "I know the feeling."

"Your family didn't seem that way." He was back at her shoulders, moving to her biceps, soothing the tired muscles there.

"My mom's generally not overbearing. Not with the boys at least. She gives my sisters hell, though." He chuckled. "No, for me it's my dad."

Bree lifted her arms as he massaged her hands and her fingers and moved down to massage the small of her back. She felt him shifting again behind her, but didn't bother to open her eyes or question him. She was thoroughly enjoying this massage and was quite content to lie there until his fingers lulled her into a blissful sleep.

Renny knew the moment he had her completely relaxed, knew the precise second that she was all his. "You said we were lovers, Sabrina?"

"Mmm-hmm," she agreed.

"For the record, I'm a very selfish lover." He pushed her nightshirt up until her bikini-clad bottom was on display and traced a finger beneath the band of soft material. "I don't like to share."

Bree felt the jolt, recognized the shift from medicinal

strokes to tempting touches. Yet she was still unable to move. Unable or unwilling? "Then we're in agreement. We'll be exclusive lovers."

Renny pulled her panties down and off her legs. "Exclusivity it is." His hands molded each of the heavenly mounds as his thumbs came close to entering her crease. "I require something else from my lovers, though."

Bree turned her head from one side to the other, acutely aware of her vulnerable state and loving it just the same. "And what's that?"

Renny spread her legs and traced a finger from her smoldering center up to where her buttocks met her back. She gasped and he licked his lips in anticipation. "Everything," he whispered, then stroked his already condom-clad erection and centered himself above her.

"Everything?" She couldn't think straight, erotic thoughts becoming jumbled with coherent ones, and she struggled to maintain her focus. "What does that mean?"

"It means that while we're lovers there is nothing you will deny me." He slipped his hands beneath her and angled her for his entrance. "Everything that you are, every thought you have, every word you utter becomes a part of me and I you." He rotated his hips while holding hers still. He watched as she gripped the sheets beneath her and struggled to speak.

"I can't…give you…everything," she moaned.

He stilled above her, pulled almost completely out of her until only the tip rested at her entrance. She bucked and tried to push back to bring him inside her again. He shook his head even though he doubted she could see him. "I want it all, Sabrina. While we are lovers I want all of you. I won't settle for anything less."

Her insides were quivering, her juices pooling at her center as his manhood teased her. She came up completely on her knees, looked at him over her shoulder and saw that he was deadly calm and more serious than she'd ever seen him before. "Renny," she whispered.

"No, Sabrina." He shook his head. "Not now. Now it's just you and me and I want all that you have, all that you are. Right now. Tell me I can have all of you."

Bree shook her head, unable to stop the building sensations inside or control the warning bells and simple whispers in her mind. She wanted him so completely, so why shouldn't she give herself the same way? Because it wasn't safe. Even as she answered her own question he leaned forward and grabbed her breast, squeezing her nipple through the cotton of her nightshirt.

"Tell me, Sabrina. Or I can't do this anymore."

There it was, the ultimatum. She hated an ultimatum— hated being tempted by one. But her walls contracted as she pushed her bottom back only to have him move just out of her reach again. And she realized she hated that more. "We're lovers," she breathed airily.

"And?" He now guided his erection up and down her center, passing her opening and grazing her clit.

She shook, heat racing through her with abandoned fierceness. If she grabbed those sheets any tighter she'd surely rip them. "And while we're lovers," she paused. He was spreading her juices everywhere, up the back, down to the front, his fingers dipping inside her, and she moaned as he rubbed her now aching walls. "While we're lovers," she gasped, "I will give you—"

He was near to bursting himself, so she really needed to hurry this up. His fingers moved faster inside her and he heard the hitch in her breath. "You'll give me what, Sabrina?" He heaved with longing for her. "Dammit, tell me!"

"Everything," she sighed as the orgasm took her and she began to rock against his hand. "I will give you everything," she repeated and repeated until her legs had finally stopped shaking.

Renny didn't even wait for her to recover before pushing

her down onto the bed and thrusting completely inside her. "Yes, baby," he whispered in her ear as her walls gripped him and he stroked her with urgency. "Everything. You'll give me everything. Yes." He was sinking, falling faster and harder than he ever had before and he didn't care.

There was nothing that could stop what was happening between them and nothing he would allow to get in his way. This was where he belonged. They were a perfect fit and as she began to move with him he knew she'd felt the same thing.

She was giving him everything; with every stroke she matched, every wicked promise he'd spoken in her ear and she'd answered, she was giving him all that she had and he loved it. He absolutely loved it all.

And when he was empty and still lying warmly inside her, it hit him that he loved her. He loved Sabrina Desdune. He loved his bodyguard.

"Military backgrounds are almost impossible to dig in to." Sam paced the floor in Lynn's living room. "I can't find out much except that he was dishonorably discharged and divorced earlier this year."

Renny sat, his legs spread wide, his elbows propped up, his fingers steepled at his chin. "So he was married?"

"Yeah. The terms of the divorce were irreconcilable differences. The ex-wife, Joanne Richmond, now resides in Florida with a healthy alimony check coming each month."

"So what was Sabrina's involvement?"

Sam shrugged. "You haven't been able to get it from her, either, I see."

"No." Renny shook his head. Admittedly, he hadn't really brought the subject up. At night when he and Sabrina were together there was no one but them. Another man didn't dare enter the picture. He relished his alone time with her, felt her slowly occupying a bigger space in his heart, his life, with each passing day. Another reason why putting an end to this threat against her was so imperative.

"Outside of this dilemma we've also decided to beef up security tomorrow night at the gallery. There was a note taped to the door at your condo. It was one of the invitations to the opening with a red *x* marking the *yes* in the RSVP area."

That caught Renny's full attention and he stood to face Sam. "When?"

"I found it this morning. I assigned another guard to Alex so I could work this thing with Bree, too. But you said the moving guys were coming, so I didn't want them to be there alone. Luckily, I got there before them and confiscated the note."

"So it'll be tomorrow then." His jaw clenched but he found himself looking forward to the confrontation. All this hiding and looking over his shoulder was becoming a royal pain. He wanted Sabrina as his woman, not as his bodyguard. And he definitely didn't like thinking of her dodging bullets or any other dangerous pastime, no matter how much she seemed to thrive on the adventure. In the past weeks he'd begun to suspect that her love of danger came from an embedded need to rebel against her family. Whatever they thought she couldn't do she seemed hell-bent on doing. Well, he was hell-bent on stopping her. He'd just go about it another way. The direct approach of denying her would not fly; she'd only push harder. Her family hadn't seemed to notice that yet.

"I'm not sure. It could be a smoke screen. Make us think the hit is tomorrow, we lower our guard when it isn't and then they attack. The gallery's taken on most of the publicity in the last few weeks, leaving the merger in the business section. But until that's over and done with the threat is still alive and viable."

"You're right. So everybody's got to be on guard. Watching everything incoming and outgoing. Protecting what's mine is vital at this point." Renny had moved to the window and was looking out at the night sky wondering who lurked in the dark.

Sam had been trying to find a way to ask his next question calmly, but figured it was just going to come out and Renny would take it however he wanted. "Does my sister fall into the category of what's yours?"

Renny turned slowly. He'd wondered when Sam was going to get around to asking his intentions toward Sabrina. From the closeness of their family, he was sure Cole or even Mr. Desdune had told him something about the two of them. Not to mention the fact that it was probably obvious, at least that's what Renny's siblings thought. "Just ask your question, Desdune." He would give a truthful answer.

Sam nodded. "Are you sleeping with my sister?"

"Yes."

Sam's jaw clenched. "And where is that headed? Will she be the next headline in the papers?"

Renny shook his head. "I'm in love with her."

"That doesn't mean she won't become a headline."

"I won't allow that to happen."

"And how do you plan on stopping it?" Sam began to pace. He wasn't sure how he felt about Renny being in love with Bree. He'd almost conditioned himself to believe it was a fling. What if Bree loved him, too? This wasn't good at all. "She's not like those other women you date, Renny. She shouldn't be dragged through the mud. She's fragile. If you break her heart, it'll kill her." He stopped abruptly in the middle of the room, his hands fisted at his sides. "Then I'll have to kill you."

Renny took the man's words and knew he was as serious as Renny would be if it were one of his sisters. But all he could offer him was the truth, what he felt in his heart. "I don't give a damn about the press. I live my life for me. Sabrina is very important to me and I won't let anyone hurt her."

Sam swore. "You don't even know her. You don't know what she's been through or what she needs."

"I know that she's a strong woman with a good head on her shoulders. I know that her family doesn't give her half as much credit as she deserves. I realize that something happened to her in North Carolina and believe me I'm going to get to the bottom of it. But I also realize that she's an independent woman who has been sheltered all her life and just wants to prove that she can make it on her own. I'm willing to give her that. I haven't fired her as my bodyguard because of that. But don't for one instant think that I'll let her get hurt on my account."

"I know she's strong," Sam almost whispered. "I've always known it. But she's the baby. It's our job to protect her."

"No. That's my job now. You just need to love and respect her."

Sam saw the determination in Renny's eyes and realized that the man was totally serious about this. He must really love Bree. "Don't let my dad hear you say that." He grinned and extended his hand.

Renny relaxed a bit and took that outstretched hand. "I hear you on that one."

They shook hands.

"But if you hurt her..." Sam started.

"Don't worry, she's safe with me."

Chapter 11

The red gown molded against every curve and juncture of Bree's body, the material gliding across her skin like fresh rose petals. As she examined herself in the full-length mirror on the back of the closet door she noticed that the lightweight outer layer sparkled subtly as she turned this way and that. The draped neckline was a modest length while the back took a deep plunge to the point that underwear was not possible.

Her stomach was still doing flip-flops over that fact and she prayed nobody else noticed. Especially her mother. Renny had invited her entire family to the opening. Why, she had no idea. Even though in the past couple of weeks they'd all grown pretty close and at dinner last night you would have thought they were either all related or had known each other for years and years.

She slipped on the strappy pumps that Adriana had insisted on then surveyed the makeup that Lynn had applied for her only a half hour earlier. Her lips shimmered with cherry gloss

amazingly looked plumper, more voluptuous. Her eyes had
been heavily lined with copper shadows. Her cheeks appeared
higher as a result of the blush, while borrowed diamond and
ruby studs twinkled at her ears. Lynn had also taken the
liberty to brush her hair until it hung down her bare back like
a dark mane. Studded clips held the mass away from her face
even as wispy tendrils were left loose and dangling precariously at each ear.

Nervous fingers went to the matching diamond necklace as
she stared in amazement at the woman in the mirror. She'd
never looked so…so glamorous before. Her hands ran the span
of the soft billowing material of the dress and she felt a shiver
of anticipation. What would Renny think when he saw her?

He'd been barred from the room, forced to dress in the tiny
guest bathroom. On a ragged oath Renny swore as he bumped
his knee for the billionth time on the sink pedestal. He'd
already decided that when this mess was over he wasn't returning to his condo; instead he'd spoken to a developer about
building him a house. A home that he could hopefully start
his family in. That might take a few months yet, so he was
still looking for an apartment until that time. But staying with
Lynn, no matter how welcoming she was or how happy
Jeremy was to see him when he came home in the evenings,
was not an option.

Expertly he looped and tied the tie, then buttoned the high
vest before donning the single-breasted tuxedo jacket. He
didn't dress up often, but looking in the small mirror he
conceded to cleaning up well, when needed. He'd already
brushed his hair until it was smooth and almost gleamed in
the fluorescent lighting. With a couple extra strokes of the
brush he tended to his light mustache and shadowed goatee.
Decidedly finished dressing, he adjusted his pants and opened
the bathroom door. He had his accessories bag in his hand and
was headed to the bedroom that he and Sabrina had been

sharing to deposit it and withdraw her so they could be on their way. It wouldn't look good for the owner and his date to be late for the opening.

Bree had just taken a step toward the door, ready to go downstairs and wait on her date that she believed was still in the bathroom. She held the small purse in her right hand after she'd slipped her gun and cell phone safely inside. There was absolutely nowhere she could conceal her weapon on her person. This dress was unforgiving in that regard. She was just about to reach for the doorknob when she saw it turn. Her heart lurched. This was the moment of truth. On instinct she backed up and waited with bated breath for him to enter.

Opening the door and making his way into the room, Renny was about to call out to her, but his accessories bag fell to the floor just inside the threshold and he cursed again before kneeling down to pick it up. He caught sight of shoes that looked like colored stilts disappearing behind shimmering red material. Like a man in a trance his eyes traveled north, taking in every seductive curve, every swish and sway of the material before stopping at the most kissable lips he'd ever seen.

He swallowed. Hard. All the blood rushed from his head to his groin in seconds, leaving him breathless.

Instinctively, as if beckoned, his eyes returned to her breasts, where pebbled nipples peeked through the material. He took a deep breath and willed his legs to raise him up, to carry him closer to her. "You are stunning," he said in a gruff voice.

She giggled nervously. "Stunning? Are you serious?" She'd admitted to herself that she looked good, but stunning was a long shot. Still, he was looking at her and slowly moving closer like a man who knew what he was talking about.

She took a moment before he was too close to quickly examine his attire. The tuxedo was Christian Dior. She knew because she'd carried it to the car when they'd stopped at the men's store to pick it up this afternoon. Every cut, every angle seemed to be made especially for him. His shoes, Dolce & Gabbana, shone right up to the bow tied at the top. On his right ring finger was a gold and diamond encrusted insignia ring with his mother's Brazilian crest embedded in its center. On any other man it would have seemed gawky and ornate, but on Renny it was the perfect blend with his charming yet forceful good looks. She released a low cat whistle that she knew was out of character for her ensemble. "Can a man be stunning?"

He smiled as his hand extended and he toyed with a tendril of hair that seductively grazed her collarbone. "Stunningly handsome, I believe."

Her smile faltered when his fingertips touched her skin. "Then that's what you are," she whispered.

"That means we're the perfect match." He saw something in her eyes shift. "For tonight at least." There it was again. Almost unnoticeable, something had changed in her. He wondered briefly if she'd finally opened herself to the possibilities between them.

"We should go." Nervous and afraid she was going to say something to embarrass herself, Bree tried to move around him.

Big mistake.

Renny caught a glimpse of the back of her dress and raised a brow. "Not just yet. Turn around and let me see this dress."

There was a small train in the back, one that Bree knew by the end of the night would be on her nerves, so she took a few steps away from him and turned around. Heat pooled between her legs and she knew the exact moment his gaze rested on the small of her back where the dress ended its alluring drape.

"Damn, are you planning on torturing me all night with that thing?" He was close now, but careful not to step on the dress. It took no effort at all to slip his hand inside until he felt the warmth of her skin. Nudging her hair aside with his cheek he placed light, wet kisses along her back.

Bree sucked in as much air as she could, else she was sure she would have expired right then and there. "Do…you… think it's…mmm…too much?"

Renny growled and removed his hand from her skin because if he didn't they would definitely be late. He wrapped his arms around her waist and pulled her back against him as he continued to nuzzle her neck. "Too much of a good thing never hurt anybody." Even though he was so hard it was almost painful.

Bree was so focused on the exquisite feelings coursing through her that when her purse began to vibrate in her hand it scared her and she jolted.

"What's wrong?" Renny asked, pulling slightly away.

"Huh?" She was confused for a second until it vibrated again and she frowned. "Oh, it's my phone." Digging her hand in her purse, she retrieved it and pressed Talk without looking at the number displayed. "Hello?"

"I'm looking forward to seeing you again, Sabrina."

"Harold?" she whispered before she realized that was the wrong thing to do. Renny's hands tensed around her just before she felt him draw away and come to stand in front of her.

"Yes, sweetheart. It's me. Did you like the flowers I sent?"

She hadn't heard anything from him since he'd sent the flowers and she'd almost believed that he'd changed his mind and decided to leave her be. "No, I didn't like them. They were inappropriate. Just like you calling me is inappropriate."

"Shh, darling. It's okay now. I fixed everything for us. It's okay for us to be together now."

"What? How did you fix it?"

Before she could hear the answer Renny grabbed the phone. "Colonel Richmond, it's a pleasure to finally speak with you."

"Who is this? I want to talk to Sabrina!" Harold screamed into the phone.

"That's not going to be possible now or ever, Colonel."
Renny gave Sabrina a steely glare when she looked like she
was going to reach for the phone again. "Now I want this to
be the last time you contact her in any way. Is that understood?"

Renny's question was answered with a low grumbling
laugh that soon escalated to a sick, ugly pitch that had his
insides clenching.

"In just a short time there will be no need for me to contact
her because she'll be with me, where she belongs."

"If you come anywhere near her—"

Harold cut him off. "Shortly. I promise you it will be shortly."

"Richmond!" Renny yelled just as the line went dead. He
tossed the phone across the room until it shattered against the
wall. Then he grabbed Sabrina by the shoulders, giving a
little shake. "I want you to tell me everything about you and
this man and I want you to tell me now, Sabrina!"

"Renny," she whispered, shaking her head.

"No! No! You will not deny me. Not again. I want to know
what happened between you two and why he's come back
for you."

He was angry; his eyes showed it, and his voice left no
further doubt. "It's…nothing. It's over. And…and…I don't want
to talk about it."

He released her because he knew that with the rage soaring
through him he'd likely hurt her by squeezing her so hard. He
walked away, taking deep breaths as he did. "Sabrina, this is
ridiculous. I told you I needed everything. That I wanted everything from you. You said you would give it to me. I've been
patient. I've tried to wait until you were ready. But you have
no intention of ever telling me, do you?"

Bree went to the other side of the room to retrieve her phone
and attempt to put it back together. "There is nothing to tell,
Renny. It's my past. I don't ask you to rehash your past for me."

"My past isn't hunting me down!" he yelled.

"Oh, it isn't? Then who the hell masturbated on your bed, leaving you a little souvenir?"

"I don't have any idea who would have done that. And I'm not the one shaking like a leaf when flowers are delivered or I receive a phone call, now, am I?"

"Well, go ahead and shout the roof down, you two." Lynn entered the room in an elaborate silver creation. "I can hear you clear down the hall in my room and I had my door closed. What seems to be the problem?" She looked from Renny to Bree.

Embarrassed and furious with Renny for putting her in this position, Bree stuffed the remnants of her phone into her purse and moved toward the door. "Nothing. There is no problem." She tossed Renny a heated glare that soon softened with the curve of her lips into a shaky smile. "Everything is fine. Renny and I just needed to clear the air a bit. I'll be waiting downstairs." Then she was gone.

Lynn didn't believe that any more than she believed in Santa Claus and the Tooth Fairy. "You want to tell me what's really going on?"

Renny dragged a hand down his face. "Harold Richmond called her again and I tried to press her into telling me what happened between them."

Lynn shook her head. "Stubborn as a mule, that's what Gramma Ruby says about her."

Renny gave her a grim look. "Maybe I should call Gramma Ruby and ask her for a potion that'll make her talk."

"You don't even want to go there." Lynn laughed. "But let's not deal with this tonight. This is a big night for you and your career. Let's just go and celebrate that." She moved closer to Renny and linked her arm in his. She'd liked him from the start and after having him stay here and watching him fall deeper and deeper in love with her baby sister she'd already started treating him as a brother. "She'll come around."

Renny walked alongside Lynn. "Let's hope it's not too late when she does."

An hour and fifteen minutes into the evening and Silhouette was a smash. Cameras hadn't stopped clicking and the champagne hadn't stopped flowing. The gallery was jampacked with art critics, agents, artists and the media. Bree had never smiled so much in her life. Her cheeks were hurting, she was tired of standing on these stilts and she was hungry. Nerves had prevented her from eating all day and being on Renny's arm while he was constantly being interviewed prevented her from partaking of the buffet there.

"This is lovely, dear." Beatriz gave her son another kiss on the cheek. "I am so proud of you."

Marvin had approached with his wife. Over his shoulder Sabrina saw Luke, Sam's replacement. Somewhere throughout the crowd were Sam and Trent and the rest of the Desdune Security crew. A part of her itched to meet up with them to go over the game plan and layout of the gallery one more time. But Sam had been clear that she was to stay as close to Renny as she possibly could this evening. And so she'd been doing just that.

"I have to agree. While the pieces require a certain taste, it seems that you've hit on something with this particular crowd. I look forward to seeing a positive article about you in the morning paper," Marvin said.

Renny grinned. "For a change, I do, too."

Beatriz shifted her assessing gaze. "And, Sabrina, you look beautiful tonight."

Bree ran her tongue quickly across her teeth. That was the only way she was going to manage another smile. "Thank you, Mrs. Bennett. A contribution from your daughters and my sister."

"They did a marvelous job. Isn't she gorgeous, Marvin?"

Marvin had noticed how good Sabrina looked the moment his son walked in with her on his arm, just as he'd noticed the totally smitten look his son had on his face. There was definitely something there and he wondered if Renny was smart enough to identify it and move forward. While he didn't exactly agree with her line of work, her family seemed to be a solid one, a fact he'd concluded after his investigation of them and then meeting them earlier this evening. They were a lively bunch and they supported their children. To Marvin, that was good enough. "Yes, she looks stunning. Nobody would ever guess you were a bodyguard."

Bree smiled genuinely at the compliment. "Thank you, sir."

Renny, however, had winced at the mention of Sabrina's official title. Ever since their first night together he'd thought of her as a woman, not a bodyguard. In fact, he'd gone through great pains to forget that was her job. To acknowledge that fact would remind him of the constant state of danger she was in and how much that irritated him. His arm tightened around her as if by instinct and he glanced around the room again. He'd been doing that most of the evening.

"Excuse me?" Yolanda said, appearing suddenly as if she'd been standing close by all along.

Bree looked at her nemesis draped in a stunning turquoise confection this evening that glittered and sparkled more than the twinkling lights strategically placed throughout the room. She gave Bree a cursory glance before settling her high-beam smile on the Bennetts and then, of course, Renny. "I think they're ready for the unveiling now."

Renny agreed. The opening was only slotted to last three hours, something decided at the last minute because of the security issues. He'd reluctantly agreed, but then recognized the advantages. One, he'd be home early with Sabrina; two, by giving the customers a little bit at a time it would increase their curiosity and most assuredly bring them back faster; and three—he thought with an inner grin—he'd be home early with Sabrina. "I think you're right. Why don't you have them refill everybody's glass and we'll move to the center podium and get ready?"

"Fine. Mr. and Mrs. Bennett, if you'll follow me I'll make sure you're situated right up front so you won't miss a thing."

As Marvin and Beatriz prepared to follow her Renny grasped Yolanda's elbow. "Find the Desdunes and make sure they have a good spot, as well."

Yolanda's frown was brief and didn't quite reach Sabrina personally, but she'd seen it nonetheless. "I can do that, Renny," Bree offered, not because she particularly wanted to save the woman any trouble, but more so because she didn't want her parents having to deal with such an unsavory creature.

"No. I need you by my side for the unveiling and its dedication." His eyes met hers and he felt the swarming of emotions that had been brimming in him since he'd awakened this morning. He had so much he wanted to tell her, so much he wanted to share. He'd finally decided what he wanted for them both, and the sooner he told her the better.

"But—" Bree tried to argue.

Yolanda waved a hand. "Nonsense." She tossed Bree a cool glare. "It is my job." And then she was off.

Bree raised a brow and looked at Renny. "I hope I don't have to deck her again. This dress is not fit for fighting." Absently she smoothed a hand over her hip.

His heated gaze followed that movement and he accepted the urge to pull her close. Around him he saw the flash of more cameras and knew the headlines would be juicy tomorrow. Deciding earlier this evening that he truly didn't care since this time they'd be right on the mark about his obsession with this woman, he let his hands find the smooth skin of her back and held his breath only a moment while she hesitated in reciprocating the embrace.

Sliding her palms from his chest to his shoulders and wrapping her arms around his neck, she let her gaze rest on his.

"That dress is made for one thing and one thing only," he murmured, his face moving closer to hers.

Her breath hitched. "And what's that?"

He passed her lips and moved to her ear, lowering his voice to a sexy growl. "To drive me absolutely crazy." One hand moved farther down to the small of her back, a finger daring to go beneath the silky material. "My God, Sabrina," he gasped. "You're not wearing anything under here, are you?"

Bree shrugged, nuzzling closer to his neck, seductively rubbing against his growing arousal. "Nothing would fit."

"Mmm." His growl and his erection grew until he knew he had to release her or his unveiling would come second to the shocked stares at a fully aroused nonstatue. "Later we're going to discuss you and your lack of undergarments," he said as he pulled away from her.

He was as hot for her as she was for him, and that thought only made her hotter. "You sure we'll need to discuss it? I was simply thinking of an unveiling of my own."

He raised an eyebrow. When she said tempting things like that it heated his blood, as well as astonished him. No one would ever guess she was a little on the freaky side. But he was more than fine with that being his secret. "We can discuss it after your unveiling." He laced his fingers with hers and started moving to the main room. "Long after," he added over his shoulder after a few steps.

Bree smiled, biting on her lower lip in anticipation.

"Ladies and gentlemen," Yolanda began from her position behind the podium. "All evening I've been asked about the covered piece to my right and all evening I've been telling you how special it was and how much you were going to love it."

She had the crowd's complete attention. Bree looked out into the audience and saw first her parents, hugging each other closer, still so obviously in love. Then she saw Cole with some woman on his arm—a different woman than had been on his arm only thirty minutes ago. Lynn was standing more to the center of the front row with Adriana and Gabrielle standing with her. The three musketeers, Bree thought with an emotional tug. The remaining Bennett men stood to the left of them, tall, strong and oh so good-looking. The single ladies in this room were probably having a field day. Sam held his position near the entrance, looking quite debonair himself in a tuxedo, while Trent and the other crew secured the doors and outer perimeter. Briefly she wondered if anyone was walking the length of the gallery including the back offices, but at the sound of the audience's applause her thoughts shifted back to the matter at hand.

"I present to you Mr. Lorenzo Bennett, sculptor and owner of Silhouette Art Gallery."

Renny released her arm to move closer to the podium and Bree found herself clapping, her heart filled with pride.

"Thank you," he said humbly, then cleared his throat before beginning again. "This piece was the final one added to the collection and that's because I didn't start it until late. The inspiration came to me one afternoon at my father's house when I received a bit of disturbing news wrapped in an unbelievable package."

A hush fell over the room and Bree continued to look out at the crowd only half paying attention to what Renny was saying.

"Have you ever received a gift that was wrapped in such a way that you thought you couldn't possibly want whatever it contained? Or have you received something and been so intrigued by its clandestine wrapping that you couldn't help peeling it away in search of the prize inside?" Renny looked at his parents, then at the Desdunes before turning slightly sideways.

She was standing right beside the piece, only a step or two away from it. He thought that positioning ironic, then exchanged that feeling for one of fate. "When I sat down to work that next day my mind was already filled. Filled with a vision, a silhouette if you will, and my fingers simply began moving. With each passing day the strokes became more impassioned, more sensual. I recognized the urgings and wanted solely to act on them."

Her hands were at her side. Then because she didn't like standing still, she clasped them and unclasped them again. He smiled.

"But something told me that moving too fast would destroy the piece. Speed would increase the likelihood of mistakes and I wanted this to be just right." He looked out into the crowd, reveled in the anticipation that loomed around him and smiled slowly—that smile the papers had reported as being devilishly charming—and watched as on cue the cameras flashed again. "It was only two days ago that I completed this piece, that I felt it was exactly right, representing all the emotion and depth of the feelings I'd poured into it."

He moved away from the podium, carrying the microphone with him, and continued past Sabrina, stopping in front of the covered piece. "The title of my collection is Breathless Passion. This piece encompasses that meaning, but surpasses it hands down. I call it My Woman, My Love." At the last words he'd grabbed the covering and whisked it from the piece, exposing it to the entire room.

The silence vanished and was replaced by oohs and aahs and a few tiny gasps. Sabrina was still canvassing the room as Renny's words invaded her mind, washing over her as if he were seducing her right there on that stage. That was ridiculous, she knew, and she attributed it to her simply being horny. But then she caught Gabrielle's huge smile and Lynn's hand going over her mouth, then Adriana's approving glare and she turned to the sculpture.

Her mouth fell open.

There lying on a chair with him holding on to her legs, kissing her ankle as he guided himself inside was a face so like her own a blind man could have seen it. It wasn't the position or even the fact that her parents and his parents and half of Greenwich were now viewing her in this position that bothered her. It was the succinct emotions etched on each of the faces. Did she and Renny look like that when they made love?

She clearly remembered being in that particular position a time or two recently and felt the heat infuse her cheeks. As if she were summoned to do so her eyes found his.

He'd been waiting, holding his breath with her reaction to the piece and what the dedication had meant to him. Now he saw the shock, the questions, the denial and yes, the longing in her. He dropped the cloth and moved to her quickly, handing the microphone to an equally astonished and now fuming Yolanda.

Bree didn't hesitate, but let him take her in his embrace. He had hugged her many times before, had even cradled her in the night. But none of that had the meaning, the intensity that this moment held. She didn't know what to say, didn't know what this meant.

He needed to be alone with her badly, but knew that wasn't about to happen. Instead he took her hands and led her a few feet from the podium while his guests were gawking at the piece. Cupping her face in his palms, he kissed the tip of her nose, then her lips. "Do you like it, baby?"

Bree was holding on to his wrists, her eyes momentarily closed. "Like it? It's breathtaking. And unbelievable. I thought…I mean, when did you have time to finish it?" They had been away from his apartment for a while now and he hadn't gone back.

"I had it delivered to Lynn's and she let me use her basement to work." He was cupping her neck now, his tense muscles relaxing a bit.

"But when?"

He knew she was wondering when he'd found the time. She was with him all day and all night, she'd assumed. "Afterward, baby. While you slept."

Realization dawned on her and she felt the prickle of tears, but she wouldn't let her emotions get ahead of her. She had to be clear; his words were still running through her mind and what she'd thought she'd heard still baffled her. "But what you said up there…" She bit her bottom lip. "I mean, what you said about the inspiration and the feelings that went into the piece. And…and…the title."

"All of that was—"

In the next moment there was a flicker, and then they were thrust into darkness.

The building was instantly abuzz with noise, the feel of panic filling the room. Instinctively, Renny grabbed Bree's arm. "Stay close to me," he murmured, then turned to walk through the crowd. He knew this building front to back. If it was a power outage he could get to the fuse box before anyone else here. But the heat that filled his chest and grasped at his throat warned him that it wasn't just a blown fuse.

With her handbag on her shoulder Bree undid the clasp and pulled her tiny revolver out. One hand clutched the back of Renny's jacket as they moved through the crowd. A visual was clearly out of the question, but all her other senses were acute—actually some night vision goggles would have been good right about now. Still, they made their way through the crowd of people who were in a full-fledged state of panic by now.

Someone was here. As they moved through the room Bree felt the menacing presence and braced herself for the worst. He had said for her to stay close to him. Well, that was her job and she hadn't planned on running away. She wasn't wearing an earpiece to connect her to Sam and the others. With her position by Renny's side for the night they'd thought that would be a bit alarming to the guests. She'd agreed and now it appeared that she and Renny were on their own.

He was moving toward the back of the gallery. They'd stayed along the wall where he could use the socket fixtures and architecture to mark their progress. Pushing past the bodies that seemed to swarm them, he didn't stop moving. He couldn't stop. The darkness brought certain danger, not only to his guests, but to Sabrina. That had him moving even faster, eager to relight the room. Whoever it was would have to come out and play like a big boy now.

Bree wasn't afraid, yet the continued darkness and the absence of any immediate action because of it alarmed her more. If they cut the lights the next viable action would have been gunshots or a scream that someone was hurt. There had been no shots and so far she was almost positive that no one was hurt, only startled. People continued to press into her. She strained her eyes around them for a glimpse of anything. A light, a flash, anything that would give her some idea of what to expect next. Her training allowed her to remain calm while her feelings for the man in front of her had her heart pounding as she feared for his safety.

How could she protect him if she couldn't see the danger coming? What would happen if the person hit the mark? Quickly becoming frustrated, she closed her eyes, willed herself to calm down. Her hands were sweating and the gun suddenly felt heavy. Shaking her head, she berated herself, increasing her hold on the gun and adjusting her fingers on Renny's jacket.

But at that precise moment a cluster of people pushed into them and the connection was severed. In an instant Bree found her fingers grasping in midair, the gun still in her hand, but her hold on Renny gone. Panic clawed at her fiercely as she kept her feet trained in the direction she'd previously been traveling. People pushed against her shoulders, causing her to stumble backward in those damned heels a couple of times. "Renny!" she called out to him, but of course only received the answer of the crowd.

"What's going on?"

"I can't see anything!"

"Get me out of here!"

People were all around her; everyone, that is, except for Renny.

"Renny!" When she was able to begin walking again she continued on the path she'd assumed they were on before straining to hear if he was calling her, as well. "Renny!"

Placing her free hand along the wall, she tried to get an idea of where she was in the gallery. She'd been there so much in the past weeks that surely she could find her way… find her way where? She didn't know where Renny was, didn't have a clue who had turned out the lights or how she could get them back on. *Okay, calm down, Desdune. You're a trained soldier. You can do this.* With the words of her little pep talk, she stiffened her spine and continued to move. She'd get to his office. There were flashlights in the bottom drawer of his desk. She knew because she'd put them there herself for lack of a better place to store them when they'd come in.

She felt the curve of the wall. That curve led to the long hallway toward the back of the gallery where the offices were. Pushing her way through people that shouldn't have been in this area at all, she kept her hand against the wall feeling for the doors while counting them off in her head. "Renny!" she called again just in case he'd had the same idea she did. Just as she got to the third door she fumbled for the knob, cursing. It would undoubtedly be locked and with these shoes on she definitely couldn't kick it in. But she was surprised when the knob turned and the door opened.

Quickly stepping inside, she used her free hand to hold up the side of her dress and moved across the floor. She wasn't three steps into the office when someone grabbed her from behind. An arm clasped around her throat, pulling her hard against the body of the assailant.

"Get off of me!" Bree yelled, thinking that it was maybe one of Sam's men. "It's me, Bree. Let me go!" She struggled against the hold, not applying any defensive moves because she assumed the person was working with them.

"So it's you?"

Bree froze. It was a woman's voice, deadly calm, but laced with the distinct edge of lunacy.

"I've watched you for a while now. You're so not his type." The woman used her other hand to trace up and down the front of Bree's body. "You seem to fit what he usually looks for in the physique of his women, but there's something different about you that just doesn't ring true."

Taking advantage of the woman's obvious preoccupation with who she was, Bree thrust an elbow into her stomach. Then when the woman had doubled over she grabbed her wrist, spinning herself around until they faced each other. Moonlight spilled in through Renny's open blinds and Bree could make out the silhouette of a woman, but the facial features were a blur. "Who the hell are you?"

She recovered quickly and brought her free hand around to slap Bree soundly across the face. It wasn't so much the force of the blow but the shock that had Bree rocking back on those killer heels. Her legs gave out as the couch was right behind her and she fell backward, dropping her gun to the floor. The woman didn't waste a moment before jumping on top of her, grabbing her at the neck.

"He's mine! He was mine before you came and just as soon as I get rid of you he'll be mine again!"

Bree grabbed at the woman's wrists futilely, for she had a strong grip and Bree's mind was blurring from the lack of oxygen. All her training had come down to this one moment. This had been the only time that she knew she needed to fight for her own life, not just for the lives of her countrymen. She was shorter than the woman, so she snaked her legs up until her foot was planted against the woman's thigh and then she pushed with all her might. Either the force of that push or the spike of that heel in her flesh had the woman releasing Bree's neck and falling back.

Bree pounced, nailing the woman to the floor, then returning the slap she'd delivered to her a few minutes ago. "You're crazy!" Bree bellowed as the woman swung fiercely at her.

Hand-to-hand combat it was and Bree certainly did not have a problem with that. She could have used tae kwon do or any of the other maneuvers she'd learned, but this chick was asking for a good old-fashioned ass whuppin' and Bree was aiming to give it to her. They tumbled over the floor, sending things crashing down around them while they threw blows that would have made a man shriek. Bree heard the rip of material and tasted the saltiness of blood in her mouth but didn't release her hold on the woman and didn't stop hitting her.

At some point the lights came on but the women were still swinging. A man would have paid good money to see a chick fight like this. Then out of nowhere something hard crashed against the right side of Bree's head and she felt darkness bearing down on her again. She had the woman by the neck now, pressing down hard enough to cut off her circulation. Then she felt her hands slipping away, her body slumping until it fell against the floor. She heard voices, some in the distance—the crowd still trying to get out of the gallery—and some closer, a man and a woman arguing, saying they needed to get out of here.

Then it was quiet.

Chapter 12

The lights had been on for about fifteen minutes and Renny's heart had made a steady pattern that assured him a heart attack was imminent. People were everywhere, trying to get to the door as fast as possible. He remembered the moment he'd turned back and didn't see Sabrina behind him; remembered the sick feeling that had swarmed him at that realization.

Still pushing his way through the people, he bumped into Sam first.

"Get to your office, everybody's meeting there," Sam notified him.

"Where's Sabrina?" Renny hoped she'd found her brother and he'd steered her to safety.

Sam looked baffled a moment. "She's not with you?"

"No. We got separated in the crowd." His eyes moved quickly around the room, seeing nothing but heads and bodies pressing together toward the entrance. What he didn't see was a red dress.

"Dammit! I told her to stay with you."

"I'll look for her." Renny was about to go back into the crowd when Sam grabbed at his jacket.

"No. You go ahead to your office, I'll look for Bree."

"Renny! Renny!"

Both he and Sam turned toward the voice to see Gabrielle squeezing through people to get to them. She fell into Renny breathing hard, her eyes erratic. "Renny, come quick. It's Bree!"

The two men looked at each other briefly before following Gabrielle to the back of the gallery. With every step, Renny felt his head pounding. His heart rate no longer registered, it thumped so quickly in his chest. He should have held tighter to her, should have made sure she was safe. The moment he entered his office and saw her lying on the floor he could have bashed his own head in for his stupidity.

She was lying on the floor, her head propped up in Lynn's lap. Her eyes were closed, her body completely limp. With three steps he fell to the floor beside her, lifting her hands in his, forgetting anybody else was in the room except the two of them. "Sabrina? Sabrina, baby, answer me."

"Somebody get me some ice," Lynn yelled.

Sam rushed into the room right behind Renny, his lips going into a tight line at the sight of his sister on the floor. Gabrielle and Adriana stood right behind Lynn while Rico had just exited the room to get the ice she'd asked for.

In about two minutes the elder Bennetts and Desdunes made their way into the office.

"What the hell happened here?" Lucien deposited his wife in the chair before pushing past Sam, Adriana and Gabrielle to get to his daughter.

"I don't know. We came in here to get away from the crowd of people and we found her on the floor," Gabrielle offered.

"Was there anybody in here with her?" Marvin asked.

"No. She was alone," Adriana said.

"Sabrina? Sabrina?" Renny was still calling to her, rubbing her arms and praying she'd open her eyes. If she'd only wake up, curse at him or even yell about all the attention they were giving her; something to let him know that she was all right. He couldn't stand the sight of her like this and felt his fear steadily turning into anger. "Did you call an ambulance?" he asked nobody in particular.

Lynn rubbed Bree's cheek. "Yes, the paramedics and the police are on the way."

Trent appeared in the doorway with Rico right behind him with the ice. "Sam, I need you outside."

Sam looked from Bree to Marvin to Trent. Then his father's hand appeared on his shoulder. "Go ahead, son. Do your job. We'll tend to your sister."

"I shouldn't have given her this job," he said quietly.

"Don't worry about that now. Just go and take care of your business." Lucien knew the guilt his son was feeling because he was feeling massive waves of it himself. This had been precisely the danger he'd tried so hard to keep his daughter away from. But Bree had always been stubborn. He moved to the chair, where his wife whimpered quietly.

Marvin Bennett came to them. "I'm sorry. This is all my fault."

Lucien remained quiet while Rico and Alex came to stand on either side of their father. "It's nobody's fault but the person who did this to her," Alex responded. "None of us would have allowed Sabrina to get hurt."

"Mr. and Mrs. Desdune, we really do apologize," Rico echoed.

"Please. Please, stop it," Marie interjected. "I know my child and I know that there is nothing she wouldn't have done for her job. There was no way anybody could have stopped her from being here or doing what she thought she had to do.

And she'll be just fine. Just got a knock on her head from what I can see. Even that's not enough to hold my Bree down for long."

Beatriz went to Marie kneeling on the floor in her two-thousand-dollar gown to take the woman's hands in hers. "You're right, Marie. She'll be just fine."

"We've got a man and a woman outside. Danforth saw them coming out of your office a few minutes after the lights came on and followed them out. He put them in one of the unmarked cars. I can go question them while you take care of things here, but I wanted you to know," Trent told Sam as they stood in the hallway.

Uniformed officers had arrived by now and were escorting the guests safely out of the gallery. Sam's first impulse was to let Trent go ahead and question them, but then he remembered who Trent was. Trent was his friend. A man who'd come all the way across the country to help him out, a man he was seriously considering going into business with. But he was also a badass. One mean ex-military man with no patience. If Sam wanted the witnesses intact he should probably do it himself. "I'll go and question them now."

"What about Bree?" Trent inquired.

"With all the family she's surrounded by she'll be yelling and cursing soon enough. But if I don't have some answers for her when she comes through she's going to skin me alive."

Sam clapped his friend on the shoulder. He was worried sick about his sister, but even more so he was angry at who had done this to her. He'd question the man and the woman all right, and Lord help them if they had anything to do with it.

Renny rode in the ambulance with Sabrina with all the family following closely behind them. She stirred once while they were inserting the IV. "I don't like needles," she whispered.

Renny smiled in relief. "So I've finally found something that you're afraid of."

She didn't respond. Her eyes fluttered closed again, but he felt good that she'd spoken. From what the paramedics were saying around him it was probably a concussion. Her vital signs looked good and even the brief bout of consciousness was a good sign. They put an oxygen mask over her face and he watched as her chest rose and fell with her now steady breathing. Thoughts of what could have happened in his office swarmed through his head. Who could have done this to her? Had she and Yolanda gotten into it again? Or had it been someone waiting in his office for him and she was caught in the cross fire?

Either way he was making himself sick with guilt. At no time had he ever thought this tiny woman would consume him this way, but ever since he'd first glimpsed her in his father's study she'd been etching her way into his heart. Not purposely, of course, and that was most likely why she'd been so successful. She was his bodyguard. Yet somewhere along the way that had changed.

With a definite pull in his gut, he knew that this bodyguard stuff had to come to an end. He would not tolerate her purposely putting herself in danger, could not tolerate the fear it produced in him. As soon as they were married he'd make this perfectly clear. As they pulled into the hospital parking lot, he felt a grim smile surface as Sabrina's turned her head, lifting her hand to take the oxygen mask away.

Who was he kidding? Telling Sabrina what to do was not going to be an easy job. But he would do whatever he must to keep her safe.

Bree heard their voices although they sounded as if they were in a tunnel a thousand miles away. She knew she wasn't in her bedroom at Lynn's house, but wasn't quite sure whose bed she was lying in. She remembered the opening at the gallery, the beautiful sculpture of her and Renny and the woman in his office.

Her eyes shot open. "Renny!" she gasped as if it were her last breath, then choked as more air entered her lungs.

"Hey, baby, you decided to join us." Sitting on the side of her bed, he took her hand in his and kissed her palm.

"She's in your office! She's after you!" Dammit, why couldn't she breathe right? Why did she sound so, so irrational?

Rubbing her hands, he tried to calm her. They'd left Sam and Trent at the gallery questioning people, so he was sure they'd get to the bottom of things soon enough. Right now all he wanted to do was make sure she was okay. "Calm down, sweetie. It's all over now."

Bree tried to get up from the bed. "No! She's in there!"

"She must have left after she knocked you on the head," Lynn replied, rubbing her sister's leg.

Bree turned in Lynn's direction, then winced from the pain. "What?"

"Yeah, you've got one hell of a lump, kiddo. Didn't I teach you to stick and move?" Cole joked with the relief they were all feeling.

With her free hand Bree attempted to touch the source of pain that now threatened to blind her on the left side. Renny moved her hand away. "It's okay. The doctors have given you something for the pain. The swelling will go down soon."

Again Bree closed her eyes, trying to take deep breaths, to get all the swimming faces in her head to stand still. They were all there. Renny's parents, her parents, Renny's brothers and sisters, her brother and sister. Wait… "Where's Sam? Is Sam all right?" She tried to get up again.

Renny gently pushed her back on the pillows. "Sam is just fine. You're the only one who won't be going back to Lynn's tonight."

"Now that she's up and seemingly back to normal, I think

we should all head out of here before my threat wears thin and the doctors call the authorities," Marvin suggested.

And one by one each person in the room kissed Bree goodnight, sharing some comment or sentiment that pushed her close to tears.

And while they did, Renny stood with Alex and Rico, who wanted to know his plans where Bree was concerned. His brothers were pleasantly surprised when he admitted he planned to keep her.

Shaking hands and hugging were something the Bennett boys did on a regular basis. They were very close, and in times like these, the bond only increased. Renny was glad his brothers were on board with his decision about Sabrina. Since they had all agreed to disagree about his business choice, he really didn't want to have to argue with them over his choice of a wife, as well.

Finally, he and Sabrina were alone.

Renny was back at her bedside, sitting down and taking her hand in his. Leaning forward, he kissed the edge of her lip that sported a tiny cut, then rubbed his free hand along her bruised cheek. "You scared the hell out of me," he whispered.

Because she'd experienced that same fear when she couldn't find him, she didn't squabble, only squeezed his hand. "I'm sorry."

"Don't." With a finger he traced her lips. "I should have protected you. I failed you this time and look what happened."

"Renny, you didn't know. Besides, I'm—"

"You're my bodyguard, I know. But I won't let it happen again, you can be sure of that."

Bree let herself be enveloped by the comfort of his words, then remembered with startling clarity. "It was a woman. She was waiting in your office."

He instantly thought of Yolanda. "Do you know who it was?"

Bree concentrated on the female's face and still couldn't get a clear vision. "No. I've never heard her voice before, either. But…she knows you," she said slowly. "She wants you."

"Larice Taylor Summerfield and Terrence Blount," Sam stated matter-of-factly that next afternoon in Lynn's living room.

The doctors had released Bree that morning and she'd refused to get back into bed before nightfall. As a compromise Lynn brought down pillows and a blanket, making her a bed on the couch.

They'd had lunch and the family trickled in accordingly. Now they all sat around the room listening to Sam and Trent intently.

"Who the hell are they?" Adriana asked flippantly.

Both Sam and Trent looked to Renny.

His fingers had clenched on his glass of lemonade at the sound of her name. "I met her over a year ago at one of the company functions. We went out a couple of times and then I forgot about her." Even to him that sounded a bit callous, but it was the truth.

"How did they get into your office? That's what I want to know," Lucien said.

"The lock to Renny's office was picked," Trent answered. Renny looked at him sharply. "Don't worry, I had a locksmith come in and change all the locks first thing this morning." He tossed Renny a ring of keys.

"Did you say Summerfield?" Marvin asked slowly.

Sam nodded. "Yes. She's Roland Summerfield's daughter."

"Son of a—"

"Marvin!" Beatriz interrupted with a hand to her husband's arm.

"Roland Summerfield, your old army buddy?" Rico questioned his father.

"And a minor stockholder in Coastal Technologies," Trent added.

Adriana turned to Trent. "What does all this mean?"

"It means that Roland's been behind this all along. The jealous fool!" Marvin was up and pacing the room now.

"But he wasn't alone." Abruptly Trent looked away from Adriana. "There seems to have been two motives in the works here, both of them highly personal against members of the Bennett family."

Alex sighed. "Dad, I think it's time you tell us the truth about you and Summerfield."

Beatriz looked at her husband before taking a breath to speak. "I met Roland and Marvin at the same time," she began slowly. "Roland was a gentleman and I liked him. But Marvin was—"

Renny gave a slight smile. "A Bennett man to the end."

Beatriz returned her son's smile with all the love she had in her heart for her husband. "Yes, he was. I loved him the moment I laid eyes on him."

"Summerfield thought I stole your mother from him and has hated me ever since," Marvin finished.

"Then why allow the deal with Bennett and Coastal to go through?" Gabrielle shifted in her seat.

"He doesn't hold enough shares to have stopped it," Rico added.

"It was never about the merger. That probably only spear-headed his plan for revenge," Sam stated.

"So who's this Blount person and what was Roland's daughter's part in the plan?"

Bree sat up, momentarily dizzy from the motion. Instinctively Renny moved to her side, placing a hand on her shoulder. She felt his nearness and wanted to turn into the comfort, but the memory of fighting with his former lover only hours before held her back.

"Larice was simply obsessed with Renny. She's always

been obsessed with the Bennett clan just like her father. She hated that Roland had never loved her mother the way he loved Beatriz and wanted to get back at him by sleeping with one of the men that could have been his son. Instead she fell in love with Renny and was angry that he brushed her off," Trent surmised.

"Good ole Bennett charm," Adriana chirped.

"It wasn't like that," Renny said in defense. "We went out maybe two or three times and that was it. I didn't call her and she didn't call me. If she was obsessed, why wait until now to get in touch with me?"

Gabrielle rose, moving lithely to the window. "It's simple. Now there's competition."

All eyes fell to Bree.

"You've been seen with Bree more in the last two weeks than you've ever been seen with another woman before."

Adriana followed her sister's line of thought. "And Bree was actually staying with you for a while."

"But that was work related," Bree interjected.

"That was impossible for an outsider to decipher," Lynn added. "Even family could see there was more going on between you two than work."

Renny looked down at Bree and she fidgeted.

Sam felt Bree's embarrassment. He could tell his sister wasn't quite comfortable with the fact the she'd gotten involved with a client, a big no-no in their business. Still, he couldn't help but notice the depth of Renny's feelings for Bree and wondered if Bree could see that, as well. "At any rate, we have Larice and Blount, who I guess was supposed to be her date for the evening. He works at the local paper and had an invitation to the opening. That's how Larice got in. He claims he didn't know about Larice's ulterior motives, but the cops are holding him for accessory to the assault because he's the one who hit Bree." At his side, Sam's bandaged hand flexed in pain. The moment Blount had admitted to hitting his sister he'd planted one firmly across his jaw. Trent had stood to the side watching, waiting for Sam to continue with a look of pure pleasure in his eyes. That alone had stopped him.

Renny stood, anger evident in his stance and tone. "He hit Sabrina?"

"Relax, man, her big brother squared that away already." Trent nodded in Sam's direction.

"So, where is Roland Summerfield? Have you arrested him?" Marvin asked.

"I've already got someone trying to locate Summerfield. And as an extra precaution I got the local cops to put an APB out on him," Trent spoke up. "As soon as he's spotted he'll be brought in for questioning."

"Well, I'm relieved that's over." Marie stood, putting Jeremy down on the floor to play with his assembly of trucks. "Now we can get on with our lives."

"It's not over until Summerfield is caught," Marvin said solemnly. "As long as he's free there's danger."

The room grew quiet as everybody let his words sink in. It was, unfortunately, true. Summerfield was still a very real danger to them.

Bree lay in the room she and Renny had been sharing for weeks now, staring up at the ceiling. So much had changed since that day they'd come here. Then she'd been fearless, ready to face anyone who threatened Renny in any capacity. After all, that was her job.

But in the past weeks she'd allowed herself to experience a host of new things. She'd opened herself physically to a man, something she was sure she could never do again. Renny was so different from Harold. His touch, his words and even his actions mimicked the man he told her he was. He hadn't dropped her after sleeping with her one time, he hadn't immediately started looking for someone else to warm his bed. There was no armed guard making him stay at Lynn's night after night and at any time he could have found his own apartment and moved out. For that matter he could simply have gone to stay with his parents. But he didn't, he stayed with her.

Bree had to admit that she liked being at the gallery with Renny. And he seemed genuinely interested in any comments she made.

For the first time in her life, she felt like she was truly doing something she wanted to do, instead of something that would prove her family wrong. While she'd enjoyed her time in the armed forces, her initial interest had been simply to spite the people that loved her but refused to let her grow up. All those years she spent training and fighting another country's war she never felt the sense of accomplishment she was looking for. And sadly, she still didn't feel as if her family had respected her any more. A part of her realized that it was simply their way of loving her and that it would probably never change. Her rebellion now seemed immature and a waste of precious time.

She heard the door open and her heart welled with expectation. He'd seemed distant at dinner and when all the family had gone home he'd retreated to the basement, she supposed to work. Lynn had helped her get ready for bed and she'd lain there for what seemed like hours waiting for him.

Renny didn't go directly to the bed although instinct told him she wasn't asleep. He undressed in the darkness and was prepared to grab a pillow and sleep on the floor when the sound of her voice stopped him.

"Why didn't you call her again?"

He froze. Of all the things he'd thought of her saying to

him the moment he came into this room, that wasn't one of them. "I wasn't interested in her."

"Then why go out with her at all?"

He dropped the pillow to the bed and sank down on the side with his back facing her. "She was an attractive woman. When an attractive woman comes on to you, you don't turn her away. At least not at first." He took a deep breath. "For a minute I thought there could be something there, but then after talking to her, spending time with her, I knew it wasn't possible. So I didn't call her again. I figured she felt the same because she didn't call me, either."

Bree shifted slowly, trying to sit up against the pillows. "Is that how it was with all of them?"

Renny gave a wry chuckle. "There weren't as many as people think, but yes, sometimes it was. Sometimes the attraction lasted long enough for us to sleep together, but then there was nothing else so I moved on. It was never my intention to purposely hurt anyone. And to their credit, most of the women I've been with knew the score early on and accepted things as they were. I didn't leave a long trail of broken hearts."

Silence filled the room.

"Am I different?"

Her voice seemed so tiny, so fragile in the dark room. Renny turned to face her then and reached for her hands. "You are not like any woman I've ever met before, Sabrina. I knew that the moment you stood up to me in my father's study."

Bree released a nervous laugh at the memory. "You didn't think a tiny woman like me could protect you."

Some of the tension in his shoulders was released at the sound of her laughter and he idly rubbed his thumbs against the skin of her hand. "I sure as hell didn't. Then you pushed me out of the way of that speeding car and I had to rethink my assessment of you."

"But you weren't attracted to me like you were to those other women, were you? Not initially, I mean." She knew now without a doubt that she had the ability to excite him beyond words.

"I was attracted to you on a much higher level than physical. You intrigued me. Everything about you was so different from what I've seen in women. My sisters are very feminine, my mother, too. So seeing a woman, a soldier, a bodyguard was different. And you were so serious about your job and so sure of yourself and your abilities. I was in awe."

Bree smiled, so completely unaware that he'd noticed so much about her. "I thought you were the playboy the papers said you were."

"And now?" He wasn't surprised that he needed desperately to know what she thought of him now.

"Now I know that you're a good man. You're fiercely loyal to your family and your work. And you do care about other people's feelings and opinions of you despite how hard you try to appear otherwise. You don't deserve all the negativity that surrounds you."

Renny grinned. "Then how about you write an exposé on that and sell it to all the tabloids?"

"I'll do better than that." Scooting closer to him, she wrapped her arms around his neck. "I plan to show the papers and the rest of Greenwich that the elusive playboy billionaire heartbreaker can be tamed."

Settling his hands around her waist, he let himself be drawn even closer, tracing his lips along the line of her jaw. "Oh, he can?"

"Mmm-hmm," she moaned. "And I possess just the right amount of femininity and military training to do it."

His lips were on her neck as she arched back farther, his

thumbs swiping over her nipples. At his touch she grew wet, anticipation quickly building.

"I don't know which part of you excites me more." His kisses turned into gentle nips of his teeth, his palms now splaying possessively over her breasts. "The woman or the soldier."

Tired of the intrusion of the shirt, he pulled it quickly over her head, his mouth immediately seeking her puckered nipples.

"Mmm. I think you like them both." She held his head firmly in place as his tongue and teeth catered to her expertly.

"It's you, Sabrina." He left a trail of hot kisses as he made his way back up her neck and to her lips. "Each part makes you who you are and you are the woman I want." His tongue dipped deeply into her mouth, coaxing hers to respond in kind. "You are the woman I love."

Chapter 13

The next morning Bree had just walked into the kitchen where Lynn and Renny sat at the table, staring at a large vase of roses. Without a word, she walked over and snatched the card from the bouquet.

We will be together soon, my love.

Renny, who had moved to stand behind her, reading over her shoulder, yelled.

"If I ignore him he'll go away," she said slowly, only half believing her own words.

"He's not going away, Sabrina! And he thinks you're still going to be with him." He spun around until he faced her. She turned away. He stepped in front of her. "Is he right? Are you planning on going back to him? Is that why you won't tell me about him?" he yelled.

Her whole body shook. He was angry and his reaction to

the flowers angered her. Biting her bottom lip for control, Bree leveled her gaze to his. "There's nothing to tell."

Renny forcibly pushed away from her. "So you keep saying."

He stormed out of the kitchen with Lynn quickly moving out of his way.

Bree dropped her head into her hands and sighed.

"You're not being fair, Bree."

"Lynn, I just don't want to talk about it." And that was the truth. She didn't want to have to tell anyone how stupid she was or how that stupidity had cost her something dear to her. She didn't want their pity, nor did she wish to endure the embarrassment again.

Lynn folded her arms and moved closer. "Well, that's just too damned bad, isn't it?"

Bree's head shot up at her sister's angry tone.

"It's not just about you anymore. It's time for you to grow up, Bree."

"What? All these years I've been trying to grow up and you and the rest of the family have told me to slow down. Now it's finally time for me to grow up?"

"That's right. That's exactly what I said. All your life you've complained about how people treated you and how everybody perceived you. But did you ever stop to think how you were treating the people who loved you? The people who were only looking out for your best interests?" Lynn paused. "No. You didn't."

Lynn dragged her fingers through her hair. "We tend to take your selfishness with a grain of salt and keep loving you because we're family. But that man that you just brushed off, he's not going to take it, Bree." Her voice softened. "You're going to lose him if you continue to keep him at arm's length. He loves you, Bree."

She didn't like what she was hearing mainly because it rang too true. Bree rose, paced the kitchen slowly, trying to grasp a rational solution. Lynn always had her back, always. Until now. "It doesn't matter anymore, so why should I have to relive it all again?"

Lynn touched her sister's shoulder. "Because this time you don't have to relive it alone. He's trying to be here for you, to protect you. Just like we've been trying to do all your life."

Bree whirled around a little too fast and felt unsteady on her feet. "I don't need protection."

Lynn put both hands on her shoulders just as she wobbled. "You sure about that?"

As he drove throughout the city with no real destination, Renny's mind whirled. He'd already called Sam and told him about the flowers. Now more than ever he was determined to find Harold Richmond. He was ready to lay it all on the line for Sabrina, but the effort would be futile as long as that man was in the picture.

He wasn't sure of Sabrina's feelings for him because she hadn't told him. No matter how many times he confessed his love to her last night she hadn't reciprocated. Could she still be in love with this other guy? No, that was impossible. There was no way she could give herself so completely to him and love another. She just wasn't like that.

His cell phone rang, snatching his mind momentarily away from Sabrina. "Speak," he answered gruffly.

"I was just wondering." Rico spoke slowly, not bothering to say hello. "You never take a woman to your condo and you rarely introduce them to the family."

Renny sighed. The last thing he wanted to deal with right now was his reputation with other women. "And?"

"So how did Larice know where you lived? How did she get your cell phone number that you change every six months? Assuming she was the one who called you about Adriana being stranded."

Reluctantly Renny began to listen to his brother's ramblings.

"And while news of the gallery opening was public, weren't invitations sent at the absolute last minute?" Rico continued.

"To a confidential list of people," Renny finished the thought. "So how did she know Blount was invited and that she could come with him?"

"Exactly," Rico answered.

"An insider," Renny stated glumly.

"Right again. The question is who?"

Renny had driven to the gallery. Not real sure of his reasoning, only knowing that he had to do something to keep his mind off Sabrina or he'd go insane. Rico had just given him that something.

Putting the car in Park, he let his head fall against the headrest and pinched the bridge of his nose. "I don't want to think about this right now."

For the first time since this conversation began, Rico really listened to the sound of his brother's voice. "Where are you? Is everything okay?"

"I'm at the gallery and everything's just peachy."

"Yeah, your sunny disposition is glowing right through the phone," Rico answered sarcastically. "Now cut the BS, is Bree all right?"

Tearing his hand from his face, he slammed an open palm on the steering wheel. "She's just fine. I'm the one going crazy."

Rico chuckled. "Women'll do that to you."

"How do you know? I don't recall meeting many of your girlfriends, either."

"That's because I'm the discreet one in the family."

"Whatever. Listen, I'm going to check on some things here and then I'll probably head back to Lynn's by dinner. I'll think about this and give you a call later."

He disconnected the phone and was about to walk through

the door when he remembered a call he had retrieved from his office voice mail this morning. Quickly he dialed another number. It was answered on the first ring. "Yeah, it's me," he said slowly. "Contact Duel Couriers and tell them you work for me. Check all the deliveries made this morning, then meet me at the gallery. I'll explain when you get here."

Yolanda was on the phone at the front desk, but upon seeing him enter she hung up. "I didn't know whether to expect you or not."

Her tone was clipped and as he walked closer he noticed the dark circles beneath her eyes.

"I wanted to check on things. When I phoned yesterday you said we had some orders."

Looking away from her, he reached for the inventory book lying on the desk.

Yolanda took a step away from him.

Out of the side of his eye he watched her. She seemed jittery, nervous as if she was hiding something. "Did you fill all the orders?" he asked absently. While there were six orders in the books, he already knew they'd been shipped as the courier had left a message on his office line earlier this morning confirming it.

Yolanda ran her fingers through her hair. "Yes, I did. How's Sabrina?"

Renny straightened and looked at her, Rico's words rumbling through his head. "She's resting. How are you? With all that happened the other night, I didn't get a chance to ask."

"I'm fine." She walked around him until she now stood on the other side of the desk. "Just fine."

He nodded. "Good."

She wrung her hands until he thought she'd rub her skin completely off. He made a big production of going through messages and flipping through the mail before returning his gaze to her. "I'd like to go over the guest list for the opening." Her hands froze. "We should probably send some sort of thank-you, don't you think?"

"Uh, yeah. A thank-you card would be good. It would show we care and extend the offer for them to come back."

Her voice sounded almost normal except for the high pitch. Renny knew enough to now be suspicious.

"Great. Get the list and meet me in my office in five minutes." He walked away before she had the chance to speak. He had planned to look at the list only to find out which newspaper Blount was affiliated with so he could ensure the man's termination. But Yolanda's weird behavior raised other questions.

He unlocked the door to his office and stepped inside, immediately flocked by memories of Sabrina lying on the floor. Some of his things were still askew and he bypassed them to take a seat behind his desk. Propping his elbows on the blotter, he let his head fall into his hands as he thought of the way he'd stormed out of the house this morning.

He was an idiot. She'd been through so much already because of him. How could he simply yell and walk out on her? He should have tried harder with her. Questioning her about Harold Richmond was difficult for him, so he could only imagine how it made her feel.

"I can get a cleaning crew to come in," Yolanda said as she picked up papers that had been knocked to the floor.

"No. Leave it." Raising his head, he saw her look of confusion. "Where's the list?"

She crossed to the desk and handed him the papers. He pretended to scan them and then on a hunch asked, "There was a Larice Taylor Summerfield here, but I don't see her name on the list. Is she a friend of yours?"

Yolanda hesitated. "I, um, I've never heard of her."

"Really? Have you ever heard of Roland Summerfield?" She blinked. Renny thought he saw a moment of recognition.

"No. I have not."

He rubbed his chin. "That's strange." He flipped through the papers.

"Wh-what's strange?" she stuttered.

"I distinctly remember seeing the name *L. Taylor* on the delivery log. Did she order something at the party?"

Yolanda shrugged. "Not from me." Then she raised an elegantly arched brow and with a smirk added, "Perhaps Sabrina took the order."

"Perhaps." Lifting the phone from its cradle, he thrust it toward her. "Why don't you give her a call to see if she received it?"

"I'm sure she did. We've been using the best courier around."

"I know, but I'd just like to double-check."

Yolanda shifted in the chair, her legs uncrossing, then crossing again. "She's probably not even at home at this time of day."

"Really? You think so. You must know her schedule pretty well."

She paused, then angled her head until shiny platinum curls slid off one shoulder. Folding her hands neatly in her lap, she replied, "I told you I don't know her."

"Then tell me why you sent an invitation to her and Terrence Blount to attend the opening." With a flick of his wrist Renny let the papers slip from his hand. "Tell me how she knew where my office was and how she got in here. You don't have a key, but it doesn't matter since the lock was picked. Maybe you could answer those questions for me."

The air fairly crackled with tension as they stared each other down. Yolanda chuckled. Deciding to give up the pretense, she flashed Renny a million-watt smile. "Maybe you can tell me why you brought her here?" she countered.

"Excuse me?"

"Don't play dumb, Renny. It really doesn't suit you. Silhouette was our baby, our dream. We were going to be so great together. Then your family friend appeared."

"You're talking about Sabrina?"

"Yes, your precious Sabrina. The one you let harass me and then had the nerve to tell me to learn to get along with."

Like neat little blocks things began to fall into place. "You felt threatened by Sabrina, too." It was his turn to laugh then. Yolanda's smile disappeared. "This is amazing. What did you and Larice plan to do?"

Her fingers clenched the handles of the chair as she tried like hell to resist throwing something at him. How dare he be so smug? How dare he laugh at her? After all she'd done for him, all she'd done for them both! "Larice." She said the woman's name through gritted teeth. "She was pitiful. After everything you'd done to her she still wanted you. I told her she could have you. I don't beg for any man." She pinned him with a cold glare. "But I wanted my place at Silhouette. I worked too damned hard for this for Sabrina to come in and push me out of the way. Instead, I knew the only answer was to get rid of her."

Although inside he simmered with rage, Renny still looked at Yolanda with only a smirk. "Because she knocked you down?"

Her eyes closed until they were mere slits, and then she lifted her chin. "No, because she interfered. She didn't belong here, didn't belong near you. So you dressed her up the other night, she's still a frump and not good enough to run in our circles. Frankly, I'm glad Larice got a piece of her. I only wish she and that fool Terrence would have been bold enough to finish the job."

In a flash Renny was around the desk, grabbing her up by her wrists. "You better be damned glad they didn't finish the job!"

"Oh, yeah?" Yolanda tossed her head back so that her hair was down her back, defiance etched in every pore of her face. "And why is that? Because you now fancy yourself in love with her?" Then she laughed, a cruel cackling sound that had Renny tossing her to the floor.

"Oh, how the mighty playboy has fallen. Who would ever have guessed a little spit of a woman could bring you down when the best have tried?"

He moved away from her then, unable to trust that he'd adhere to his father's training to not hit a female. "It would be in your best interest to keep your mouth shut."

Yolanda stayed on the floor, her skirt twisted so that it bared her long legs. "And why is that, Mr. Bennett?"

"Because anything you say or do from this point on may be held against you in a court of law." Trent came through the open door, gun drawn.

Bree sat in a lounge chair on Lynn's back porch. Lynn had gone to work and Jeremy was at the sitter's. It had taken almost an hour for her to convince Lynn that she'd be all right by herself.

Her mind drifted between memories of North Carolina and Renny's whispers of love. Lynn was right. It was past time she stopped thinking about herself. She loved Renny and she recognized the differences between the two men. She had no idea what Harold was up to, but figured Renny had a right to know what happened between them. She'd asked about his past relationships and he'd told her. She owed him the same in return.

He'd been gone most of the day and she was worrying herself sick about his safety. Roland Summerfield was still on the loose, so the Bennetts were still in danger. Sam had called an hour ago to say that he'd just left Renny and that he was perfectly all right. Still, she'd feel better when she could see that for herself.

The sun was just setting as her lids grew heavy. There was a light breeze, but she'd brought a throw and now huddled beneath its warmth. In a moment she'd go inside and start dinner for her and Lynn and for Renny, if he returned.

"You shouldn't be out here by yourself."

She started at his voice, then relaxed with the sight of him back in one piece.

"Sorry." He took the seat next to her. "How're you feeling?" He'd had a day of revelations, but prayed that it didn't show.

"I'm good." She made a big production out of smoothing the blanket down, then decided to give up the pretense. "I'm better now that you're back. I was worried about you."

He nodded. "I was worried about you."

"About this morning…" she began.

Renny shook his head. "You don't have to talk about it if you don't want to."

She looked at him quizzically. He wanted to know what happened, but he'd let her keep the secret if that's what she wanted. Lynn would be pleased. She was so right about Renny.

"No. It's time I was honest with you."

He sat back in the chair, allowing her the time and space she needed. What she was about to do wasn't easy for her.

"Harold was my commanding officer. We trained and did maneuvers together. I knew he liked me right off the bat and as soon as I got over the initial shock, I realized I liked him, too." Twiddling the fringes of the throw between her fingers, Bree tried to steady the incessant pounding of her heart. What would he think of her once he knew the whole truth?

"We were in the same unit, so any type of involvement was out of the question. When he was promoted to colonel it sort of opened the door for us."

"I thought the military frowned on relationships between soldiers."

It did and that was part of the shame she bore. "We were

very careful, for the first year at least. Everything was wonderful that first year." Taking a deep breath, she summoned
the strength to continue. "Then word somehow got out that
the white colonel was dating a black soldier." She shrugged.
"Our secret was out."

The fact that Harold was white shocked him a bit, but not as
much as the fierce need to wrap Sabrina in his arms and end this
ordeal for her. He remained still. She needed to purge herself as
much as he needed to hear the rest. "And then what happened?"

"It seems that little bombshell was only the tip of the
iceberg. The rumors swirled and traveled around until Harold's wife heard them all the way in Raleigh."

Renny sat up. "He was married while he was involved
with you?" He racked his brain to remember the information
Sam had come up with on the colonel. While the man's race
had been overlooked, they'd known that he was divorced and
that he was dishonorably discharged from the service. They'd
also learned his age. Harold Richmond was older than
Renny's father, which clearly meant he was too damned old
for Sabrina. That temper he'd been known for throughout his
family was about to be released. Taking deep steadying
breaths, he tried like hell to keep that from happening.

Bree wouldn't look at him, couldn't imagine what he was
probably thinking about her right now. "You'd think I'd know
a married man when I saw one." Her fingers moved rapidly,
twirling and untwirling the fringe. "Joanne Richmond, his
wife of twenty years, made her first appearance on the base."
An overwhelming tightness clutched her chest as she mourned
for the young woman who had been so stupid to fall in love
with an older man, an older married man who happened to be
her commanding officer. Before she could stop them, tears
streamed slowly down her face.

Renny made a move toward her, then held back. Could he
touch her without hurting her more? The anger he felt was

directed solely at Harold Richmond, but he was having a hell of a time keeping that in check. Seconds passed quietly and he finally reached for her hand. "Sabrina, you have to know that it wasn't your fault."

"Ha," she fairly yelled, attempting to choke back the tears that came so freely now. "Not my fault? I was a bright-eyed soldier enamored by the decorated colonel that paid some attention to me. Some real attention." She didn't move her hand from his, but she did sit up straighter in the chair before dropping her legs to the floor and turning to face him. "All my life I'd been doted on and watched extra carefully because I was the baby. Even my teenage dates had been supervised by my parents or my siblings. It was like living in the world's most glorious prison. Going into the military was the first independent thing I'd ever done." The tears grew bothersome, so she swiped them away with the back of her hand.

"I was Private Sabrina Desdune, not the little sister, not the baby daughter. I loved the freedom. I loved the challenge." Keeping her eyes trained on his, she continued quietly. "And then I loved him."

Her words sliced through him and he closed his eyes with the pain. Then he clasped both her hands in his and looked at her, this time with all the love he felt brimming in his heart. "You were young and impressionable. He took advantage of that."

"No." She began shaking her head.

He tugged on her hands. "Yes," he said forcefully, ceasing her head from shaking and drawing her eyes back to him. "I understand about wanting freedom. I've longed for it for a good portion of my life, as well. And it came, I earned it. And so did you. But that didn't give him the right." Drawing his lips into a tight line, Renny reined in his control. "It didn't give him the permission to touch you. He was older. He was your commanding officer, dammit! He should have known better!" he yelled.

She'd seen him angry earlier, had watched as Harold's flowers had transposed the loving, compassionate man she knew into a seething, dangerous man that she almost feared. At that very moment she realized his anger was spawned from his love for her and she all but melted in shame. How could she deserve such a love like this after what she'd done? The tears came again full force. "She said I ruined their marriage. That I ruined their life. They had two children. She took them away and refused to let him see them. I was responsible for that."

Renny moved to the chair to sit beside her, keeping her hands in his. "No. He was. He ruined his marriage by not being faithful. He ruined their life because he was foolish. She blamed you because she loved him, too. But she was wrong, Sabrina. It wasn't your fault because you didn't know."

"But I can't say I would have stopped if I did know." And that was the burden she'd borne all this time. She remembered loving Harold with such a fierceness that she thought she would have done anything for him. Now, however, those feelings compared to what she felt for Renny didn't feel like love at all.

She'd looked up to him, admired him and was in awe of the fact that a man like him would want a woman like her. Maybe it was just infatuation, like a schoolgirl crush, only she'd given that man her innocence—a piece of herself she could never get back.

"You would have stopped." He wrapped an arm around her, pulling her close against his chest. Kissing her hair, he tried to take away all the years of hurt and guilt she'd experienced. "You would never have knowingly gotten involved with a married man. You're too good a person for that. I believe that with all my heart and you have to believe it, too."

As much as she hated tears, Bree couldn't stop the dam from breaking. All this time she'd been trying so desperately to keep this secret for fear that it would change his perception of her. But it seemed he already had an impression of the person she was, and no matter what she said or what she'd done, he didn't seem all that eager to change that. Could she love this man any more? Wrapping her arms around him, she let herself be comforted finally. She let Harold and what he'd done to her become a part of her past, the past that she would from this moment on leave behind.

"Thank you," she whispered.

Pulling back a few inches but keeping her tightly in his grasp, he looked down at her tear-streaked face. "For what?"

"For understanding. For not judging me."

He smiled. "I judged you wrong before when I thought you were a weak little woman. I have no intention of making that mistake again. I know who and what you are and nothing is going to change that." He kissed her forehead this time, her eyelids, her cheeks, then finally, lovingly, her lips.

Bree sighed as she melted into the warmth of his mouth, wondering what she'd ever done to deserve such a man and praying she'd never do anything to lose him.

Chapter 14

Roland paced the floor, his mind whirling about his next move. The merger had gone through. It was done. Bennett Industries and Coastal Technologies were now one, retaining the name Bennett Industries because Marvin Bennett had the controlling shares in the new multibillion-dollar company.

Once again his nemesis had come out one step ahead of him. He had the woman, the money, the family that Roland had always wanted. And the one thing that he'd thought would forever remain his now dangled on one of Bennett's hooks. His daughter had been arrested, accused of breaking and entering and assault. He wasn't entirely sure what had possessed Larice to go to Renny Bennett's gallery opening, especially after he'd assured her that he was taking care of the Bennett family.

But Larice hadn't listened. She'd had it bad for the younger Bennett son and Roland had known this. Yet he'd underestimated his daughter's intent when she'd told him she wanted the man by any means necessary. Never in a million years would he have thought she'd resort to violence to get him. But then he had never really understood Larice. Because she was a girl, they'd never been particularly close and after his wife's death she'd seemed to hate him more often than not.

Now she'd barricaded herself in her apartment, hiding herself from the world and thinking whatever disastrous thoughts she could come up with next. He knew the Bennetts were probably watching her like a hawk now that they'd undoubtedly made the connection, so he didn't go to her. But he had sent messages. He'd e-mailed her, text messaged her and had received the same response. *It's all your fault.*

She blamed him and he blamed Marvin Bennett. This all began with the man he'd once called a friend. And now it would end with him.

Despite her substantially smaller lump on the head, Bree was determined to go to the press conference with the rest of the Bennett clan.

"You couldn't talk any sense into her?" Alex asked when Renny walked into his office with her trailing behind him.

Sam simply smirked and turned his head. "You don't know my sister very well, Alex. Once she's set her mind to something it's like parting the Red Sea to get her to change it."

"Tell me about it," Renny murmured. He still wasn't keen on the idea of her being here, but the argument had lasted well into the night and finally he'd given up. It was either that or lock her in the bedroom and even then he knew she'd find a way to get out and then there would definitely be hell to pay.

"Good morning, Alex." With a sugary smile Bree stood on tiptoe to kiss his handsome cheek.

Alex couldn't resist, he smiled down at her. "You've got one hard head, little woman."

He'd taken to calling her that and Bree admitted she kind of liked it. "Not really, I just have a job to see through."

"And after this job she's retiring from the security business," Renny added with a serious glare in her direction.

Bree took a deep breath. They'd discussed that last night, as well. He didn't like her career choice and while she was initially up in arms and ready to do battle over it, she'd given a career change some deep thought herself. "Not exactly."

Sam looked from Renny to Bree in question. "Then what exactly? You're quitting the family business so soon?" Not that he was the least bit upset. As good as Bree was at what she did, he had no problems with her leaving the firm. He had no desire to see his sister lying unconscious again. The bruise on her forehead still angered him.

Bree smiled. "I received a really good offer from this art gallery that doesn't have a manager and is in dire need of a security supervisor."

Rico had just entered the room with a cup of coffee in hand. "So you've crossed over to the art world, too?" Shaking his head in Renny's direction, he took a seat. "I knew the two of you were going to be trouble."

Trent entered, sobering the entire office, with the jeans and the tight T-shirt he wore, his gun holster open for display and his jacket in his hand. "Ready to go over the game plan?"

It was ten minutes to one. The press conference was scheduled to begin promptly at one-thirty and be over at two o'clock. Private interviews had already been granted to the two biggest newspapers in the city and scheduled for later that afternoon.

The front of the Bennett Tower was secured. Two armed guards stood at the glass entrance doors with officers in unmarked cars parked strategically throughout the block. Inside, plainclothes cops stood among the crowd with press badges blending in seamlessly while keeping a close eye on their surroundings.

Sam stood with Alex. Trent stood with Rico. Marvin had his women surrounding him, Beatriz, Adriana and Gabrielle, while suited guards formed a semicircle around the entire group. Renny stood beside Sam with Bree between the two of them.

She'd worn a straight-cut business suit, her gun tucked in the waistband of her pants at her back, another at her ankle. Her earpiece was in place as she heard the conversation of the outside guard conferring with Sam and the inside guards. Renny held her hand so tightly she feared at any moment she'd lose circulation in the entire limb.

At precisely one o'clock, Darren Lithgow, Coastal Technologies' CEO, was at the microphone. Cameras flashed and reporters immediately fired off questions.

"It is my great honor to finally announce that it is official. Coastal Technologies and Bennett Industries have successfully completed the largest communications merger of all time."

Applause sounded around them. Marvin smiled, and Beatriz held his hand as she beamed with pride. Adriana and Gabrielle smiled at each other, then out among the crowd. The older Bennett boys shook hands while Renny nodded to each of them.

Darren spoke for another few minutes answering questions and making light jokes before introducing Marvin. At her side Bree felt Sam tense. She looked to him, but he stared straight ahead. She looked to Trent, who was scanning the other side of the room. Through her earpiece it was quiet.

She turned her attention to the podium, then to watch the man whose son had stolen her heart. He was a tall man, a broad man, a handsome man just like his sons. He commanded your attention and appealed to your senses. He spoke in a melodic rhythm keeping eye contact and ensuring your interest. But as his hand lifted to adjust the microphone, Bree saw the flash of a red light and knew the moment of dread had finally come.

Marvin was smiling, about to go into his thanks to his family for support. The microphone had been positioned lower as Darren was shorter than he was. He simply needed to adjust it, to say his part and they'd be on their way. He didn't like that his family was all here, that they were all out in the open for Roland to attack. He'd make this short and sweet.

Renny felt her tense and looked down at her to see what was wrong. Her eyes were fixed on the podium, on his father. Then she shifted, pulled away from him in an attempt to make her way closer.

In that instant sparks crackled in the air, spewing from the microphone. The guards that had surrounded the Bennett women quickly pulled them back while Bree pushed past Sam and Trent. Renny grabbed her arm just as she would have reached out to pull Marvin away from the podium. Flames ignited quickly, engulfing the entire podium in a matter of seconds. Sam and Trent reached Marvin just as the flames licked at his suit.

For the second time, screams erupted in Bree's ears as she felt herself falling to the floor. Renny fell heavily on top of her with two guards flanking around him. Alex and Rico had been likewise covered as all hell began to break loose. Guns were drawn, plainclothes officers moved throughout the crowd and firemen were dispatched. The doors were ordered sealed as another officer stepped forward with an extinguisher.

Bree looked up from her spot on the floor to see the snowy-white substance arching through the air. She squirmed and struggled because she could also see the flames still eating the material of Marvin Bennett's suit.

"Keep her here," Renny told the two guards around him without even looking at her.

In an instant he was gone and when Bree got to her knees to follow him she felt the heavy hands of the guards on her arms. Giving them a blistering look did no good and while she could probably have taken at least one of them down, the pounding of her heart, the fear etching slowly throughout as she watched Marvin engulfed in flames held her still.

Out of the corner of his eye—and why he saw this above all the other pandemonium in the room, he'd never know—Renny saw a man dressed in all black making his way to the elevators. Although he'd never seen the man in person he knew without a doubt who it was. Roland Summerfield.

He was running within minutes heading for the elevators himself. Bennett Towers was a thirty-story building, Summerfield could easily get lost inside and make it out of one of the other exits. Renny wasn't about to let that happen.

Bree saw him leap from the platform and immediately reached for her gun. If he wasn't going to check on his father, there was a good reason, a reason she knew could cost him his life. Retrieving her weapon, she jerked free of the guards and stared at each one of them. "You can either follow me or shoot me." And with that she turned and ran toward the elevators.

They had cameras planted all over the building and as she ran Bree pulled the mouthpiece out of her shirt collar. "Where are elevators one and two headed?"

Renny wouldn't know where the previous elevator stopped, so she had a better chance of getting to Summerfield first. Slamming the palm of her hand against the up button, she waited impatiently for a response.

"One's on twenty-seven and…"

She climbed into the elevator with the two other guards right behind her as silence filled the earpiece. "And?"

"And two is on twenty-seven also."

Her heart lurched as she pressed Twenty-seven. Thoughts of Renny in danger ran rampant through her mind and she gripped the gun tighter.

Renny stepped off the elevator and watched as the one next

to him had just closed the doors. He looked down one side of the hall, then the other. His father's office was on this floor. That's where Summerfield was headed. Running down the hall, he pulled off his jacket and increased his speed, determined not to let this man get away.

He entered the office searching for Summerfield only to find it empty, but just as he was about to turn around and head back out he came face-to-face with the barrel of a gun. Behind it was a look of pure hatred. Dark eyes filled with such rage and disdain that it almost took his breath away.

"If it isn't Marvin's baby boy."

Renny backed up a step, his hands flexing at his side. The man, Roland Summerfield, was his father's age, tall in stature, lean in frame. It would be no battle at all for Renny to take him down. The only obstacle—the black gun aimed at his head.

"It's nice to finally meet you, Mr. Summerfield." He would keep a calm head. This man was clearly near his breaking point.

Roland looked him over. Marvin and Beatriz had done well. "So you're the one my daughter is in love with. You have your mother's eyes," he said more quietly than he had spoken before.

For a brief second Renny glimpsed another emotion in the man's face. Love? Desperation? Resignation? "That's what she says."

"Beatriz was beautiful."

"Yes, she is." Renny inched closer as the extended arm with the gun in hand shook.

"I loved her."

"I can understand why." He could almost reach out and snatch the gun.

Bree sprinted down the hall, the silence causing her to panic, to lose all the military training of objectivity. She had to get to Renny, had to make sure he was all right. "Renny!" she yelled as she burst through the door.

"Sabrina!" Renny's gaze flew to the door.

Roland turned, aimed and fired.

Renny heard the shot, saw the moment the tiny ball of fire was released from its barrel and jumped on Roland's back. The gun slid across the floor as Renny pummeled the back of the man's head. Roland twisted and the men began to tussle.

All Renny could see was Sabrina standing in the doorway; then he heard more shots and he hit the man with more force than the last time until the thin frame had gone limp beneath him. Vaguely he felt hands at his back pulling him, dragging him across the floor. But her name echoed in his head, the shocked expression on her face floating throughout his vision.

"Renny, baby. Are you all right?"

It was her voice. He felt a hand on his cheek and realized it was her touch. Only Sabrina could light his fire that way, only she could get his blood heated with one stroke against his skin. His eyes opened, cleared and adjusted on the small round face in front of him. He lifted a hand, rubbed his thumb over the high cheekbone and sank into the deep ocean of her brown eyes. "Sabrina?"

She took a deep breath and decided not to fight the tears that threatened to fall. "You big idiot. You scared the daylights out of me."

"Me?" Renny sat up straighter. "You're the one who came barging in here when there was a madman with a gun." The gun. The shot. His hands moved over her quickly. "Are you hurt? Do you need an ambulance?"

Through her tears she swiped his hands away and chuckled. "No, silly. He's a horrible shot. His bullet landed in the wall about a foot away from my head."

At her words Renny pulled her to him tightly. "I told you to stay there. I told them to keep you there," he whispered into her hair.

"How could I stay there and watch you run off?" She

breathed into the crook of his neck, so thankful that he was safe. "I'm your bodyguard, remember."

Bree was exhausted. As much as she hated to admit it, her concussion and then this afternoon's exertions were simply too much for her to handle right now. Glen, one of the guards on Sam's payroll, had brought her home while Renny and his family followed his father to the hospital. Sam and Trent took Roland Summerfield to the police station.

For some reason Lynn felt the need to be at the hospital with the Bennetts, so Jeremy was already en route to her parents' house by the time she got home.

"I've made you a bed on the couch because I know you're never going to lie still in that bed until you receive word on Mr. Bennett's condition. I'll have my phone and I'll call you as soon as I can." Lynn said all this in one breath as she slipped her arms into her jacket.

Bree would have questioned her, but simply collapsed onto the chair instead. Besides, peace and quiet would do her good right about now. She'd fixed herself a cup of tea and now sat with her legs propped on the chair, the phone within arm's reach.

Laying her head back against the pillows, she allowed her mind to recap the events of the past few weeks. Her life had been a roller coaster of emotions and events in that time. She'd walked into this job thinking it would be the best distraction for that disastrous time in North Carolina and from the moment she set eyes on Renny he'd taken her mind off the past.

She wanted to be with Renny. She wanted their life together. The idea of a family of her own had crept up some time in the past few days as her head continued to throb from the vicious blow she'd received. But more than ever, with each morning she helped Jeremy with his breakfast and watched him leave for day care, she knew she wanted children of her own. That wasn't going to be possible if she was gallivanting around, throwing herself in front of bullets and whatnot for the sake of a job.

She'd just settled into a cozy little daydream of her and Renny, a beautiful house of their own filled with his artwork and three little boys that looked just like him. She would have been in a deep slumber when the doorbell ringing both startled and irritated her. Seconds passed and the bell rang again, insistently this time. Tossing her feet off the side of the chair, she wondered if maybe it was one of the guards coming with news of Mr. Bennett's condition. She was at the door, her hand on the knob, when she realized that Renny or someone else would simply have called her with that news. But with Roland behind bars her guard was down, so she pulled the door open and stared into familiar eyes.

"Hello, Sabrina."

He smiled as if this were a casual visit, as if she would be elated to see him. Instead her fists tightened at her sides and her shoulders squared. "Harold."

"You look tired." He reached out to touch her face, but she moved beyond his reach. "You're still very beautiful, but you haven't been taking care of yourself."

"What do you want?" She wasn't in the mood for his sweet talk and he was definitely full of that. She remembered the times he'd been able to talk her into phone sex with that sexy voice.

"I've come for you," he said simply.

She cocked her head to the side wondering if he was serious. His ocean-blue eyes sparkled while his ebony hair ruffled in the light breeze. She remembered thinking the first time she saw him that he'd looked just like Superman and shortly after that he'd become just that in her life. She shook her head to clear the foolish thought. "That's ridiculous, Harold. It's over between us. It has been for some time now." When he didn't answer, but simply smiled at her, she added for good measure, "How's your wife?"

His smile slipped and he took a step closer to her. "Joanne won't be a problem for us anymore."

Bree tried to block his entrance, but he pushed past her so quickly she almost lost her footing. "I don't want you here."

"That's fine," he said, looking around the foyer. "The sooner you get your things together, the sooner we can get going."

Was he serious? Bree chastised herself for asking that stupid question. Of course he was serious and arrogant and always the commanding officer. "We're not in the service anymore, Harold. You can't just order me around."

Harold turned to face her, enamored with the innocent beauty once more. She'd been fresh as the morning dew when he'd first seen her. He'd known right off the bat that she'd been untouched. That thought had aroused him beyond belief and sparked his need for her. When she didn't turn away his advances, he began to crave her, just the sight of her at first and then more, he desperately needed more. And when she'd finally given it to him he knew he'd love her forever. "Once a marine always a marine, Sabrina."

"You're crazy." Bree brushed past him, intending to get to the phone to call the police and have him removed from the premises, but he grabbed her arm, turning her back to face him.

"No. I'm not crazy." He grasped both her arms, pulling her close until her breasts rubbed against his chest. He fought off a moan as his groin sprang to life. "I'm in love with you. I can't live without you."

He'd grayed at the temples in the time they'd been separated and thin lines had begun to form at the corners of his eyes. He was still handsome, now dangerously so. "You are a married man, Harold. I can't be with a married man." Her voice sounded unsteady to her own ears as she prayed she wasn't losing her grip with him.

"I'm not married anymore. I told you Joanne wouldn't be a problem." He pulled her closer, reveled in the soft curves moving against his body. He lowered his head to kiss her, but she turned away and he nuzzled her neck instead. "It's just you and me, Sabrina. I need you so much. Feel how much I need you." He pulled on her hand, placing it over his erection.

Bree tried to pull away, refused to grip the rigidness. His touch repulsed her. The fact that he thought things were okay between them made her even sicker. "No!"

"Yes! You still love me. I know you do. And I forgive you for what you've done with that man. I know it was only to get back at me. But that's all in our past. We can start over tonight." His hands were roaming up and down her body, his mind revisiting the times they'd made love, and he cringed thinking he wouldn't be able to resist taking her right here and now.

Bree allowed her body to go slack as he caressed her, then with a swift move punched him in the throat, stealing his breath, and hurried beyond his reach. "No! You're wrong. I don't love you. I never did. You were an infatuation, a figment of my imagination, and now that's over. I'm happy now without you."

Still gasping for his breath, Harold let her words register. She was turning him away. That was impossible. She loved him, she'd told him so. "Sabrina," he gasped.

Bree moved and reached for the phone. "No, Harold. This has got to end here and now. I'm calling the police."

But Harold had other ideas. He jumped on her back, knocking the phone off the hook so that it tumbled across the room. Bree fell onto the sofa with Harold on top of her. She struggled to break free, but felt his protruding arousal inching between her legs.

"You remember this, too, don't you, Sabrina? You remember how good we were together."

"No! Get off of me!" Bree screamed at the top of her lungs, hoping, praying someone would hear her.

"Oh God, I need you, Sabrina." He wasn't going to be able to wait. With an arm pressed securely on the back of her shoulders he held her still while his other hand unzipped his pants. "It's been so long, baby. So very long."

She heard the zipper and felt icicles of fear slide down her back. He wouldn't rape her. He couldn't be that out of touch that he'd do something that stupid. When she felt his hands at the band of her pants she knew that's exactly what he planned to do. "Harold! No! Please! No!" Again those incessant tears crept up only to spill into hot rivulets down her face. She didn't have all her strength, her head was throbbing, her limbs tired from today's earlier exertion, but she knew she had to do something to stop this madness.

"It'll be quick, baby, this first time." He felt himself close to exploding just from the way she wriggled beneath him. "Then we'll go back to my hotel and I'll take real good care of you."

Bree kicked and twisted, making him lose his grip on her pants before he could get them down over her hips. He pulled her hair and she screamed.

"Now that's enough! You didn't fight when he touched you!"

Bree was crying in full force now, her vision blurred, her scalp burning, but she continued to fight, to move and squirm until Harold pushed his hands down her pants and groped her bottom with enough force to have her gasping for breath.

"Don't make me hurt you, Sabrina. Joanne made that mistake," he breathed into her ear. "Please, I don't want that to happen to you. Baby, please be still. I just need you real quick, please."

His fingers were moving between her legs searching for her entrance and she squeezed her thighs together tightly. "No! No!" Then her thoughts shifted from herself to the man she truly loved, the man she needed now more than ever. "Renny, please," she whispered.

Harold heard her words just as his fingers slipped inside her. Bree screamed at the contact, knowing that it was only a matter of moments before Harold took her completely. Then as suddenly as she'd felt his heavy form atop her it was gone.

Renny had stepped out of the car and heard the screams coming from the house. Not bothering to question his own tired limbs, he broke into a run and pushed through the half-opened door. His heart hammered in his chest and all but plummeted when he saw the man on top of Sabrina. Instead his vision turned red and he reached for the man's neck, pulling him off her and tossing him to the floor.

Harold rolled over quickly, ever the soldier, and looked into the face of his temporary replacement in Sabrina's life. "You son of a—" He was on his feet in seconds only to catch Renny's vicious right blow and fall back against the bookcase.

As Renny closed in, Harold reared back, extended a kick that landed in Renny's midsection, bending him over in pain. He pounced on Renny's back with long, swift blows designed to break him down. But Renny was strong even if he wasn't a trained soldier. One solid punch to Harold's exposed groin had the man falling to his knees instantly. And then it was on.

Renny kicked him and watched the blood spew from his mouth. "So you want to force yourself on a woman!" he roared as the bottom of his foot came down on Harold's ankles. "You're a sorry excuse for a man and somebody should have kicked your ass a long time ago!" But that was okay because he planned to administer that whipping himself tonight.

Bending down, he lifted Harold at the collar and threw him across the room until his body slammed against the wall and he slid to the floor. Renny felt as if he were reenacting a Floyd Mayweather fight as his fists connected repeatedly with Harold's face. All he could see was the man on top of

Sabrina, all he could hear were her screams. She was crying. Yelling his name, calling out to him. He was supposed to be protecting her. She was the bodyguard, but she needed him to protect her, to save her from this nightmare.

He continued swinging until her voice sounded closer, her crying seemed to cease and she touched him.

"Stop it, Renny! Stop it, baby, he's not worth it. Please stop it," Bree whimpered from behind him. While Renny and Harold had been fighting she'd pulled herself up from the sofa and called Sam on his cell phone. He and Trent were on their way here, anyway, and should be coming through the door at any moment. But from the way Renny was beating Harold, Bree didn't think the man would live that long if she didn't do something.

"Come on, baby. Come with me now." She pulled on his shirt, urging him away from Harold's battered body. "Please, Renny. I need you to come with me."

His knuckles throbbed, his head screamed with rage. "Sabrina," he whispered as his shoulders slumped in defeat.

"That's right, baby. Come on with me."

He turned to her then, scooping her up in his arms and holding her so tight she almost couldn't breathe. But the contact felt so good, Bree wrapped her arms tightly around his neck and sobbed. "I love you, baby. I love you so much."

Renny rocked her in his arms. "I won't let him or anyone else hurt you, Sabrina. Not ever."

"I know. I know."

"I'll be *your* bodyguard," he told her with all the emotion he felt. He would protect her for the rest of their lives.

Epilogue

Nine Months Later

In the backyard of their multimillion-dollar estate, Renny and Bree hosted their family's summer cookout. The grills were smoking, tables heavy with food while Earth, Wind & Fire's rhythmic tunes blared from the speakers.

Carrying a bowl of fruit to the table, Bree looked around at her family and extended family. Marvin Bennett, now her father-in-law, had healed well after miraculously only suffering first-degree burns on his hands and parts of his arms. Visions of that horrible day still crept into her mind sometimes. Beatriz looked ever beautiful in her flowing white sundress and her long hair.

Her father was busy giving Renny a crash course on the proper marinades and smoking times for spare ribs and beef. Jeremy chased a big red ball over the lush green grass as the sun beamed down over them. She was really happy as she plucked a ripe piece of cantaloupe and stuck it into her mouth.

"Whatchu see, chile?"

Bree didn't startle and didn't have to turn to know Gramma Ruby was standing right behind her. The aging voodoo mistress had come up from Louisiana for her wedding in January and hadn't returned yet, saying she had business up here to tend to. Bree had to admit, she kind of liked having her around.

"I see all my family enjoying themselves and eating me out of house and home." She grinned.

Ruby shook her head, placing a hand on Bree's shoulder. "No. What do you really see?"

Instinctively she knew what Gramma Ruby meant and she relaxed herself, scanning the yard once more. What she saw this time was drastically different from what she'd seen only moments before.

Lynn sat on the step of the gazebo, Rico leaning against the frame looking down on her. Trent, who was returning to Las Vegas shortly, sat across the table from Adriana staring besottedly while she sipped from a glass of lemonade. Jeremy continued to play with his big red ball, this time with Sam—who was happily single these days—running alongside him.

Then walking through the midst of her new visions was the man she loved more than anything else in this world. He wore white shorts and a tangerine-colored polo. There were some men that looked damn yummy in those bright colors, and Renny was definitely one of them. He'd let his beard grow in, a look that both suited him and warmed her. Without a word he reached for her and she took his hands, walking into the cocoon of his love, going up on tiptoe to share a quick kiss.

"Did you see it?" Gramma Ruby asked.

Not leaving Renny's embrace, Bree turned and nodded to her grandmother.

"It's your job to spread it around."

Bree smiled. "It feels so good. I'll make sure I do just that."

Dark, rich and delicious…how could she resist?

NATIONAL BESTSELLING AUTHOR

ROCHELLE ALERS

The Sweetest Temptation

Book #2 of The Whitfield Brides trilogy

Faith Whitfield's been too busy satisfying the sweet tooth of others
to lament her own love life. But when Ethan McMillan comes
to her rescue, he finds himself falling for the luscious pastry
chef…and soon their passions heat to the boiling point!

Meet the Whitfields of New York—experts at
coordinating other people's weddings, but not so great
at arranging their own love lives.

Available the first week of July wherever books are sold.

ARABESQUE®

www.kimanipress.com   KPRAI020708

Bound by duty…or desire?

forget me not

NATIONAL BESTSELLING AUTHOR

ADRIANNE byrd

Detective Jaclyn Mason's investigation of her partner's murder plunges her into a world of police corruption—so she seeks help from her partner's best friend, FBI agent Brad Williams. Brad ignites passion beyond Jaclyn's wildest dreams…but can he overcome her fragile trust to convince her that it's true love?

"Byrd proves once again that she's a wonderful storyteller."—*Romantic Times BOOKreviews*

Available the first week of July wherever books are sold.

ARABESQUE®

www.kimanipress.com

KPAB1050708

Every marriage has a secret—or three...

USA TODAY BESTSELLING AUTHOR

BRENDA JACKSON

JUST DESERTS

Book #3 in The Three Mrs. Fosters miniseries.

Danielle's husband's death shattered her dreams of
motherhood. Now she had a chance to salvage those dreams.
But would a marriage of convenience to Tristan repeat the
mistakes she'd made with her first, hasty marriage?

The Three Mrs. Fosters:

Alexandria, Renee and Danielle are three very different
women with one thing in common: their late husband!

Coming the first week of July wherever books are sold.

KIMANI™
ROMANCE

Welcome to the Black Stockings Society—
the invitation-only club for women determined
to turn their love lives around!

Power Play

Book #1 in a new miniseries
National bestselling author

DARA GIRARD

When mousy Mary Reyland discovers her inner vixen,
Edmund Davis isn't sure how to handle the challenge. Edmund
enjoys being in charge, but the new sultry, confident Mary
won't settle for less than she deserves, in business or pleasure....

Four women. One club.
And a secret that will make their
fantasies come true...

Coming the first week of July wherever books are sold.

KIMANI™
ROMANCE

www.kimanipress.com   KPDG0740708

The laws of attraction…

PROTECT
and
SERVE

Favorite author

Gwyneth Bolton

Detective Jason Hightower has waited fifteen years to find
out why Penny Keys left him. Penny hasn't returned home
to face her difficult past…or the man she still loves.
But Jason wants answers, and this time nothing
will keep him from the truth.

HIGHTOWER HONORS

FOUR BROTHERS ON A MISSION TO PROTECT, SERVE AND LOVE.

Coming the first week of July wherever books are sold.

KIMANI™
ROMANCE

www.kimanipress.com   KPGB0750708